AVALANCHE

A Stone Mountain Mystery

Dear Seigel Family
Enjoy
Kristina

Kristina Stanley

AVALANCHE
A Stone Mountain Mystery #3

www.KristinaStanley.com

FIRST EDITION Trade Paperback

Imajin Books — www.imajinbooks.com

June 25, 2016

ISBN: 978-1-77223-248-6

Cover designed by Ryan Doan — www.ryandoan.com

Praise for Avalanche

"A mountain as deadly as it is majestic; characters far too familiar with the Seven Deadly Sins and murder—Kristina Stanley's *Avalanche* has it all. This fast-paced mystery is as thrilling as a heart-stopping run down the slopes." —Gail Bowen, author of the Joanne Kilbourn Shreve mysteries

"Layer upon layer, like snow building for an avalanche, Stanley weaves a story that keeps you guessing. You can't turn the pages fast enough." —Jeff Buick, author of *Bloodline*

"*Avalanche* smashes and uproots relationships in Stone Mountain Resort, leaving devastation in its wake. With as many layers as winter's snow, this whodunit will keep you turning pages and guessing to the end." —James M. Jackson, author of the Seamus McCree Series

For my brothers, Peter and Michael, with love.

Acknowledgements

Mathew, the love of my life, eagle-eye editor, and constant supporter is the person I need to thank first.

A heartfelt thanks goes to my friends for life who read, reread, commented and commented again: Liliana Conn, Michael Conn, Janice Janczyn, Sue Kreiling, Debi Sarandrea and Adrienne Stewart.

A special thanks goes to Monica Conn and Fred Conn for helping me name characters in the early days. The characters Monica Bellman and Fred Morgan are named after my niece and nephew and together they named Roy McCann.

For expert advice in his field and for reading for accuracy, Andrew Nelson, Association of Canadian Mountain Guides Ski Guide, Avalanche Forecaster and Educator.

I would like to thank Humber School for Writers through which I received feedback from Joan Barfoot and Mary Gaitskill.

And of course, thank you to Cheryl Kaye Tardif and Imajin Books for believing in me.

CHAPTER ONE

Fearless of skiing in the backcountry, Roy McCann climbed to the summit of Stone Mountain Resort and paused at the entrance to the Dragon's Bowl. His muscles ached, and his calf cramped from the strenuous ascent. He released his boot from the binding of his touring ski and stretched his foot toward his shin, fighting the developing knot.

The first glow of morning light reflected off the run, and Roy searched the shadows for signs of another person. A two-kilometer crescent started above the tree line and ended in the forest, providing a steep powder run for only the most advanced skiers and snowboarders. The terrain also provided infinite hiding spots. *So where?*

The avalanche warning sign hanging from an orange safety line displayed a considerable danger rating. Logic said he should turn back. Not a chance. His need to finish what he started was stronger than logic.

He surveyed the precipice above the bowl. An overhanging mass of hardened snow extended along three-quarters of the ridge, but the band of uncertainty was small. He could manage the terrain.

Prepping for a downhill run, he removed the climbing skins from the base of the skis. He ducked the line and traversed to his favorite entry point into the bowl.

The sun rose over the peaks, and his headlamp automatically switched off. Twelve hundred meters below, the chairlift operators began their morning ritual. The lifts rotated, and the rhythmic hum of machinery drifted toward him. His shift with ski patrol started at eight, so he'd better get his ass in gear. He'd done his best.

He jumped off the edge and attacked the run. Powder sprayed above his knees as he glided through each turn. A skier's dream.

Several seconds in, the whumph of packed snow fracturing echoed across the Purcell Mountain range.

Avalanche!

He jammed the edges of his skis against a mogul, stopped and checked the cliff directly above him. The morning sun glistened off the snow, momentarily blinding him. The rumble of a slide pummeling everything in its path reverberated through his bones.

Which way?

An ash-gray cloud of snow exploded over the cliff, blocking out the sky. Too late. Ice chunks, trees and mountain detritus surged toward him, sounding like a vat full of boiling rocks.

He pushed with his poles and took off. Crouching, he picked up speed.

The avalanche closed in. He glanced left and right, searching for an escape route, but dense forest lined both sides. He raced toward the edge of the run, aiming for shallower snow.

Wind blasted past him, and snow grabbed the back of his skis, shot putting him forward. He flung his hand toward the on button of his transceiver, but it wasn't there. He'd been in such a hurry earlier he'd shoved the equipment into his backpack instead of putting on his harness. *Dumb*.

He hit the ground chest first, air expelling from his lungs. His muscles fought a losing battle for control, and he plummeted. Desperate to stay above the turbulent snow, he swam. Sunlight flashed on and off each time his face breached the surface and was dragged under again.

Snow mixed with fragments of mountain pounded him from every angle, rag-dolling him end over end, snapping a bone in his right arm. A rock snagged his backpack and ripped the straps off his shoulders. A branch tore his upper lip in half.

He glimpsed a person blurred by a curtain of snow. He screamed, but the roar of the avalanche swallowed the sound.

Buried alive.

An immense pressure came from everywhere and nowhere at the same time. His left hand cupped in front of his mouth, providing a small pocket of air. His right arm burned as if it had been pulled from its socket. His boots pressed against his feet, making it impossible to wiggle his toes.

The pulse in his neck pounded. *Slow your breathing.*

In less than fifteen minutes the snow would solidify into an ice mask, creating a sealed cavity around his face and cutting off his clean air supply. His own breath would slowly kill him as his oxygen transformed into carbon dioxide. The deeper he breathed, the faster he would die.

The unattached half of his lip blocked one nostril. He worked his tongue, creating moisture in his mouth, tasted blood and spat. Saliva dribbled from the corner of his mouth to his ear, telling him he lay with his face toward the surface.

He scratched his fingers against the packed mass in a feeble attempt to dig himself out. To break the silence, he closed his eyes and hummed his mother's favorite tune.

His sister flashed in front of him like images on a movie screen. He owed Kalin…a lot. Maybe he deserved this.

"It'll be alright." But he knew it wouldn't. Every night demon his brain had ever conjured up, every imaginary villain who chased him because of what he'd done joined him now.

At seven thirty-two a.m., Roy's headlamp burst to life, eerily illuminating his surrounding snow coffin.

CHAPTER TWO

Once she knew the thing, she couldn't unknow it.

Kalin Thompson submerged into the steaming water and waited for dawn. The hot tub, nestled behind her chalet at Stone Mountain Resort, invisible from the road or from neighboring homes, gave her a place to think, gave her time to figure out how to tell her husband of seven months her news. Ben didn't like change, and this would be a doozy in his world.

If only her brother hadn't been such a jerk last night. What a disaster. Before she'd had the chance to tell Ben her plans, Roy had shown up and started an argument that ended with Ben telling Roy to move out of the house. Roy had poured what remained of his beer into the sink and stormed to his ground-floor bedroom. Kalin stomped upstairs and feigned sleep when Ben arrived.

The Purcell Mountain range was the first range west of the Rocky Mountains, and kilometer after kilometer of forested terrain inhabited by wildlife stretched before Kalin. She turned off the jets, closed her eyes and listened to the forest awakening. Somewhere in the distance, an avalanche rumbled.

A twig cracked and an edginess spread through her. Another snap from behind. She scanned the forest, laughed at herself for being nervous and sank lower in the tub.

She tried to ignore the willies but had to look again just in case. Her eyes locked with the opaque eyes of a cougar, and she let out a tiny squeal. In a blur, the cougar disappeared behind a tree, almost as if it had never been there.

Kalin eased to the side of the tub closest to the house, barely causing a ripple, and backed onto the deck. *No sudden movements*. Step by step she worked her way toward the house, treading slowly even though the snow froze the skin on the soles of her feet. She opened the door a crack and slipped inside.

"Ben, get up. There's a cougar out back," Kalin yelled. She'd left her husband tucked in their sleigh bed on the second-floor loft with his head buried beneath his pillow.

Ben raced into the living room, his cheeks flushed from sleep, his brown hair mussed, and in sock-covered feet slid to a stop on the hardwood floor, inches from Kalin. Not anticipating the quick stop, Chica, their yellow Labrador, bumped into the back of his legs.

The muscles on his bare chest and stomach rippled with tension as if ready for battle. Nothing was stopping her from grabbing his hand and dragging him back to bed. Makeup sex was always good, but she remained by the door with the interior lights off where she had a clear view of the hot tub.

When Kalin didn't move, Ben asked, "Is it still there?"

"I can't see it."

"Why were you in the tub?"

"I needed to think."

Ben caressed her cheek with the back of his fingers. "Maybe it's not the best idea to go outside by yourself in the dark."

She ignored the tension remaining from the previous night and enjoyed the heat of his hand. "What should we do?"

"Get naked?"

She suppressed a laugh. How had he known what she was thinking? She rested her palm on the curve of his lower back and pulled him close. "I meant about the cougar."

"Nothing. It's probably moved on already." Chica stood by Ben's side at the window, emitting a guttural growl. "Or not."

Chica pressed her nose to the glass, leaving smudge marks, and barked several times.

A white rabbit bolted from behind the hot tub, zigzagging for the trees. The cougar exploded from its hiding spot and snatched the rabbit by the neck. A quick death. No cruelty intended, only a meal required. In a flash of movement, the cougar disappeared again.

"Wow," Ben said. "Did you see how fast it was?"

So much for sympathy. "Can you feed Chica while I get dressed?"

"So no getting naked?"

"Unfortunately," Kalin seductively sucked his earlobe and let it go with a smack, "you don't have time before your shift."

Ben touched his lips to hers, sighed, then said, "I'll watch to make sure the cougar doesn't come back. Although," Ben raised both eyebrows twice, "you do look sexy in that red bikini."

Kalin smiled as she jogged up the steps to the bedroom. She returned wearing slippers, charcoal-gray fleece pants and a lilac sweater. She wanted to talk to Ben before she put on her suit and he asked questions about her business attire.

"I've been promoted," Ben said.

Her news would have to wait. "Why didn't you tell me last night?"

"Roy interfered."

She wrapped her arms around him, ducking slightly to nuzzle her nose in his neck, and his stubble tickled her cheek. Her gut wrenched. The anxiety of sharing her news turned to dread. *Conflict, here we come.*

"That's wonderful," she said, but her words didn't match the emotions swirling inside her like snowflakes in a storm. Being the youngest director on the team, Kalin had been surprised by the phone call she'd received earlier in the month. Thirty-one years old, a booming career and married to the hottest guy at the resort should have made her happy. But what if there was more?

"Did you know?" Ben asked.

As the director of human resources and security at Stone Mountain Resort, Kalin should have known, but she suspected she'd been kept out of the loop because she was married to the candidate. "No, I knew Turner offered the director of mountain ops to Oliver. I hadn't heard if he accepted."

"He did. And right after, Turner called me in. I thought I was being reprimanded for something, he looked so serious. Then he told me Oliver was the new director, and I would report to him if I accepted the promotion. Like I wouldn't."

Ben broke the seal on a new can of coffee, and the aroma wafted toward Kalin. While he prepared the coffee maker, she studied the mountain chalet they'd built. Today was their fourteenth day in the home they'd designed together.

Ben drummed his fingers on the granite counter top, and his gorgeous brown eyes darted around the kitchen, making her suspect he had more to announce.

"Turner's expanding the role. Avalanche forecasting will report to me. I'll be in charge of search and rescue, too."

Kalin laughed at his enthusiasm. How could she wreck his day when he'd just been handed his dream job? "You'll be great at it."

A familiar pit of fear awakened in Kalin. She'd been a widow when she met Ben, and she couldn't survive another immense loss, but he knew how to be safe in the backcountry, and she should stop worrying. "I thought I heard an avalanche earlier."

Ben reached behind Kalin's head, pulled her hair free from her ponytail and let his fingers linger on the curve of her neck. As if he read her thoughts, he said, "I'll be careful."

"I know. I'm proud of you."

"There's one more thing." In a gesture characteristic of nervousness, Ben ran his finger along the hairline scar on the underside of his jaw. "This means Roy will report to me."

"Are you sure that's a good idea?"

"He's your brother. And after last night, I don't know, maybe we can get past the crap of the last couple of weeks. Besides, I recommended him for the job. I can't fire him because I'm the new manager."

"Did you hear him leave earlier?"

"Hard to miss the slamming door."

Maybe Roy would surprise her and things would get better. "I'll defrost a couple of steaks. Let's celebrate your promotion with a nice dinner."

Chica's tail thumped, and Ben rubbed her head. "I think she understands the word *steak*."

With open eyes, Kalin leaned forward and pressed her lips onto his. Her body ached for him, but she needed to change into a suit soon.

"Man, I love your one brown eye, one green eye thing. You have no idea how beautiful you are. Rain check on getting naked?"

The warmth of his compliment made her smile. How could she tell him she wanted to leave Stone Mountain?

"You know this means you can't seriously consider the job at White Peaks, right?"

Ben's phone rang, and he took the call. "I'll be right there."

"What?" Kalin asked.

"My new role starts right now. The avalanche you heard was in the Dragon's Bowl. I gotta go."

* * *

Kalin watched Ben's truck trundle along the snow-covered Black Bear Drive until his taillights were pinpricks, then jogged up to the loft. She was not going to worry. The avalanche happened before the resort opened for the day, and all Ben needed to do was assess the surrounding terrain.

Once dressed, she stood before the full-length mirror attached to her closet door and checked her suit from several angles. She only owned one now that she worked in a ski resort. Maybe with the change in blouse, she'd look different enough from the previous interviews.

She'd kept the first and second interviews for the general manager role at White Peaks a secret from the president at Stone Mountain. James Turner was a boss who expected loyalty. The interviews had been with the human resources director, then the outgoing general manager. Going from being a director responsible for four hundred winter employees to a resort that hired over a thousand seasonal employees was a bit of a jump. Her security team patrolled the fifteen hundred guest rooms at Stone Mountain. She didn't know how many rooms White Peaks had, but the number had to be much larger. The change would be a challenge, but she could do it. Couldn't she?

In a few minutes, she would log into a video conference with the board of directors.

Her cell rang just as she did up the top button of her suit. She checked the name on the display. The resort's finance clerk.

"The safe is empty," Helen Armstrong said.

"How can that be?" Kalin asked.

In a frantic voice, Helen explained what happened. "Can you come in…Please?"

"Hang tight. I won't be long."

As the senior finance clerk, Helen counted the resort's money before she prepared floats for the various outlets around the resort. Her attention to detail made her good at her job, but she had to be mistaken. Kalin couldn't put a major theft on her résumé, not now, not when she needed a good reference.

She called White Peaks and postponed her final interview. She did her best to explain the situation without exposing proprietary details.

A total of fifteen minutes had passed when she rushed into the finance center in the administration building. She found Helen slumped on the carpet, facing the empty safe. "Who else knows about this?"

"No one," Helen said.

Helen's softness in appearance matched her personality. Her fit body carried curves that made her appear more feminine than athletic. An odd fit for a ski hill. She wore her hair tied tight behind her head, and only enough makeup to highlight her doe-like eyes.

"Are you okay?" Kalin asked.

"I don't know what to do."

"We'll figure this out." Kalin extended her hand to help Helen get off the floor.

Like a wolf sensing weakness, Jessica Scott appeared in the doorway. She stood with her hands on her hips and glared at Helen. "I thought Eric was on shift today."

Jessica carried herself like a runway model. All angles. No curves to soften her look. Her blonde hair fell straight, ending halfway between her shoulder blades. Not one kink in sight. Precisely laid blush accentuated her sculpted cheekbones. Although Jessica was physically beautiful, Kalin thought Helen's personality made her the more attractive of the two.

From her place on the carpet, Helen answered her boss without looking at her. "He asked me to sub for him."

Jessica leaned forward. "Why are you sitting on the floor?"

Red crept up Helen's neck to her face and turned her cheeks a blotchy crimson.

"Helen?" Jessica asked.

Helen swung her hand in front of the empty safe. "The money's gone."

"What do you mean *gone*?" Jessica strode to the safe, grabbed the door and swung it wider. "And what's Kalin doing here?"

Poor Helen. Kalin watched her carefully. Helen didn't look her boss in the eye. Instead she stared at the wet footprints left by Jessica's winter hiking boots on the threadbare carpet. Even wearing jeans, Jessica looked elegant.

Helen had been a senior clerk for five months, and with her lack of education, she'd been lucky to get the job. Kalin had risked hiring her because she thought her honest and detail oriented. And even though it shouldn't influence a hiring decision, she liked Helen.

"It's not my fault," Helen said.

Jessica took a deep breath. "I didn't say it was. What happened?"

"I don't know. I opened the safe and found it empty. When I locked it last night, it was full." Helen rose and wiped her palms on her denim skirt. Black leggings covered her shapely legs. She wore flats and a plain beige sweater.

"Stop with the whipped puppy look. You need to get yourself together. How much money was in the safe?" Jessica asked.

Kalin pulled Jessica away from Helen, giving Helen some space. Jessica was Roy's girlfriend, and Kalin didn't want to hear from him later that she'd given Jessica a hard time, so she kept her voice polite. "Jessica, calm down. Okay? Yelling at Helen isn't going to help."

With a shaky voice, Helen said, "I won't know for sure until I total the receipts from last night's cashouts, but I think…" Helen swallowed. "I think around one hundred thousand."

"That can't be right. It's too much for one day."

Orderly piles of receipts from the weekend covered Helen's desk, and by the time she finished reconciling, Kalin expected she would know to the penny how much money had been stolen.

Helen intertwined her fingers and pressed her palms together. "It's from Saturday and Sunday. Plus the cash I keep for the floats."

"What are you talking about?" Jessica asked.

"I didn't take the money to the bank on Saturday. I–"

Jessica arched her perfectly sculpted eyebrows. "You what?"

"The bank requested I hold on to the money until today. They said the bank drop was broken."

"You've got to be kidding. Look, Turner will want to know the exact amount you lost, so hustle up and get the reconciling done."

"But…I didn't lose the money."

"I need to tell Turner soon," Jessica said.

"We still have a problem," Helen said. "I'll start reconciling now, but I can't finish until I get the receipts from night audit."

Jessica's lip curled, and she exhaled in a growl. "Have you called Simon?"

"I haven't had the chance yet."

"Call him now. I'll talk to Turner, then come back to help you. Get an accurate count done within an hour."

Having a cavity filled would be better than joining that conversation. Turner, the president of the resort, wasn't known for accepting mistakes or failure well. And a theft would definitely fall under the failure category. Failure to secure the safe. As director of security, this was her fault. "Want me to come with you?" Kalin asked.

Jessica eyed her for a moment. "No. Turner won't like that you knew before he did. I'll go."

Kalin didn't exactly trust Jessica to give Turner an accurate account of the theft. Who knew what she would say without a witness? "You don't need to take the blame for this alone. I'll come."

CHAPTER THREE

Ben arrived at the mountain operations building and found the Stone Mountain ski patrol team assembled and in full regalia. He took in the people he was now responsible for with new eyes. Every patroller wore a red ski jacket bearing a white cross on each sleeve. On each chest hung an avalanche transceiver and a VHF radio. Matched with black ski pants, black gloves, black helmets and black backpacks, they looked professional and inspired confidence.

The only issue was the rank odor of so many sweat-infused jackets in one room. Ben ignored the smell, knowing he was probably just as offensive, and dumped his fleece on the bench in front of his locker. His volunteer fire department T-shirt stretched across his chest and arms, and he flexed his biceps. Could anyone tell he was nervous about his new role?

"Listen up, everyone," Oliver Ward said. "As of now, Ben's the new manager of ski patrol and search and rescue. He'll be reporting to me in my new role as director."

After a few cheers, slaps on his back and congratulations, Ben said, "Let's get to work." He turned to Oliver. Two newbies in their roles. Maybe Oliver was nervous, too. "What's the status?"

Oliver bent and snapped each buckle into place on his left boot. "We're ready to check out the terrain surrounding the Dragon's Bowl." He rubbed his ear, stopping at the missing lobe, the lobe he'd lost to frostbite a couple of years ago during a search and rescue mission. The wooden bench he sat on wobbled on the uneven concrete floor as he buckled his second boot. He twisted his head toward Ben. "Is Roy with you? He's not answering his phone."

"Nope. He left the house before I got up this morning." Ben opened his locker, pulled out his equipment and started his meticulous routine of gearing up. To say Kalin's relationship with her brother was complicated was an understatement. Ben heard Roy leave well before dawn and hadn't tried to stop him. But where was he now? Coming to work late was not a cool move.

And there was Kalin to worry about. She liked to hide in the hot tub when she needed to think. He should've asked her what was on her mind instead of being preoccupied with his promotion and the argument with Roy.

So much of Kalin attracted Ben. He liked the way she always walked with purpose as if she had somewhere important to be. Her mixture of curves and muscle was sexy as hell. He loved the dimple that appeared on her left cheek when she smiled and how her nose wiggled when she talked. Sometimes he couldn't believe she'd chosen him. He'd make her proud.

An elderly man with a silver Husky clipped to a leash stood outside the glass door and knocked. All heads turned toward him.

Oliver opened the door, letting a gust of cold air rush into the room. The chill made his skin redden, and the freckles across the bridge of his nose faded with the color change. "Can I help you?"

"Bishop, sit," the man commanded. "Name's Bryan Nelson. I'm staying at the Evergreen. I heard an avalanche a while ago. You guys set one off?"

"No," Oliver said. "But there was a slide in the Dragon's Bowl. We're getting ready to check it out."

"Someone might have been on the mountain this morning."

Silence crept across the room as, one by one, each patroller focused on Nelson. The Dragon's Bowl covered seven hundred and fifty acres of difficult terrain.

"I was walking Bishop," Nelson nodded toward the Husky, "around five thirty, and I think two people were trekking up the ski hill. I saw two headlamps, but one was way up the mountain. I'm not sure if it was a reflection or a light from a person."

The team erupted into a frenzy of motion.

Ben grabbed his skis from the rack at the side of the room. Roy's assigned spots contained an empty slot. "Oh, crap."

"What?" Oliver asked.

"Roy's touring skis and poles aren't here. He can't have—"

"Dawn patrol?"

"Who the fuck knows with Roy? I hassled him about not taking the job seriously. Maybe he's…Christ. I don't know."

Oliver leaned close to Ben's ear. "Keep it together. You can do this."

Ben took a deep breath. "Anyone seen Aiden?"

As the lift manager, Aiden Price needed to be informed if ski patrol initiated a search and rescue mission. Ben would leave only two patrollers to monitor the eight ski lifts and one hundred and twenty ski runs on the mountain.

"He's not in yet," one of the patrollers said.

Before issuing commands to the group, Ben locked eyes with Oliver.

"You're in charge," Oliver said.

Ben gave one curt nod and faced the team. "Call in everyone," he said to the administration assistant who'd been hovering in the doorway nearest his desk. "Then see if you can find Roy. Also check if anyone else is missing." To the rest of the team, he said, "Let's go."

He tightened his helmet strap and bolted toward the outdoor shed that stored the snowmobiles.

Time had just become the enemy.

* * *

Twenty minutes later, Ben surveyed the destruction caused by the avalanche. A sea of knocked-down trees, ripped by the roots from the ground, covered the terrain to the right of the Dragon's Bowl. The forest to skiers' left remained pristine. If Roy had been on the demolished side of the run, for sure the avalanche crushed him. Ben's gut wrenched, but his job demanded he suppress his emotions and get on with the search.

"Everyone turn your beacons to receive mode." Ben pointed toward the toe of the avalanche. "Let's start there."

The team zeroed in on the spot. Each held a receiver aimed toward the surface. No one spoke. Boots crunching on snow, the swish of ski pants rubbing together and heavy breathing disturbed the silence.

The thunder of a helicopter distracted Ben. He crouched, tucked his chin to his chest and waited for the helicopter to land. The blades whipped wind and snow in all directions. The side door opened. A man with two search dogs jumped to the ground and duck walked away from the blades. Once they were at a safe distance, the helicopter took off.

The handler released the dogs and commanded them to start at the toe. The dogs ran in a zigzag pattern with their noses to the snow, barking repeatedly, moving from lower to higher altitude. The red vests the dogs wore kept them visible but didn't hamper their movements.

"I've got a signal," a patroller said.

Ben clomped over chunks of snow and joined the searchers. Each person held a receiver close to the ground, taking one careful step forward after another.

"Here," another patroller yelled.

The patrollers closest used their probes and searched beneath the snow. Minutes passed, but they found nothing.

"Over here," the dog handler shouted. "They've got a scent."

Fifty meters away, the dogs scratched at the surface, tails wagging, indicating a find.

The patrollers who were probing near the transceiver signal walked toward the dogs.

"No," Ben said. "Keep to your area." He radioed the rescuers higher on the mountain to join the dog handler.

A patroller in the toe of the avalanche waved at Ben. "I've hit something."

Ben grabbed his shovel from his pack and connected the two ends together. Even though his body ached to slam the blade into the snow, he shoveled carefully. "I can't find anything. Keep probing."

Ben shoveled more snow.

Clunk.

The tip of his shovel rested on a solid object.

"Careful now," Oliver said.

Ben removed snow surrounding the object, and part of a transceiver peeked through the surface. Dropping to his knees, he dug with his hands, feeling for Roy's face. "Step back. I need some room. We don't know which way his body is oriented."

A few more scoops of snow out of the way, and Ben stopped digging. He leaned his head into his hands and closed his eyes.

"What?" Oliver asked.

Ben turned to his boss. "It's his transceiver. It's been ripped from him."

Oliver leaned over Ben's shoulder. "Is the whole pack there?"

"Just the pocket."

Several members of the rescue squad were perched on snowmobiles at the top of the bowl, waiting for instructions from Ben. He waved them over and showed them where to probe. "Concentrate on any change in texture below the surface."

Infused with the energy of desperation, the rescuers formed a line crossing the run. With heads down, each person pushed a probe carefully through the snow.

Down slid the probes. Up came the probes. One careful step forward, down slid the probes again. A dance of grace in grim circumstances.

Frozen breath puffed in front of Oliver's face, hiding his expression. "Call Roy again. That could be anybody's gear."

Ben did as his boss instructed and tapped Roy's name on his cell display. The call switched to voicemail. He looked at the team and shook his head. Closing his eyes for a moment, his eyelashes froze together. He pinched his lashes between his thumb and index finger and melted the ice. A gust of wind, bringing in a storm as if it were a bad omen, stung his cheeks.

* * *

Ben leaned close to Oliver, cupped his hand around his mouth and said, "We're only focusing on Roy, but what if two people were up here?"

Oliver lifted the earflap of his helmet. Ben knew since he'd lost his lobe, the cold bothered him. He'd had extra thick flaps custom made to protect his ears. "There's been no sign of anyone else."

"I think we need to expand the search, just in case." Using his radio, Ben asked the team on the upper quadrant to return to where he sat on his snowmobile. Once every member waited before him, he checked his watch and wrote the time in his notebook. "Let's start the grid search again but a little farther up."

If the avalanche buried Roy, he'd run out of time, but they had to try. Even if it was only to find his body. Fucking hell. Why had he argued with Roy?

"Hey," a shout came from the dog handler. "We found part of a backpack."

The temperature on the thermometer attached to Ben's jacket zipper read minus twenty-seven degrees Celsius. The burn of frostbite stung his cheeks. Without thinking, he took a deep breath, and the cold air made him cough.

The dog handler passed Ben the scrap of backpack.

Ben worked his jaw in frustration. The scrap had a Canadian flag sewn onto the canvas. A beaver was embroidered onto the corner of the flag. Without the beaver, the flag could have belonged to anyone, but Kalin and Roy had a tradition of putting the flag together with the beaver, representing Canada. Their stepdad had started the tradition when they were young, and they'd carried it on as they grew older.

His training taught him that once buried, the heat of a person's breath solidified the snow, cutting off the air supply. With each passing minute, the ice surrounding Roy's face became thicker. The rescue team continued the search, just not as frantically as before. No one mentioned the words "recovery mission", but they were probably all thinking them. Ben eyed the weather. *Safety first.*

A patroller radioed Ben from higher on the mountain. She'd been searching the terrain above the avalanche. Between heavy breaths, she said, "There are tracks directly above where the slide started."

"How close?"

"Close enough that the avalanche could have been triggered by a person."

"Roy?" Ben asked.

"We've no way of knowing."

"Did you follow the tracks to see if they disappeared into the avalanche's path?"

"The wind's too strong up here. Most of the tracks have already been obliterated. There was only a few feet and then nothing."

The glint of something shiny poking out of the snow caught Ben's eye. He sidestepped closer and pulled a bent ski pole into the air. He spoke to the group nearest him. "Use your probes here and work your way up."

Ben phoned the mountain operations administration assistant and asked him to check the number on the pole against the list of patrollers. He heard him click on his keyboard and his intake of breath.

"The pole belongs to Roy."

"Can you find Turner? I don't know if anyone has told him about the avalanche yet."

Ben turned back to Oliver. "Now we know." He called Roy's girlfriend, Jessica, and the call switched to voicemail. Then he tried Kalin and got the same result.

CHAPTER FOUR

Kalin and Jessica waited in the reception area outside the president's office. Jessica's phone rang, and she ignored it. Seconds later Kalin's rang, and she switched off the ringer without checking the display. Turner had a strict policy about no cell phone use in his office, and she didn't want to worsen his mood with a minor transgression.

While they waited, Kalin took deep breaths to settle herself. Maybe she should have called the RCMP before coming to Turner's office, and maybe she should have waited until they knew exactly how much money had been stolen. Maybe.

Her boss didn't accept mistakes, and she wouldn't be the first person to lose her job for making one. At the least, this would affect her reference check. Talk about terrible timing.

Turner had been the president of Stone Mountain Resort for six months. He'd been hired to replace the previous president, Gavin Reed, after a fire destroyed most of the lower village. Turner had taken a resort in financial trouble and created profits in record speed. A weak person couldn't have implemented the required changes. Kalin suspected he dreamt of managing a larger, more prestigious resort and needed to prove himself. Hearing about a theft this large would really set him off.

Turner walked straight past them and motioned for them to follow. He entered his office beyond the desk of his administrator.

"I need to report a theft," Kalin cleared her throat. "Sometime between closing yesterday and opening this morning, someone broke into the finance center. This morning Helen discovered the empty safe."

Turner pulled at his shirt collar, exposing the edge of a tattoo. Kalin knew two things. One, the gesture meant he was angry, and two, he'd be even angrier if he realized she'd spotted the tattoo. He kept his past private, so she averted her eyes.

"Is she telling me you lost an entire day's receipts?" Turner asked Jessica.

Jessica bit the inside of her cheek. "It's worse. We also lost Saturday's cash in addition to the money we keep stocked to make up the daily floats."

"How much?"

"Helen thinks around one hundred thousand."

"Thinks? Why doesn't she know exactly?"

"We don't have night audit's receipts yet," Jessica said.

"Well, get them."

A bead of sweat formed on Turner's forehead, surprising Kalin. She'd never seen him sweat. He snapped his gum and let out a long breath. She smelled mint mixed with a medicinal aroma.

"How the hell could something like this happen?"

Jessica flinched at Turner's raised voice. "Helen said someone from the bank called on Saturday afternoon. They told her the cash drop was broken and not to bring the money to town until they called to say they'd fixed the unit. They said most likely it would be Monday since they're closed on Sundays. So last night, the money from both Saturday and Sunday was in the safe."

"Did Helen verify the call was from the bank?"

Jessica looked to Kalin before answering, then straightened her back and faced Turner. "I don't know. I'll ask—"

"Ask? Are you kidding me? This is our biggest weekend of the year. You should have procedures in place instructing her to call the bank back. You should have told her not to leave more than one night's receipts in the safe. You're the manager. You can't leave that kind of decision to the clerks. You should know better."

Even though Jessica had been hard on Helen, Kalin couldn't stand by and let Turner yell at her. "Maybe we could find out what happened before we blame anyone?"

Jessica eased a step away from Turner. "The majority of the cash is for the floats, not from daily receipts. We probably didn't make that much in cash on Saturday. Most people pay with debit or credit."

"Are you making excuses for Helen and yourself?"

"No. I—"

"You what?" Turner swallowed and clenched his jaw.

"I don't think Saturday's take made up a significant portion of the money stolen."

Kalin could see from the way Turner's lips pressed into a white line that Jessica had made him even angrier. To take his focus off Jessica, she asked, "Should I call the bank?"

Turner shook his head. "Call the RCMP and let them deal with it."

"Should I fire Helen?" Jessica asked.

Wow. Not nice. Planting the seed of blame in Turner's mind. As Helen's boss, Jessica should be protecting her, not throwing her at Turner like a camper throwing meat to a bear, trying to change the beast's focus.

"Don't do anything yet. Call the RCMP. Let me know when they get here."

* * *

"The worst has happened," Ben said. "The avalanche—"

"Hang on." Kalin stopped in the hallway and turned to Jessica. "I'll meet you in the finance center. I have to take this."

Kalin exploded through the administration building's outer doors and faced the ragged mountain peaks. She heard wind buffeting Ben's phone. He was somewhere on the hill. "What's happened?"

"The avalanche was in the Dragon's Bowl."

"Are you okay?"

"I'm fine, but—"

"But what?" Kalin's chest rose and fell in rhythm with her quickened breathing.

"We don't know for sure yet, but…Oh, crap, Kalin. I don't even know how to say this. Roy might have been caught in it."

Kalin's heart pounded. Why had they chosen last night of all nights to ask Roy to move out? She'd heard him leave well before dawn and hadn't tried to stop him. "How is that possible?"

Ben filled her in on what he knew. "Have you talked to him today?"

"Not since last night." Kalin's mind was on fire, being hit by lightning strikes in rapid succession, processing what Ben said. She couldn't move. Her brain refused to send instructions to her muscles, so she stood on the path, staring at the snow on the ground. "Roy's safe. He has to be."

"You have to prepare yourself. The avalanche happened at seven thirty."

She resented the softness in Ben's voice. Who cared about the time? Ben shouldn't be bothering her with trivial matters. He should be searching for Roy. "That doesn't mean anything."

"It's been too long."

"You don't know that, so stop talking and keep looking for him." Kalin understood he was only telling her what he knew, but she needed to direct her anger somewhere. "I'm sorry. I didn't mean that. I'm just frightened for Roy."

"We'll find him."

"Please be careful." If anything happened to Ben, Kalin wasn't sure she'd survive. They'd only been married for seven months. That wasn't enough time together. "Are the conditions safe for you to be up there?"

"For now."

"I want you to do everything you can to find him, but…"

"I know. I'll be careful. I love you."

"I love you more."

She turned and ran back inside. She'd direct her anger at her boss. Why hadn't Turner told her about Roy earlier?

* * *

Kalin dashed into Turner's corner office only to find the spacious room empty. She had every intention of making sure he put all resources on the search for Roy. She pivoted and banged into Turner's chest as he entered his office.

"What are you doing back here?" Turner asked.

"There's been an avalanche."

"I'm aware."

"Why didn't you tell me?"

Turner closed his office door, letting the latch click gently into place. "Considering what's going on, I thought you had enough to worry about."

"Are you crazy? You had no right to hide this from me just so I'd focus on the theft and not Roy."

"Since Roy's your brother, I'll ignore your outburst."

Another mistake. She should have gone to mountain operations. Why was she wasting time with her boss? "Sorry. You're right. I'm going to mountain ops to see if I can help."

Turner sat at the round table centered on the plush navy carpet, stared at Kalin for a moment, then pointed to his guest chair. "Before you go, call Fred. I need someone from security in here now."

She overcame the physical pain of sitting, of not doing something for Roy, and lowered herself into the chair. Fred was the security manager and reported to her. "He's on vacation until Friday."

"You let him go on our busiest week?"

Kalin's legs bounced, and she pressed her palms on her kneecaps to control the motion. "His brother's getting married in Hawaii. The rest of the team is here."

"But no one senior?"

Who cared? Kalin should be at mountain ops, not sitting here discussing vacation plans. Instead of bolting for the door, she forced herself to ask, "Why do you need Fred?"

"To liaise with the RCMP. Without him here, you'll have to. Have you called them yet?"

"No, I…" She should do as Turner asked, but she couldn't focus. The view of the Purcell Mountains' cragged peaks normally dominated the room with its beauty. Today, all Kalin could imagine was Roy buried beneath the snow. She hoped for a large air pocket. Anything to keep him alive long enough to be found. "Couldn't you take care of it until I check in with search and rescue?"

By the scowl on Turner's face, she guessed he wasn't pleased with her question. She understood the extreme pressure he was under with both the avalanche and theft happening at the same time. But she was, too. He'd have RCMP, media, and staff to deal with, along with the demands of head office. To do her job well she needed to help him with the theft investigation. "Okay, I'll make sure Helen and Jessica are set, and then I'll head to mountain ops."

"I want you back by the time the RCMP get here. I need you to work with them on the investigation. Make sure there are no media leaks. And check if you can get Fred to come back early."

She nodded and bolted for the door.

"And Kalin, don't talk to the RCMP without me."

CHAPTER FIVE

Kalin needed a moment and stopped in the administration hallway. She leaned into the wall, pressing her cheek against chipped paint. *Get under control.*

"What are you doing?" Tessa Weber asked. "Standing side-pushups?"

Her recruiting specialist was trying to be funny, so Kalin held back the snap in her voice. "I need you to clear my calendar today and take care of anything urgent."

"You want me to what?"

The cochlear implant for Tessa's right ear helped her out with hearing, but she still had trouble when someone spoke too fast. She'd had the implant for less than a year, and was still figuring out how to hear things properly. Like a child, she'd had to learn what sounds were. Even something as common as a footstep or a raindrop was new to her.

In Kalin's agitated state, she'd forgotten to slow her speech a bit. "Can you clear my schedule and take care of anything urgent today?"

"Sure. What's going on?"

"I don't have time to explain. Just help me out, okay?"

In a gesture familiar to Kalin, Tessa pulled her hair over her implant. "Okay. Where do I find your schedule?"

"Monica has access to it. She can help you." Kalin relied on her HR manager for support and knew between her and Tessa they'd handle the day. Kalin had hired Tessa during last year's arson investigation after Tessa approached her with the story of her newly implanted gadget. Prior to the implant, Tessa hadn't been able to do a job that required phone interactions. The technology opened up a new career for her, and Kalin had liked her spunk and taken a chance with her lack of HR experience.

"Got it." Tessa skipped away toward Monica's office.

Kalin strode along the threadbare carpet and stopped just short of the finance center door. She heard raised voices. Not nice, but she remained in the hallway and didn't let the women know she was there.

"Did you get in touch with Simon?" Jessica asked.

"He hasn't answered his phone."

"Where are you with the reconciliation?"

"I'm trying, but without night audit's receipts, it's difficult," Helen said.

"Give me some of what you have. I'll help."

"What did Turner say?"

"That you never should have left Saturday's money in the safe. That's what he's most upset about. Because of you, the company lost two days of cash instead of only one."

Harsh. Kalin was tempted to interfere and defend Helen but not yet.

"When the bank called, I didn't know what else to do," Helen said.

"I wouldn't say that to Turner if I were you. Anyway, you should have called the on-duty manager. You should have verified with the bank they had a problem."

"But the bank called me."

"Someone called you. You don't know for sure it was the bank, and you better believe I'm going to find out what the problem was on their end."

"You're going to blame me for this," Helen said.

"Who else would I blame? Did you give the combination to anyone?"

"No, I wouldn't."

Constable Miller, together with a female cop Kalin hadn't met before, walked along the hallway toward Kalin and interrupted her eavesdropping.

Miller wore his hair cropped within millimeters of his scalp, his RCMP uniform was pressed and clean, and his arms hung wide around the weapons hooked to his belt. The strength with which he carried himself reminded her of Ben. He put his hand on her shoulder and squeezed. "You okay?"

"Not really."

"Ben will find Roy. Hang in there."

Kalin's throat constricted, and instead of answering, she nodded. She would not cry. "Hey, congratulations. I heard about your engagement to Becky."

"Thanks. This is Constable Wagner."

Wagner's RCMP cap hid her hair but not her heart-shaped face. The Kevlar vest gave her a square shape and emphasized her muscled arms. Kalin nodded at her, and the woman nodded back. What was there to say?

"Shall we go in?" Miller asked.

Kalin followed Miller and Wagner into the finance center and introduced them to Jessica and Helen.

Had anyone told Jessica about the avalanche? Informing her in front of the others seemed cruel. Jessica had only been dating Roy for five months, but the length of time might not reflect how deeply she cared for him. Kalin would wait till after the meeting when she could talk with Jessica privately.

Miller sat between Jessica and Helen. Wagner stood in the doorway with her legs wide and arms crossed over her chest, blocking the entrance.

"Now, who discovered the empty safe?" Miller asked.

With attention focused on her, Helen's cheeks flushed in an uneven tone. She pressed her palms on her denim skirt and gave Miller a timid smile. "I did. The safe was locked this morning. I think the thief had the combination."

No doubt Helen needed some support, but Kalin was unsure of how to give it to her, so she waited for Miller's next question.

Miller smiled gently at Helen as if he understood a harsh approach wouldn't work with her. "Is there a way to find out who accessed the safe?"

Jessica frowned. She pulled her long blonde hair from behind her back to the front of her chest and twisted the tresses with her fingers. "The out-of-date safe technology allows for only one combination. Newer models have a unique number for each person, but we weren't allocated the budget to upgrade. With the existing model, it's impossible to determine who opened the safe last."

* * *

Turner edged Constable Wagner out of his way and entered the finance center. "I told you to let me know when the RCMP arrived," he snapped at Kalin.

Everyone in the room stood.

Miller stepped between Turner and Kalin. She'd worked with him previously on an arson and a murder case, and he'd earned her respect. She didn't mind his alpha male instinct to protect her, especially now when she hovered on the edge of control.

Without making an issue of Turner's raised voice, Kalin introduced him to Miller and Wagner.

"Did one of our employees do this?" Turner asked.

Miller straightened, giving Turner the full force of his presence. Kalin could almost smell the testosterone.

"I can't say yet, but it does look like someone who knew the combination opened the safe." Miller's eyes darted to Helen, and had Kalin not been watching him, she would have missed the gesture.

Turner stepped toward Helen and loomed inches from her. "Unless the safe wasn't locked last night."

"I locked it." Helen stepped backward and bumped into her desk. "I never leave without making sure it's properly secured. I remember flipping the handle closed and entering the combination last night."

"So you say."

An uneaten doughnut and a cup of coffee occupied the corner of the desk. Helen must have noticed Turner staring because she threw the doughnut into the garbage and placed the coffee out of sight on the bookshelf.

Turner's cell buzzed against his hip, but he ignored the interruption.

Answer it. What if it was about Roy?

Helen intertwined her fingers in front of her skirt and turned to Jessica. "Won't you tell them I'm careful?"

Jessica looked at Turner with her eyes half closed as if she didn't care and shrugged.

"What's the next step?" Turner asked.

Kalin opened the window a crack, thinking the air would dissipate the distinctive odor of stress.

Helen lowered her head and glanced at Kalin while biting her fingernails. Helen wasn't built for this kind of pressure. If Kalin were alone with her, she might have reached over and hugged her.

Miller moved beside Turner and glanced out the window. "No access this way without a ladder. I'll have an officer check for marks in the snow."

Turner nodded.

"The doors haven't been damaged, and there's no sign of a break-in. Who has both the combination to the safe and a key to the office?" Miller asked.

"Four of us. Duncan Bosey. He's the director of accounting. Myself, Helen, and Eric Wilson. He's a junior clerk," Jessica said.

"Not you?" Miller asked Turner.

"I don't need either the combination or the keys. I don't do clerical work."

"Is the combination written down anywhere?" Miller asked Jessica.

"I keep it in a spreadsheet on my computer. Usually I change it weekly, so I need to record it somewhere."

"Who has access to the spreadsheet?"

"Only me," Jessica said. "It's password protected as is access to my computer. The clerks have to ask me if they forget the number."

"You said usually you change the combination weekly. When did you last change it?"

Kalin had missed the significance of Jessica's earlier statement and smiled at Miller's attention to detail.

"Answer the man," Turner said.

Jessica sighed. "Early December."

"What are you talking about?" Turner closed his eyes, pinching the bridge of his nose between his thumb and index finger. "You're supposed to change it every week."

"I know," Jessica said. "We were so busy over Christmas, it got overlooked."

"Let's worry about that later. Are you sure no one else has access to your computer?" Miller asked.

"I don't think so."

Turner slid his hand through his hair and made a fist. "The IT department has access to every computer on the resort. They could easily get the combination if they knew where to look."

"Did anyone other than Helen work in the finance center on Saturday or Sunday?" Miller asked.

Helen shook her head, while at the same time Jessica said, "I covered her lunch break." Jessica frowned at Helen. "She went snowboarding."

"Is it procedure to have only one person working?" Miller asked.

Jessica looked directly at Turner, not Miller, when she answered. "I asked for the budget to be increased to pay for two people to work each shift, but you denied my request."

"You know we cut back because of the fire," Turner said.

"Okay, I'd like to interview the finance center and IT staff. Is there a conference room I can use?" Miller asked.

"I'll get my assistant to set one up for you," Turner said, "but if you already know who had the combination and keys, shouldn't you be checking their bank accounts, searching their cars and homes?"

"It's too early in the investigation for that," Miller said.

"Why?" Turner said in a raised voice.

Miller clenched his jaw.

In a quieter tone, Turner asked, "Can you tell me why?"

"Because we need a warrant, and that requires evidence."

"We know one of them is the thief."

"I don't know that. I know a person, or persons, had the combination to the safe. Either the thief had a key to the finance center or the door was left unlocked. The thief may have stolen the combination, one of the staff may have written it down or been threatened to disclose it. Until I investigate further, I do not have enough evidence to get a warrant."

"So what do we do?"

"*We* don't do anything. I'll interview everyone involved. The finance center will remain closed while my team checks for fingerprints. I'll get prints of everyone who has legitimate access. Then I'll find out who is agreeable to a polygraph test. You *will* let us investigate."

"What's a polygraph going to do for us? I thought they weren't reliable," Turner said.

"The test might not be admissible in court, but if it shows a person is lying then it could be enough to get a search warrant. Anything the person says is admissible in court, so we might get something that way."

"Can we force people to take the test?"

"No. Unless we have a warrant, it's voluntary. If someone refuses, we can't really do anything."

"I can do something. Anyone who refuses will be fired."

Time to stop worrying about Roy and participate in the conversation. "We can't do that," Kalin said.

"I can do whatever I want."

"But employment standards—"

"I don't care about employment standards. I want the money found." Turner strode to the door and without looking backward, he said, "Kalin, come with me. We have things to do."

"I'll catch up with you later." Kalin rested her hand on Jessica's arm. She'd have to tell her about Roy soon.

* * *

After spending an agonizingly long fifteen minutes with Turner, Kalin waited for Ben on the steps outside the mountain ops building. Cold seeped into her dress boots, and she stomped from foot to foot. On the other side of the glass door, the ski patrol meeting space, normally a busy hub, sat abandoned. She sent the SAR team a silent thank you for searching for Roy even though arctic cold surrounded them.

Her jaw ached from clenching her teeth during her meeting with Turner. He'd dragged her out of the finance center and grilled her about the security process without a thought of Roy or the avalanche.

Ben rounded the corner, clomped over a mound of snow and reached for her hand. She held tight as if his touch could give her strength.

Her breath blossomed into clouds in front of her face, and her skin prickled from the sub-zero temperature. "Any news?"

"Nothing yet. The team's still searching. I just came off the mountain to talk with you and meet more rescuers. What's with the suit? Aren't you freezing?"

"A bit. Are the helicopters here?"

"Already searching."

"What about dogs?"

Ben canted his head toward the parking lot. A red SUV pulled into a space at the end of the nearest row. The driver disembarked and opened the back hatch. Two German shepherds wearing vests jumped to the ground and barked at their handler. Ben waved at the driver to head toward the snowmobiles waiting by the side of the building. "There are two already searching and here come two more."

"Who's on the mountain now?"

"Everyone available is searching for Roy. I get you're worried, but I'll handle this. Okay?"

Kalin bit the inside of her cheek to keep herself from saying anything rash. She shouldn't take her fear out on Ben. "Okay."

The icy air stung her hands, and Kalin shivered. She pulled her suit jacket tight over her chest.

"You're freezing. Let's go inside." Ben put his arm around her shoulder and led her into the ski patrol meeting room.

Even when empty, the room smelled of antiseptic.

"I've never seen you in a suit."

Kalin rubbed her hands together, and the heat returning to her skin caused more pain than the cold. "Now's the worst time to talk about this. The chairman of the board at White Peaks called me. I was supposed to have my panel interview today."

"You didn't say yes to the job, did you?"

Disappointed at his first response, Kalin hid her feelings. "I wasn't offered it yet. I postponed the interview because of what's going on."

"I don't want to move there. White Peaks is a metropolis. There's no village plan. It's sprawling condos surrounded by more sprawling condos. There's no community. It would be like living in a city. What if you get the job?"

Stone Mountain was Ben's life. And she loved him. "It's a long shot."

"No, it's not. You can't mean moving. We just built our house."

"And it's beautiful. It won't be hard to sell." Their first attempt at building the house had been destroyed by arson. They'd almost decided not to rebuild, but both Kalin and Ben believed in Stone Mountain and the life they'd created.

Could she really think about moving after all they'd been through? The isolated resort surrounded by crown land suited her. The town of Holden, twenty minutes away by a rough mountain road, provided all they needed.

"If I'd known you were really serious about this, I wouldn't have accepted the manager role."

Ben was right. The timing sucked. He'd worked hard to get this promotion, and he deserved the success. Oliver would be annoyed if Ben quit so soon after taking the position, but she had to see where the opportunity led.

"Does Turner know yet?"

"No."

"Aren't you worried he's going to find out?"

Since the theft and the avalanche distracted Turner, she wasn't worried. Much. "The people at White Peaks will be discreet. There's something else." Kalin told Ben about the theft.

Ben wrapped his arms around her. She folded into him and rested her cheek on his shoulder. She loved this man. He was dealing with an avalanche and still had time to comfort her. A sob built in her throat.

He pressed his lips to her ear. "You okay?"

"No. Yes. You're so unbelievably good to me."

The man with the search dogs rapped twice on the window.

Ben released her from the hug. "I need to get back on the mountain. Call if you need me."

The conversation about White Peaks would have been much tougher if Roy wasn't missing, and for that Kalin silently thanked Ben. He understood her relationship with Roy and how hard this was on her. "Be careful."

CHAPTER SIX

Jessica Scott rested her forehead against the frosted windowpane and watched Kalin walk from the mountain ops building to the administration building. Would Kalin stand up for her?

How could someone empty the safe while she managed the operation? Her office might be a hovel, but she'd earned the place. And how dare Turner treat her like she'd done something wrong? She kicked the wall hard enough for drywall to loosen and drift to the carpet.

"I hate that wall, too," Simon Crane said.

Jessica swirled. "Ever think of knocking?"

The scent of freshly shampooed hair followed him into her office. Jessica glared at him, daring him to speak. His cheeks and ears were flushed from the cold. When he'd turned fifteen, Simon acquired his perfect looks as if a magic fairy visited his bedroom one night and granted him one wish. Since then, he tried to look cool. He wore a hunting knife on his belt when everyone else carried bear spray. He refused to wear a toque when the temperature dropped below zero and everyone else dressed for the weather.

"I just got Helen's voicemail," Simon said.

As the night auditor, Simon's last duty of his shift included delivering the previous day's receipts to the finance center. Irritation understated what Jessica felt about him missing today's delivery. "What happened with the receipts this morning?"

Simon flashed his signature smile meant to disarm her, but she knew him too well to fall for the amateurish trick. She waited while he stared at her with his transparent blue eyes and tidied his blond hair with his hand.

"I'm sorry. I forgot to bring them to Helen. I went home to sleep and didn't realize—I'll take them to her now. Anyway, she should have called to remind me as soon as she got in."

"You know she's too timid for that." Jessica held out her open hand with impatience. "Give them to me."

Simon handed her the bag. "Are you pissed? It won't happen again."

"You can't rely on our history to get you out of this." Jessica had grown up in the valley with Simon. Besides a brief stint in Calgary, he'd never lived anywhere else. She'd hired him when the last night auditor quit after her husband died in some horrific accident. The woman had been one of Kalin's best friends.

She opened her desk drawer and pulled out a disciplinary form. She filled in Simon's offense and handed him the paper.

"You're kidding, right?"

"My job's on the line. I have to show Turner I'm capable."

Simon flicked the paper at Jessica, letting it flutter to the floor. "You can't."

"You owe me."

"How do you figure that one?"

"I told Kalin I did a reference check on you, so she wouldn't. As if she'd hire you after the number of times you've been fired."

"I didn't ask you to lie for me."

"Who else would hire you?"

Simon inhaled deeply, several times, as if controlling his temper. "Fine."

Jessica walked around her desk and picked up the form. Simon signed on the dotted line, and she put the paper aside to store in his personnel file. "So let me tell you what happened today."

After she finished her tirade on the day's events, Simon said, "That explains your mood."

"Don't be snide. I've had enough. Constable Miller treated me like any other staff member. I should be given more respect than the clerks. Tomorrow he's coming back with questionnaires and a fingerprinting kit. Turner's going to force everyone to take a polygraph test."

"That could be a problem for you."

"Shut up."

"Hey, if you need to talk, I'm here for you." He punched her lightly on her arm and left her alone.

The rhythmic thumping of helicopter blades drew her attention toward the ski hill. The chopper thundered past her office window. She'd been dating Roy since last summer. If a skier had an accident requiring a helicopter, he'd be busy. Still, he should be the one offering support, not Simon.

If Roy kept behaving like an ass, well, off to the dump with him. She'd caught the jerk going into Helen's place at night, too drunk to notice her a few steps behind him. When he'd left the bar, her intuition told her to follow him. Why did he have to choose one of her employees? Not that he'd ever sleep with someone as fragile as Helen.

Jessica loved skiing with Roy. He'd learned to ski with his sister when they were kids, and with his aggressive nature, he'd excelled. She didn't know why, but she liked guys with an edge.

The problem with the edge was the cuts that came along with the adventure. For the first time in her life, the beginnings of heartbreak nipped at her.

Her desk phone rang. She ignored the ringing until the call switched to voicemail. Roy never called her landline. Her cell rang. She checked the display in case it was Roy, but no luck. Ben Timlin was on the other end. Too bad. She wasn't in the mood to talk to him.

* * *

Jessica figured Constable Miller had finished interviewing employees, and she left her office in search of Helen and Eric. Her two clerks. One shy and typically nervous. The other a contrast with his loud voice and outspoken demeanor. Jessica found them and led them into the maintenance closet at the end of the hallway.

In the cramped room, Helen leaned against the shelves containing cleaning products, and as usual her face became a host to stains of red and uneven goose bumps. And what was with the flat shoes? If she was going to wear a skirt, why not wear flattering pumps to go with it?

Eric ducked his head as he walked through the doorway, shifted a mop and stood beside Helen. "Why are we meeting in here?"

"I don't want anyone to see us together."

Eric looked at her as if she was an idiot.

"If we meet in my office, anyone passing by can see through the window. Look, it's better if we keep a low profile. This has been a tough morning for all of us." Jessica rested her backside on the edge of a commercial vacuum cleaner. A plume of dust rose behind her, releasing a musty odor into the air. Grit from the machine stuck to her sweating palms. "I don't think either of you had anything to do with the theft, and I don't like the way Turner's treating us. We're not criminals."

"I agree. Turner's being a jerk," Eric said.

"Why did you ask Helen to cover for you this morning?"

Eric slid his eyes toward Helen and licked his bottom lip. "I had something personal to do."

"Which was?"

"Personal."

"I don't think the RCMP will let you get away with being so vague," Jessica said, suppressing the annoyance in her voice.

"They didn't ask if I was supposed to be on duty. Why do we have to fill out questionnaires if Constable Miller already interviewed us?"

Nice change of subject, Jessica thought. "I guess they want to look for inconsistencies or maybe they want our answers in writing. Who knows? Have either of you agreed to a polygraph test?"

Helen looked to Eric. He nodded and she copied.

Jessica hired Eric for the winter season because of his previous banking experience. Most of the time, Eric's friendly and outgoing nature drew people to him, although Jessica noticed he'd put his joking aside for the moment. But really, what did she know about him? He was confident enough to pull off the theft. All he needed to do was hide the money until he left the country at the end of the ski season. "Eric, do you want to take the test?"

"What choice do we have? Helen said Turner would fire anyone who didn't."

"If we all refuse, he can't fire the entire team," Jessica said.

"What if the cops don't catch the thief? Turner's going to think one of us did it, and he'll fire someone," Eric said. "We could clear our names, and the RCMP would target someone else."

"Our names are clear. It's their job to prove otherwise," Jessica said.

Helen fidgeted with a bottle of bleach. She picked at the label with her fingernail, ripped off the top corner and searched for a place to put the gummy remnant. She ended up squishing it in her palm. "I'm not sure it's a good idea to refuse the polygraph."

Too timid to steal from Stone Mountain and a rule follower, of course, Helen would think that way. Jessica just couldn't picture Helen sneaking into the finance center in the middle of the night. "The cops can't search anyone's place without a warrant, and since they have no evidence, they can't get a warrant without tripping someone up. I won't have our group treated this way. The cops should be looking for an outsider."

Eric lifted his chin and studied Jessica. "Since when do you care about anyone in the group?"

"Just because I don't show it, doesn't mean I don't care. Look, we're all upset about having to take a polygraph. I don't think we should let them push us around."

"But Turner will be angry if we refuse," Helen said.

Jessica studied the dust on her palm, then wiped her hand on her jeans. "I'll talk to him. Tell him no one feels right about this. Let me at least try, and if it doesn't go well, we can always do what he wants."

* * *

Jessica ignored the headache pounding its way from the base of her neck to her temples. It wasn't even five o'clock yet, so too early to go home. The theft wasn't directed at her personally, but the missing money would cause her problems. She punched the back of her office chair. The chair swiveled, and the armrest knocked her teacup onto the floor.

"Shit."

She called Roy for what must have been the tenth time, and he didn't answer. She tossed her cell at the wall, but it fell short and thumped onto the carpet. Roy had probably cut out early and headed to the bar to drink with his all-important buddies. To hell with him.

With the way Turner treated her, staying at home tomorrow seemed more appealing than coming to work. Maybe she should get back into the real estate business. She still had her license, and she got along well with the people in the local office. The flexible hours of an agent would mean she wouldn't have to miss any ski time. Maybe she could even ski more.

If she was going to change her life, a drastic change should do the trick. She should dump Roy and change jobs, except she liked her job and had worked hard to get it. Roy, she could do without.

A knock on her office door caused an uncontrollable shiver to travel from her spine to her ribcage. After the day she'd had, it couldn't be anything good. Ignoring that she was mad at him, she picked her cell off the floor and dialed Roy again, but the call forwarded to voicemail.

"Shit. Shit. Shit."

She opened the door. Aiden Price stood in front of her, wearing his lift operator uniform. Jessica had met him during her first week at Stone Mountain. In her enthusiasm to get on the slopes, she'd forgotten her newly printed staff pass. Aiden had been at the lift station and given her a complimentary ticket, making her promise to show him her pass later. An overnight powder dump smothered the runs, and she would have missed the fresh tracks if she'd had to go home and get her pass. He'd said she looked so excited about skiing that he hadn't had the heart to turn her away. They'd been friends, sort of, ever since.

Aiden's toque sat crooked on his head, and his zipper stuck halfway to the top of his jacket as if he'd dressed in a hurry. He stood silently staring at her.

"What?" Jessica asked.

"Can I come in?"

She let him pass. "Man, you smell ripe."

Aiden wiped sweat off his forehead. "I've been working hard all day. We're short on ski patrol. I had to manage the lifts and take care of the junior patrollers."

"What's going on?"

"Why haven't you been answering your phone?" Aiden asked.

"To understate things, I've had a busy day."

"Have you talked to Roy today?"

"No. Why?"

"An avalanche hit the Dragon's Bowl this morning. Roy's missing."

Jessica had seen the helicopter earlier. Her gut clenched. When he hadn't returned her calls, she never guessed he might be hurt…or worse. And why hadn't Turner told her? What a jerk.

"It's possible he went into the Bowl alone this morning before the lifts opened," Aiden said.

"I told him he shouldn't be doing that alone. And usually, he lets me know before he goes. I don't get why you think he was caught in an avalanche. There's something you're not telling me."

"A guest saw someone going up the hill early this morning before the avalanche. Search and rescue found part of a backpack with a Canadian flag sewn on the flap. The same kind Roy had."

Her heart raced. He couldn't be buried. Not Roy. "Did they find anything else?"

"His ski pole."

"Even if he was caught in the avalanche, he could be trekking down the mountain right now. You don't know he's hurt." Jessica regretted every lousy thought she'd had about Roy. If only he would walk in and she could yell at him for not answering her messages, but not this.

"You look pale. Are you alright?"

"It's been a bad day."

"So I heard. Everyone's talking about the theft. Funny Roy disappeared this morning." Aiden shrugged. "Just sayin'."

Kalin opened the door without knocking.

By the tears on her cheeks, the news was bad. Hope that Roy had been found alive crashed to the ground like a tree felled by a chainsaw, and the sharp branches stabbed tiny holes in Jessica's heart.

* * *

Kalin entered her new home, surprised Chica wasn't at the door to greet her. Talking to Jessica about Roy had exhausted her. She didn't know how to support the woman when she wasn't that fond of her. She tossed her jacket on the bench in the front hall.

"Chica?"

The thump of her tail came from Roy's room. Kalin found her on his bed, chewing one of his socks.

"Bad girl." Kalin rushed to the bed and shoved Chica to the floor. She tugged the ripped sock from Chica's jaws, and her breath caught in her throat.

Chica scrunched into the corner and wagged her tail. She couldn't remember the last time she'd yelled at her. She never yelled at her dog. Only, she was chewing something of Roy's. Kalin crouched and rested her palm on Chica's head. "I'm sorry."

Chica licked Kalin's nose. Unable to control herself, Kalin sobbed. She stroked Chica's back, and Chica nuzzled her neck. Even after Kalin had been a jerk, the dog loved her.

How many times had she wished Roy wasn't living with them, intruding on her new home with Ben? She'd taken him for granted. Kalin couldn't stand being in Roy's room. "Come on, let's go upstairs."

Her beloved dog followed, somehow knowing Kalin needed her. The hollowness of the house pressed in on her, and she crashed on the couch to wait for Ben.

A shout came from downstairs. "Kalin, it's Nora."

Nora, all of five-feet tall and carrying her son, burst into the room. Having a mind of its own, her short black hair stuck out at odd angles. And even after delivering a baby, she still weighed less than one hundred pounds. "I just heard. Why didn't you call me? I would've come sooner."

"I'm not thinking straight. So much happened today." Kalin reached for eight-month-old Ethan and hugged him. Born while trapped in the forest by a fire with a Grizzly bear pacing nearby, Ethan had been given the middle name of Forest.

Nora draped her jacket over the back of the couch. One leg of her cargo pants stuck inside a sock. She put her arms around Kalin and Ethan in a group hug. "Any news?"

Kalin felt like a giraffe standing so close to Nora. At five-foot-ten, she could rest her chin on the top of Nora's head. "Nothing. Did you hear about the theft, too?"

"The rumors are spreading. How could I not hear?"

Nora scampered to the kitchen and uncorked a bottle of white wine. "We need this."

Kalin accepted a glass and took a long sip. The cold liquid iced her throat. "What a mess."

"I hate to leave you right now, but Ian's got a World Cup race at Lake Placid. I'm heading there tomorrow."

Don't go. "What about Ethan?"

"Pete's taking him. And Susan will help out if he needs it."

Kalin smiled at Nora for calling her dad Pete. Nora had only known since last spring that he was her father and hadn't changed from calling him Pete to calling him Dad. Since she was already in her early twenties, maybe she'd always refer to him by his name. Ethan would be fine with his grandfather. Kalin just didn't want Nora to leave. She needed her best friend right now. "I'm sort of surprised he's still dating Susan."

"I'm glad actually. I didn't like her much at first, but she's Ian's mom, and Pete seems happy with her."

"How long will you be gone?" Kalin asked.

"I'm not sure. I'm going to Toronto on my way back. We should know about Janet's acquittal by then, and I want to be there for her. Either way."

Janet was Nora's birth mother and had spent eighteen years in prison for killing her own son. As it turned out, she might be innocent. Kalin hoped for Nora's sake she was and the acquittal came through.

The front door opened and closed. Chica bolted from the room. Ben's slow steps up the stairs didn't bode well. He turned the corner to their living room and faced Kalin and Nora.

He didn't need to say anything for Kalin to know he hadn't found Roy.

"I gotta go," Nora said. "I'll call you from Lake Placid." Nora lifted Ethan from Kalin's arms, squeezed Ben's shoulder as she passed him and trotted out of sight.

Kalin ran to Ben and buried herself against his chest.

CHAPTER SEVEN

On Tuesday morning, twenty-six hours after the avalanche, Kalin finished her video interview with the board of directors at White Peaks. She couldn't believe she'd remained composed.

She'd asked them not to do a reference check until she had time to talk with her boss. When they asked her if she'd told Turner, she avoided a direct answer. She said only that she wanted to follow process and formally ask him for a reference.

Would Turner be good enough to give her a recommendation? He wasn't known to support employees he perceived were going against him.

What was wrong with her? Her brother might be dead, and she was thinking about her career. She had faith Roy would be found. This was not the time to miss work. Her security manager was off the radar somewhere in Hawaii, so there was no getting him to come back early.

She arrived at the administration building just before ten a.m. and hustled to the finance center. Constable Miller and Paul Turner waited for her.

"Search and rescue will find Roy soon," Miller said.

Not trusting her voice, Kalin nodded her thanks. She had a good relationship with Miller, and kindness right now would only make her cry. She cleared her throat. "Where's your new partner?"

Miller glanced at Turner before answering Kalin. "Attending to other things."

"Still a man of mystery, I see. So, where are we?"

"An officer checked if the combination could be read through the windows. The safe's keypad can't be seen from any angle, with or without binoculars." Miller thumbed the latch on the window closest to the computer. "You might want to install higher quality locks."

Disgusted with herself for not instructing her team to secure the room properly, Kalin entered a reminder into her phone to talk with Fred as soon as he returned from Hawaii. She relied on him for day-to-day security operations, but his strength didn't lie in planning or improving existing processes. He needed direction, and his lack of strategic planning was one of the reasons she'd been promoted to director of security instead of him.

At least Turner hadn't been at the resort last winter when keys had been a serious issue. She didn't think he knew she'd been reprimanded by the previous president for not securing keys. She'd taken the blame for Fred and scored a few points with him.

"Did the thief enter through a window?" Kalin asked.

Miller turned away from the frosted pane and faced her. "We don't believe so. There aren't any marks in the snow, and without a ladder, a person couldn't climb to the window."

Even though on the same floor, the offices on the ski hill side of the building were at ground level, whereas the offices on the parking lot side were one level up. The shape of the building with the higher altitude wall built into the mountain meant employees often used the hallway as a shortcut from the parking lot to the mountain ops building, especially after a big dump of snow.

"Could the safe combination be read from the hallway?" Turner motioned to the door that reached halfway up the doorframe. Both halves were locked after office hours. The top half was designed to stay open during the day, allowing employees access to the cashier without needing to enter the room.

More than once, Kalin had seen staff chatting with Helen as she prepared daily floats. Roy often stopped to talk with her before his shift started. She seemed to make him happy. Kalin could hear his laugh echo off the walls and see him wink at Helen before he strutted along the hallway full of confidence. Why had Roy dated Jessica and not Helen?

She was hit with the awkward moment of realizing Miller and Turner were staring at her. "What?"

Turner curled his lip. "You moaned."

"Oh. Sorry. What were you saying?"

"I asked if the safe combination could be read from the doorway," Turner said.

Miller mimicked punching a keypad. "It's possible. Even if they couldn't see the entire pad, a person watching the cashier's fingers could memorize the order the keys were tapped. I'd like to interview everyone again to find out if anyone noticed someone hanging around the finance center in the mornings while Helen opens the safe. And speaking of Helen, is she around today?"

Turner circled Miller. "She won't be in until Friday. She asked for some personal time off. Why?"

Miller jutted his chin and slowly twisted, keeping his face toward Turner. "We haven't taken her fingerprints yet. Do you have her home contact information?"

"Kalin can give that to you." Turner cracked his knuckles. "Did you speak with the bank manager?"

"I did. No one from the bank called the resort on Saturday. The drop box wasn't broken," Miller said.

Kalin interrupted the male dance for power and asked, "So the call was just to get Helen to leave more money in the safe?"

"Looks that way."

"So it's irrelevant," Turner said. "Let's get back to the real point. Even if someone had the combination, they still needed a key. That limits the suspects to a small group."

"Not necessarily. In November, Jessica Scott requested a replacement key. Your locksmith's records show she lost hers and had a duplicate made."

Kalin stared at the useless deadbolt. What else had Miller found out about the inner workings of Stone Mountain? "Let me guess, she broke protocol and didn't have the locks changed."

Miller nodded.

Turner ignored him and spoke to Kalin. "How is it possible Jessica could have a new key made without you knowing?"

The resort's locksmith, Ted Brightman, was technically strong, but his thought process didn't include sharing. If she didn't ask him a specific question, he wouldn't provide additional information. "I only review the key list quarterly."

"Not the answer I was looking for."

* * *

Jessica pressed her back into the corner of her office as if that would keep her standing. Roy had spent the night on the mountain, and with the fierce cold and wind, her hope diminished.

"I have a few more questions," Constable Miller said.

Without moving from the wall, she kicked her office guest chair toward him and motioned for him to sit. She should've expected him to question her again. "Sure."

"How long have you been the finance center manager?"

Jessica raised her chin and looked down her nose at him. She knew the gesture accentuated her slim facial features. She'd chosen a red tailored sweater, with its low V-neck, and black jeans for the day. She'd even taken extra time to straighten her long hair. She needed a power look. Something that made her feel confident. "Since your girlfriend quit and moved to town."

Miller actually laughed. "Fair enough. What was your relationship with Roy McCann?"

Jessica's heart buzzed. If she'd been wearing her heart rate monitor she used while running, she bet the display would read one-hundred-forty beats per minute. She needed to sit and flopped into her chair. "He's my boyfriend. You're speaking in past tense. Has he been found?"

Miller shook his head. "I didn't mean anything by it. Search and rescue are still looking for him. How long have you been dating?"

Jessica forced herself to breathe slowly. Deep breath in. Count to four. Deep breath out. Roy was okay. He had to be. "Since the summer. Why are you asking about Roy?"

Miller rested his elbows on his knees and clasped his hands together. "Was Roy in any trouble that you know of?"

Nice try with the soft and personal voice. Miller had no right to ask about her private life, no matter how politely he spoke. Jessica flung her straightened hair away from her face, but she could tell the gesture was wasted on Miller. She pushed her chair backward, but the wheel caught on a piece of torn carpet and stopped her before she'd moved a foot from him. "I don't think so. I don't understand what you're getting at."

"Did you, at any time, give Roy the combination to the safe?"

When Aiden had come from running the lifts to tell her Roy was missing, he'd hinted he thought Roy stole the money, and now Miller was almost saying it outright. "I would never do that."

"What about by accident? Could you have written it down somewhere he might have seen it, or could he have overheard you talking to anyone?"

Outside, a group of ski patrol clomped in ski boots toward the lift. They were probably replacing some of the search and rescue team who'd already been on the mountain too long. The lack of urgency in their movements frightened her.

"Jessica?" Miller prompted.

"I'm careful with that information. Look, as the manager, I have to set a good example. My computer is the only place the combination is recorded, and Roy had no access. You should be talking to Helen."

"Why is that?"

"Ask her yourself. She might have something to say."

Miller sighed. "Did you give Roy a key to the finance center?"

"No."

"Why didn't you have the locks changed when you lost your key in November?"

"How do you know about that?"

Miller's gaze remained flat. No more soft eyes for her. "So I lost my key. That's not a crime."

"Maybe not, but according to Kalin, you ignored company policy regarding keys. Once a key is lost, the locks are supposed to be changed. I'm curious why you didn't do that. You said yourself, as the manager you have to set a good example."

"Turner has a reputation for firing people who make mistakes. He's been cutting costs since the fire in the lower village last spring. I didn't want to lose my job."

"Does the public have access to the finance center's direct number?"

Miller's change in direction threw her off balance. What did public mean? "The number is not on the Internet, but it is listed in the internal directory. Does that count as public?"

"How many people have access to that?"

"Including both seasonal and year-round employees, I'd guess somewhere around five hundred."

"Does anyone else report to you who might have access to the finance center?"

"No. Simon Crane is the night auditor, but I don't see him much at work. He's off duty by the time I get in."

"Where's his office?"

"In the lower village behind the front desk. He covers late night check-ins or guest issues until the front desk staff arrives for the morning shift. He uses a computer there to process the night audit."

"Are you friends outside of work?"

"We ski together once in a while. He's an awesome skier." A helicopter thundered past Jessica's window and flew toward the Dragon's Bowl. "Can I call and find out?"

Miller nodded.

"Ben, it's Jessica. I saw the helicopter. Did you find him?"

When she heard Ben's answer, she looked at the ceiling and blinked several times.

"Bad news?" Miller asked.

"No news. They're widening the search. I thought, maybe..." Jessica cleared her throat. "What were you asking?"

"What about Simon's wife? Does she ski with you?"

Right back on track. No sympathy for her. She reminded herself he was a cop and would investigate everyone even remotely close to the finance center. "No. Natalie's not athletic."

"That doesn't present a problem for him?"

"This is a ski resort. There's always someone around to ski with."

Miller wrote in his black notebook, flipped back a page and read something. "How long has Eric Wilson worked here as a finance clerk?"

"Since December first."

"Did you do a criminal record check on him?"

Shit. One more thing for Turner to reprimand her for. Maybe she could blame Kalin if this ended up being a problem. "Normally I would have, but he's Australian. He brought his own paperwork with him."

"Even though he's a junior clerk, I'm surprised you'd bring him on without doing your own check. Do you think he could be the thief?"

"I guess it's possible. I mean, it could be anybody, right?"

"Is he friends with Roy?"

Jessica had seen Eric talking to Roy on occasion, but she'd never seen them hang out. If only she could do something to help Roy now, instead of talking about whom he was friends with. "No."

"With you?"

"No." The back of Jessica's neck tightened, and if she didn't relax, another migraine would attack her. Miller's questions were heading in one direction. He was looking at more than one suspect. He was looking at her.

CHAPTER EIGHT

Thirty hours after the avalanche, Kalin kneeled on her office floor and stroked Chica's back. She rested the side of her face on Chica's silky belly and closed her eyes. The smell of Labrador combined with the dog's rhythmic breathing gave her some comfort.

When Jack died, he'd died instantly, making her a widow at twenty-seven. He was already lost to her when she buried his body. Thinking of Roy buried beneath mounds of frozen snow…Had he known he might die?

Ben and the search and rescue team were doing everything they could to find Roy. She tried not to think the worst but couldn't help herself. With the temperature so far below zero double digits registered on the display by her window, how could he possibly survive? Time to call her mom again with an update, even though she had nothing new to report.

The phone was in her hand when Constable Miller entered her office. Chica's tail thumped in welcome, but she stayed with Kalin. Miller shut the door, sat in the guest chair and seemed at a loss for words.

The crack between the window and the frame let in a wisp of cold air, and the space heater fought to counter the frigid temperature.

Miller rubbed his hands together as if he was cold. He cleared his throat, then said, "This is a bit awkward."

Kalin's office door opened, and Constable Wagner joined them. She remained standing and leaned back against the door.

If they'd found Roy, Ben would have told her. Kalin shoved herself off the floor, turned up the heater until the humming indicated the little machine couldn't fight much harder and took a seat in front of her desk. Her legs bounced, and she put her hands on her knees to stop the tremors. The motion made her appear nervous, but she couldn't seem to keep her legs still lately. Chica lumbered off the floor and placed her jowls on Kalin's lap. Kalin caressed her head in a silent thank you for the support.

"The timing of the theft and Roy's disappearance is a big coincidence," Miller said.

"And I know, you don't like coincidences."

"Don't joke. I'm serious."

Heat rose in Kalin's face as her anger arrived. "You think Roy took the money?"

"You have to admit, it looks suspicious. He hasn't been found. He could have triggered the avalanche to make us think he died."

Kalin closed her eyes and rubbed her palm on her forehead. "You can't be serious. He wouldn't do that to me or my mom."

"I am serious. We need to talk about the possibility."

"This is bull. Search and rescue are still looking for him. I have to believe he'll be found alive." But after Miller sowed the seed of doubt, the idea blossomed into a possibility. Would one hundred thousand be enough to tempt Roy to disappear?

"Is there anything you can think of that might be important?"

"As in, did Roy do or say anything to indicate he was going to steal from the resort? I can't talk about this." Kalin stood.

"I know this is hard, but I have to do my job."

Kalin knew Miller well. He looked at all possible suspects before narrowing the list. He couldn't ignore Roy to avoid hurting her feelings, so she settled back in her seat. Besides, Constable Wagner blocked the exit with her bulky frame.

If her choices were to believe Roy stole the money and took off, Roy stole the money and died trying to escape, or Roy was caught in an avalanche by accident, she'd choose the option of innocence. "Roy didn't take the money. I'll prove it to you."

Miller groaned. "Not again. You have to stay out of our investigations. Especially this one. You're too close."

"I'm also the director of security, and I'm not going to let my brother be blamed for something he didn't do."

"Where were you on the morning of the theft?"

"I was at home with Ben."

"Roy is living with you? Is that correct?"

At least Miller used the present tense. She wasn't ready to talk about Roy in the past tense. "He is."

Kalin's thoughts drifted to the day Roy moved in.

* * *

Twelve days before Roy disappeared, Kalin opened the front door of her new home and found him standing on her porch with a please-don't-be-mad-at-me grin. His backpack, a suitcase and a duffle bag rested on top of the snowbank beside the walkway.

"Hey."

"Hey." Kalin returned his grin with her I-know-you-want-something smile. They'd played the smile game since they were children. Without speaking, the shape of the lips told the other what was going on in the mind.

Roy tilted his head down and lifted his eyes. His one brown eye, one green eye mirrored Kalin's. "Can I come in?"

He really did want something if he was flashing his eyes at her.

"Sure." Kalin opened the door wider, and her brother stepped into the foyer. The heating underneath the slate tiles kept her sock-covered feet warm, and she was glad they'd spent the extra money on the upgrade. She didn't miss his one-dimple smile, the one he used when he wanted to manipulate her, the one that matched hers. People often asked if they were twins, but Roy was her baby brother by two years. Sometimes she had a hard time thinking of him as a six-foot tall, independent man.

Roy plunked his suitcase, duffle bag and backpack on the floor, and snow melted into puddles. Kalin fought her desire to get a mop. The water wouldn't stain the new tiles.

She heard the thump of Chica jumping off the king bed in the loft two stories up and her paws plodding down the stairs. The yellow Labrador liked her sleep, but as soon as she saw Roy, excitement got the better of her, and she jumped on him. Her paws rested on his chest, and she licked his face. Roy laughed and didn't discourage her behavior. With muscled arms, he rubbed Chica's back.

"Chica, down."

"She's not bothering me." Roy removed his toque, and his dark-brown hair curled at the base of his neck. Kalin had the same hair color, but she wore hers shoulder length and curled under instead of outward. His always seemed to be a mess.

Before sitting, Roy ran his hands over the mountain peaks carved into the top of the wooden bench that filled the foyer.

"You did beautiful work," Kalin said. "Why did you stop?"

Roy avoided her gaze by leaning forward and untying his boots. "Lost interest."

She shook off the irritation his short answer caused and reminded herself how long she'd been trying to make amends with him. "Come on up. Want some coffee?"

"Sure. What should I do with my things?"

"You can leave them there." Kalin nudged Chica to the staircase leading to the main floor but stopped when her foot landed on the first step. Roy slung his duffle bag over his shoulder and trod along the hallway away from her. "Where are you going?"

He canted his head in the direction of the guest room on the ground floor. "I'll just put my bags in the spare room."

Here it comes. "Why?"

"My landlord says he needs his place for the winter. So I've got nowhere to go."

"Did you get evicted?"

"Nice."

"I need to talk to Ben first."

"So call him."

"I can't. He's in the backcountry."

"Don't worry so much. He won't mind. Anyway, it's just until I find a place."

"At this time of year, you're going to have a hard time." Kalin's human resources team managed staff housing, and locating a room right when the ski hill opened to the public was harder than Roy imagined. The seasonal staff who didn't get a room in staff housing had already filled most of the privately rented units. She loved her brother, but he was difficult. "Did you try to find somewhere?"

Roy ignored her question and continued walking along the hallway. "Really, Ben won't mind. He's cool."

"It's still polite to ask. This is his home, too." Why didn't Roy move in with Jessica? He'd been dating her almost since the day he arrived at Stone Mountain, but the last time Kalin interfered with one of his relationships hadn't worked out well, so she'd keep her question to herself.

Before Roy moved west, she hadn't spoken to him in two years. Roy showing up at her wedding last June gave them a chance to repair their relationship. His decision to stay must have meant he'd forgiven Kalin.

* * *

"What time did Roy leave the house?" Miller asked, interrupting Kalin's memory of him.

Kalin stood and faced her office window. She placed her fingertips on the pane and held them there, letting the cold burn her skin. "I'm not sure. He was gone when I got up."

"Are any of his things missing?"

"Like what?"

"Like his wallet, or clothes or anything that might indicate he wasn't coming back."

Kalin rested her forehead on the window, letting the cold numb the pain in her eyes. "I haven't gone through his stuff."

Miller asked a few more meaningless questions, then departed with his silent partner. Had the woman joined the interrogation because Miller and Kalin were tight? Maybe he wasn't trusted with Kalin.

Her cell rang. Charlotte Summers from *The Holden Press*.

They'd met when Charlotte interviewed her about being the new human resources manager for Stone Mountain. Kalin had relocated from Ottawa, and Charlotte had been writing a series of articles about professional women moving to the area to work. Charlotte had also helped her investigate some locals Kalin had suspected were involved in the arson case at Stone Mountain the previous spring.

She hit the speaker phone icon. "Hi."

"You sound miserable," Charlotte said.

"You can tell that from one word? I guess you heard."

"I did."

"Is this an official call?"

"No. Of course not. Is there anything I can do?"

"Find out who stole the money."

"Is the theft public knowledge?"

"It's not." Kalin leaned forward and rested her head in her hands. She'd let her guard down and leaked to the media, but at least she'd leaked to Charlotte instead of a reporter she wasn't friends with. "I assumed that's why you were calling."

"No, I was calling to see how you are. I heard about Roy and the avalanche. Any news?"

"Not yet, but a day and a half is too long for him to be missing." Kalin took a deep breath. More bad weather loomed over one of the peaks to the west, straining to reach Stone Mountain as if determined to dump more snow on Roy. "Ben's doing his best, but SAR hasn't found any trace of him. They only found some of his gear."

"I'm so sorry. I wish I could help you."

The wind preceding the storm rattled the windowpane. “You can. Please forget I said anything about money.”

CHAPTER NINE

"Man, I hope that was the right thing to do," Ben said. The end of the second day searching and no luck. He'd stopped the search at dusk, debriefed the team and sent them home for food and rest. Nobody could survive thirty-six hours under the snow.

"The team won't find Roy in the dark," Oliver said.

Still hot from exertion, Ben reached around Oliver and opened the window. The cloud cover ensured no moonlight penetrated to the mountain, but he heard the trees bending to the wind's will. The incoming storm terrified him.

Ben trusted Oliver's knowledge of the mountain, the weather and the snow conditions. He'd been an avalanche forecaster at White Peaks before working at Stone Mountain, and Ben almost asked him if he'd liked living in White Peaks but remained silent. Gossip spread like a virus in the small resort.

The radar weather map showed the incoming weather. Oliver leaned back in his chair, and the smooth material of his ski pants slid on the plastic surface. He removed his toque, and sweat plastered his curly hair to his scalp. Taller than Ben by six inches, he gave the impression he looked down his nose at Ben when he spoke. "What a mess."

Ben compensated for his stature by spending hours in the gym, and his bulk countered Oliver's height. He had no issues being short, but that didn't mean he had to be small. He leaned forward and pointed at the screen. "That doesn't look good."

"Nope."

Ben studied the weather.

"How's Kalin doing?"

"The timing couldn't be worse. She should be focusing on the theft, but she's having a hard time concentrating. And I don't think it helps I'm in charge of the recovery mission."

"So you don't think it's search and rescue anymore?" Oliver asked.

"It can't be. I haven't told Kalin yet, but I want her to at least have some kind of closure. If we don't find his body, she won't even have that."

"You know every inch of snow we get makes this harder."

Ben examined the screen, looking for any hint the weather wouldn't get out of control. Roy had shown up for their wedding in June and decided to stay. Kalin worked hard at rebuilding her relationship with him, but Roy resisted her efforts. He said he came to Stone Mountain to repair his relationship with her, and he tried at first, but then spent more time drinking with his buddies than hanging with Kalin. He'd bring her in close, then push her away. Ben suspected Roy had some hidden motive for moving to Stone Mountain but had never figured out what it was.

"I've been thinking about the second person seen trekking up the hill," Ben said.

"The guy must have been mistaken. No one's been reported missing."

"What if it's someone we didn't know was around?"

"You'd think if anyone went up there and didn't come back, there'd be a person who'd come asking. And don't you think two unrelated people going up the mountain is unlikely?"

"I guess for now we can assume Roy was the only person up there."

Oliver twisted his chair away from the computer and toward Ben. "If the weather gets too rough, we have to think of safety first."

How could Ben go home and look Kalin in her eyes? Tell her the bad news? "I hear you."

"It's your call."

Of all the decisions to make, why was this one his? "We'll wait until morning. Maybe the weather forecast is wrong."

* * *

Fifty hours after the avalanche, Ben slowed his steps as he neared Kalin's office. Wednesday morning hadn't brought better weather. The storm had pounded Stone Mountain overnight and continued through dawn, giving no indication of waning.

The night before, he'd talked with Kalin for hours, debating whether or not to continue the search. She'd tucked in their bed and slid as far to the opposite side as she could without falling off. Ben suspected she'd faked sleeping just to stop talking about the weather and Roy.

Making Kalin understand his rationale topped his priority list. Knowing her the way he did, she might use the failed search as an excuse to take the new job. She'd already suggested living part time in White Peaks and part time in Stone Mountain. What if she actually made the move?

He could see her convincing herself that working there five days a week and spending two days at Stone Mountain would be okay. Five days would extend to six, then seven as she got busy. She'd take her job seriously. She couldn't stay out of the office here, so what made her think she could there?

Now he was about to motivate her to take the job at White Peaks. He reached her closed office door. Maybe she was in a meeting with someone, and he could postpone seeing her.

Ben put his hand on the doorknob but didn't turn it. Once that happened, their relationship would change forever. The poster taped to the outside of her door contained a message for employees to choose their attitude. Stuff about being present and enjoying the workday. Smiling faces of people working in a ski resort stared at him. He needed to choose his attitude and face the situation.

"You don't want to go in there?" Turner asked.

Ben hadn't heard his footsteps cross the carpet and tried not to react. His hand stayed on the doorknob. "Not really."

"I understand. Do you want me to talk to her?"

Turner's offer surprised Ben. He could be harsh, and Ben hadn't expected compassion from him. "Thanks, but no. I have to do this."

"I'll call Kalin's mother. Kalin shouldn't have to inform her."

"I appreciate that."

Turner nodded and left Ben to talk to Kalin.

His phone rang. He could've ignored the call, but answering would delay telling Kalin. "Timlin."

"Have you told her yet?" Oliver asked.

Ben picked at the tape holding the bottom corner of the poster to the particleboard door. "No. I'm outside her office now."

"Turner was just here."

"And?"

Oliver hesitated. "So you haven't talked to Kalin?"

Ben figured Oliver had something to say about her, but she was an odd subject for him to talk about. Kalin collected drama like other women collected shoes. Even when she tried to stay away from issues, they found her. "What's going on?"

"Nothing. Speak to Kalin, then come see me. We should talk in person."

Ben opened Kalin's office door and didn't find her. The smell of wet dog reached him, and Chica thumped her tail against the carpet. She lay hidden underneath Kalin's desk. He crouched and rubbed her belly.

Pinned to the undersurface of one of the shelves lining the wall above the desk, a picture of Jack smiled at him. He hadn't known she still kept her first husband's photo. He'd been hurt when Kalin hadn't changed her last name to Timlin but understood she needed a link to Jack. How could he be jealous of a dead man? If he could've kicked himself, he would've.

He needed to find Kalin, then Jessica.

* * *

Jessica stepped out of the women's washroom and found Turner blocking her exit. She had the urge to check her fly but stopped herself in time by wiping her hands on her jeans. Had he followed her? What kind of man corners a woman outside the bathroom?

The sleeves of Turner's white dress shirt were rolled above his elbows, and his muscular forearms bulged under the pressure of his clenched fists. "What the hell do you think you're doing?"

Her snide answer was, "Peeing," but she refrained. "I'm headed to my office."

"That's not what I meant, and you know it. The polygraph is an important part of the investigation. Why did you persuade your team not to take it? You're the manager. I need you to lead by example."

The toilet in the men's room flushed.

Her direct boss hadn't gotten involved or even spoken to her since the theft. A finance guy who liked to deal with numbers more than people. His mild manner often drew him away from conflict, and she suspected he was distancing himself from her. She'd do the same in his place. She wasn't going to let Turner intimidate her, so she spoke politely but with authority. "I'm sorry. It's been a tough week. I haven't been thinking clearly."

"Right. Then you'll take the test. Talk to your team, and they'll follow your lead. I'll call the RCMP and get times set up."

Jessica glanced at the door to the men's room, waiting to see who would come out, but when no one did, she said, "I'm not doing a polygraph test, and I'm not asking the others to do one either. It's an invasion of our privacy."

How could Turner hassle her instead of asking her if she was okay? He knew she dated Roy, and yet he only cared about the money. He should be offering to give her time off and asking if she needed counseling. He shouldn't be pressuring her about a stupid polygraph test.

Turner stepped toward Jessica.

She backed up until her shoulder blades were pressed against the door. Her eyes were level with his Adam's apple, and she arched her back to look him in the face. Maybe she should invite him inside the ladies' room, or maybe she should just step back through the door. She didn't think he'd follow. Even though she'd just come out of there, her bladder demanded another visit.

"It's not an invasion of privacy. It's a criminal investigation. They're not going to ask you about your private life. They'll only ask questions relevant to the theft."

Jessica glanced along the narrow hallway. At one end sat the offices of the administration staff, at the other the stairs to the ground floor. "That's not true. They've already asked me about my relationship with Roy." Jessica waited, and when he didn't answer, she shook her head. "I can't help you with this."

"Then you should know you're making a career-limiting decision."

Turner's breath caressed her cheek in an intimate way. The odor of mint, of gum used to hide a drink, filled her nasal cavities. She shivered.

Kalin approached from the end of the hallway.

Jessica almost smiled at Kalin's curled lip. Whatever emotion she felt accentuated the color difference in her eyes, and the green one pulsed emerald. Turner hadn't been whispering, and Kalin probably overheard his threat.

"Interesting place to have a meeting," Kalin said to Turner.

In his mid-forties, Turner had maintained the physique of a long-distance runner, and he looked like a runner ready to bolt. He growled and stomped toward his office.

One point to human resources, Jessica thought.

CHAPTER TEN

Ben stopped at the edge of the guest services counter. Typical of Kalin to pitch in and help others. Twenty-some skiers formed a line in front of the desk. All four tills were open and operating. Kalin worked behind a register, handing out refunds due to the closed lifts. The smile on her face hid any anxiety or sadness she must be feeling.

Behind her, three large windows faced the hill. The wind blew the snow sideways, and the snow cut visibility to three meters. A screen of snowflakes hid the ski lifts, and Ben had the feeling even though Kalin tapped icons on the till and handed out refunds, she was lost in a blur of thoughts.

He stepped behind the guest services desk and nudged Kalin on the shoulder. "Can we talk?"

She turned, and the look of expectation on her face crushed his heart. He held his toque in one hand, shifted it to the other and couldn't say the words.

"You found him."

She'd made a statement, not asked a question. Ben slowly shook his head.

"Then what? You look frightened."

The next skier in line slapped his ticket on the desk along with his credit card. "Any idea when the lifts will open again?"

"Not today, I'm afraid."

"But the conditions must be awesome."

Kalin processed the refund as she spoke. "I'm sure they are. The wind makes running the lifts dangerous. We need the weather to settle down." She handed the guest his credit card. "Thanks for understanding."

Ben took a step toward her, and she grabbed the edge of the counter as if bad news might knock her over.

"The wind hit forty kilometers per hour and has been holding steady for the last couple of hours," Ben said.

"I know that."

The space behind the till seemed to contract to the size of a gondola built for two.

Kalin waved the next guest forward. "I can't worry about that now."

Ben leaned close to her ear, speaking so only she could hear. "Since six this morning, another twenty centimeters of snow fell, and the dump's expected to continue through tomorrow."

Kalin's chest expanded and contracted in rapid succession. She stared at him without blinking.

Ben had treated people who died while he performed CPR, he told a man who was paralyzed that he would be okay, but this, this was ten times worse. He was about to crush Kalin.

"You know I have to consider the safety of the search and rescue team in every decision I make. I can't risk anyone else getting hurt."

Kalin clenched her fists at her sides and stood motionless enough to be an ice sculpture. Frost had formed around the edges of the window, doing its best to block out the view, and Ben wished it would block out the way she looked at him.

Unclenching her fists, she opened the till to get cash for the snowboarder who stood in front of her. "Thanks for your patience." She missed the woman's hand and several coins clanged onto the counter. "Sorry."

"The risk of another avalanche in the Dragon's Bowl is high." Ben took two deep breaths, cleared his throat and said, "I've called off the search."

Silence greeted him. He expected Kalin to say something. Her face drained of color, and he thought she might faint. He raised his arm to hug her.

"Don't touch me."

"Kalin, I had no choice."

"What did Oliver say?"

Ben could tell Kalin the decision had been his boss's. Or Turner had forced the issue. Anything would be better than admitting he'd been the one, but he couldn't lie to her. "He agreed with me."

"Did you have to convince him?"

"No one on the team wants to stop, but everyone knows we have to."

After processing one more skier, Kalin turned to the guest services supervisor standing beside her. "I need to close the till. Can you handle things?"

Without waiting for an answer, Kalin stepped away from the desk, pulling Ben with her. "I'm calling Mom. And you should go tell Jessica." She dialed, and the call switched to voicemail. Kalin hung up without leaving a message. "She must be on the phone."

"Turner is probably talking to her now."

"I need to go." Kalin put her palms flat on Ben's chest and shoved.

* * *

After getting bad news from Oliver about the weather, seeing Ben look miserable, speaking with Jessica and having Kalin almost reprimand him, Turner stared at his office phone, dreading the call he was about to make.

Phoning Roy McCann's mother and saying her son was missing was one thing. Telling her the rescue team had shut down the search, that her son was probably dead, was another matter entirely. He could have asked Kalin to tell her mother, but he wouldn't shirk responsibility.

He'd been caught off guard by Kalin and forgotten to talk to Jessica about the lost key. That discussion would have to wait. And Kalin. What the hell was he going to do about her?

He knew how his wife would react to the upcoming call, and it would be horrific. Crystal took the slightest negative comment a doctor made about their son as a personal attack. He couldn't count the hours he'd spent consoling her after a difficult discussion with one of Warren's doctors. Warren's condition hurt him, too, but Crystal's needs came first, and the emotional demands exhausted him.

Turner completed a few unrelated calls, asked his assistant if anything needed his attention, and when he couldn't procrastinate any further, he picked up the phone. Still, he sat, contemplating the words he would use.

Constable Miller hadn't stated it outright, but Turner thought the police suspected Roy of stealing the finance center money. Once the weather cleared, Turner would order the team to resume the search. They might find the missing money or at least Roy's body, but he would tell Mrs. McCann none of this.

He took a deep breath and dialed. "This is Paul Turner calling from Stone Mountain."

"We've been waiting for your call. You've found him. I knew he would be okay."

Even though he couldn't see her face, he could hear the desperation in her voice. "I'm sorry. We haven't found him."

"Then why are you calling?"

Turner clutched the edges of his cell, stretching the skin over his knuckles, making the bones protrude. "I need to inform you I called off the search this morning. There is a treacherous storm, and it's too dangerous for the rescue team to be out in the current weather. The risk of another avalanche is high."

"You still don't know the avalanche buried Roy. What does Kalin say?"

"I'll talk with her."

"You didn't include her in the decision?"

"She's not part of the search and rescue team."

"What about Ben?"

"Ben and his boss made the recommendation. I agreed with the assessment."

"I don't believe you. Ben wouldn't do that. Roy is still alive."

"The temperature has been well below zero since the avalanche, and two and a half days is a long time to be out there."

"I don't care what the weather is. Roy's strong. He cycles, he kayaks, he skis. He's in good shape. He'll have set himself up on the mountain. Made a snow cave to protect himself. You can't call off the search. Roy is still alive. He's waiting for you."

"I'm very sorry. Once the weather improves, I'll instruct the team to resume the search, but I think you need to prepare yourself for the worst."

"You don't know Roy."

"I am sorry, Mrs. McCann. There is nothing more we can do right now. This is a tragedy, but I need to stress that Roy entered a closed area. The signage was explicit, and the run was roped off. I can't put the rescue team in any more danger. I will call you when I have any further information, and please call me if you want to talk or check on the status. I'm here to help you."

"I don't need your help. My son does."

Oh hell, what else was he supposed to do? Roy was almost certainly dead, and he needed to focus on the theft. The stolen money would lower his bonus, and he could not afford the loss of income. He had his son to care for.

The bills grew monthly. Every time they drove to Calgary for treatment, the extra costs for hotels, food and gas were not covered by insurance. Soon they'd have to move to an urban area. As Warren's disease progressed, they'd need to be near a multidisciplinary treatment center. Until now, he'd appreciated having a stay-at-home wife to care for Warren. Until now, they hadn't needed the money.

Cystic fibrosis had been unknown to him. He hadn't understood the disease when the doctors diagnosed his son. Now he knew Warren would have a difficult and short life. Telling Crystal his bonus might be in jeopardy could push her over the edge.

He opened the bottom drawer of his desk and slipped a flask from behind a file. He unscrewed the cap and sucked back a long swig. The liquor burned his throat but eased the stress.

"Mr. Turner?"

He slipped the bottle back behind the file and retrieved a piece of gum from his top drawer. Where the hell was his assistant? She was supposed to block people from randomly entering his office.

He turned toward his door and found a woman who wore her hair waist length and tied in a single braid resting on the front of her shoulder. She looked eighteen, but Turner had the feeling she was in her mid-twenties. Her brown eyes opened wide. Had she seen the bottle? "Yes."

"Charlotte Summers." She reached forward to shake his hand, and without thinking he extended his. "*The Holden Press*."

He let go of her hand as if she'd covered her palm with poison. "I'm busy right now. I don't remember setting an appointment with you."

"I was up at the resort and was hoping to get a few minutes of your time."

"We've already made a statement about the avalanche."

"I was wondering if you could confirm the amount of money stolen."

"How do you know about the theft? We haven't released any details."

Charlotte shrugged. "Word travels quickly in our small town."

Wrong answer. He'd find out who leaked to the local newspaper and fire that person. "I've no comment."

"Are the theft and the avalanche related?"

"Why would you ask that?"

"I can't be the only one thinking—"

"The theft is confidential at this point. Search and Rescue are doing their best to find Roy McCann. Now, if you'll excuse me, I've a meeting to attend."

CHAPTER ELEVEN

Kalin grabbed her ski jacket and exploded through the outer doors of the guest services building.

"Wait," Ben yelled.

Talking to him was not an option. She needed to move. To get far away from him. Her breath snagged in her throat, and she gagged. She ran toward the mountain operations shack, heading for a snowmobile. The wind drowned the sound of Ben's voice.

Just outside the shack, a snowmobile sat unattended with the key in the ignition. Through blinding snow, Ben's silhouette ran toward her. She didn't care.

One turn of the key, and the engine ignited. She twisted the throttle, jerked forward and aimed toward the Dragon's Bowl. At the high speed, snow stung her eyes. The sharp pain felt good. A distraction from agony.

She reached the edge of the cat track that wound to the summit and turned north. Roy was waiting for her, and she was going to find him. She couldn't leave him buried.

Without a helmet and gloves, her skin froze.

The trail ahead turned sharply to the left, and she hit the curve too fast. The rear of the snowmobile slid sideways and hit a tree. The machine reverberated but kept moving.

She throttled up, leaned forward over the windscreen and squished her knees against the cold leather seat. Bouncing and sliding to a higher altitude, closer to Roy with every second, she ignored the danger.

The snowmobile flew over a mound of snow, landed hard and her chin hit the top of the windshield. Blood splattered on the screen. She wiped her chin and kept going.

How could Ben leave Roy buried on the frozen terrain? Didn't he care about her?

Frantic to get to Roy, she increased speed. Her safety meant nothing if she could reach him.

Almost blinded by the wind and snow, she lost track of the path. Both lengths of the snowmobile's skis detached from the ground, and she was airborne. The snowmobile landed with a thud in deep snow. Kalin launched over the windshield and slammed onto her back.

Like an overturned turtle, she couldn't get up. Everywhere she pushed, she sank deeper. She thrust her head from side to side, gulping air. She was going to be buried just like Roy. The snow would cover her, too. She screamed.

A ghost appeared over her. Death had arrived to claim her.

"Grab my hand."

"Get away from me!"

"Kalin, it's Ben. Let me help you."

With frozen fingers, she wiped the snow off her eyes. The madness settled, and she reached for Ben.

He pulled her forward, and she leaned into his chest. She closed her eyes and sobbed. "This can't be true."

Ben put his gloved hand under her chin and lifted her face. She winced and shoved his hand away.

"I need to check your face."

"Don't touch me," she said but pulled him tighter.

"Please, just let me see how badly you're hurt."

Kalin shook her head. "I need to find Roy."

Ben tightened his hold on her and put his lips to her ear. "I'm sorry. You can't imagine how sorry."

"Then why did you call off the search?"

"When you have time to think, you'll understand. It's too dangerous for the others. And we can't help Roy now."

"Yes, you can."

"You know he's gone. If I thought there was even a small chance he was alive, I wouldn't quit."

Within seconds of snow gathering on their clothes, the wind whipped the flakes away. Ben released Kalin and held both of her hands. She let him lead her to his snowmobile.

"I'll come back for yours later."

Kalin mounted the sled behind him, put her arms around his waist, tucked her hands into his pockets and rested her head on his back.

* * *

Four gurneys filled half of the ski patrol clinic, each separated from the other by a beige curtain. The other half of the floor contained Ben's office and a sanitary cleaning station. A cupboard of medical supplies covered one wall, and windows facing the ski hill provided the view. A slight odor of disinfectant lingered.

Cotton pads covered with Kalin's blood littered one gurney. She'd let Ben clean the wound and had agreed to have one of the patrollers drive her to the hospital. By the amount of blood, Ben figured she needed stitches.

He unlocked the door, the door to the first office of his career. The hub of ski patrol functioned from there. And he'd been useless. His beautiful wife almost killed herself because he bumbled the way he told her the news. He was such a jerk.

The outer door opened, and he listened to approaching footsteps.

Oliver appeared. "Let's go into your office."

Ben stepped backward, closed the door behind his boss and sagged into his chair.

Oliver remained standing, played with his ear without a lobe and stared out the window. "What happened?"

Ben related the story, including the crashed snowmobile.

"Do you want to go to town?" Oliver asked.

"Kalin wanted me to stay here in case the weather changes and we can restart the search."

"Not likely. I can't believe the weather."

"Then you think I made the right call?" Ben only second-guessed his decision to call off the search because Kalin reacted so badly.

"I think the weather's getting worse. There was no other choice."

Ben tapped his monitor and the computer came alive. The current weather report appeared on the screen. "I know. I guess."

"We've known each other a long time."

"Is something wrong?" Ben asked.

"I'm going to tell you something I've said I wouldn't."

The message must be bad, or Oliver wouldn't be hesitating. "Okay."

"I need to ask you not to tell Kalin."

"That's hard to promise when I don't know what you're going to say."

"I know, but…Well, Kalin can be headstrong, and I don't want her telling Turner about this. I'm making a choice I shouldn't."

Ben examined his fingernails. If he promised Oliver he wouldn't say anything, then he'd stick to his word. They'd been through many difficult situations over the last eight years together, and clearly Oliver trusted him. He didn't want to have a secret from Kalin, especially now with their strained relationship, but Oliver thought he needed to know whatever this was. "Will I be disloyal to Kalin if I don't tell her?"

"I don't think so."

"I'll keep it to myself then."

"Turner came to see me. He thinks Roy is the finance center thief."

"Crap."

"He thinks Kalin might be involved, too."

"You can't be serious."

"I think *he* was."

"Kalin would never risk her job here." The instant he said the words, White Peaks came to mind. In Turner's eyes, Kalin thinking of leaving her job would make her look guilty.

"That's why I thought you should know."

"Why would Turner tell you? I don't get it."

"Because you're married to her, and he wants me to keep an eye on you."

"He thinks I'm involved?"

"He didn't say that, but he doesn't want you searching the mountain alone."

"This sucks."

"He wants me to report anything you tell me about Kalin or Roy that might be related to the theft. Even though Kalin is the head of security, he doesn't want her investigating."

"Thanks for letting me know."

"What are you going to do?"

"Try to persuade her not to investigate." Ben turned back to the image on the screen. The reports showed the wind getting stronger overnight.

CHAPTER TWELVE

In answer to the bell, Jessica shoved open her front door with her hip, pushing against the wind that threatened to shove her back into her suite. Snow whipped across her driveway, blocking out her view of the road.

All she'd wanted was a bit of sleep, but she couldn't even have that.

"I saw something on the night of the theft," Aiden Price said.

Aiden huddled on Jessica's front porch with his arms crossed tightly over his chest, and cold air blasted past him into her hall. Somehow he appeared insignificant wearing personal clothes. His lift manager uniform gave him credibility, and Jessica suspected that was part of the reason he often wore the getup, even when he wasn't on duty.

"Turner called off the search, and the money's still out there," he said.

"You mean Ben called it off. How could he do that to his brother-in-law?" Jessica leaned on her open front door with a quilt hanging over her shoulders and squinted against the raw weather. Her frustration at Turner for cornering her outside the washroom had grown from anger to fury. Finally, exhaustion had wrapped around her like a sleeping bag with a stuck zipper, and she hadn't been able to summon the energy to go to bed. Instead, she'd camped out on her lumpy couch and fallen asleep. "I'm tired. Do we really need to do this now?"

"Don't you want to know what I saw the morning the money was stolen?"

"Fine. Come in." Jessica stepped out of the way. Her skis and poles hung on the wall rack to the right. Her helmet, goggles and gloves covered the entrance side table. Gear she would never use with Roy again.

Aiden knocked snow off his gloves and stamped his feet before stepping across the threshold. He pulled the door closed, shutting out the howling wind.

Jessica's cell chimed, and she answered on the first ring. "Hey."

"Nice meeting you had with Turner today," Simon said.

Without moving the cell away from her ear, Jessica clicked the volume button on the side of her phone to low. "What do you mean?"

"I was in the can. I heard every word."

Aiden raised his eyebrows and gestured with his hands for Jessica to hurry up.

"I can't talk right now," she said.

"Do you know if I'll be asked to do a polygraph?"

"No, and I don't care."

"If Turner fires you, can I have your job?"

As if Simon could jump from night auditor to finance center manager. "I can't believe you called me for that. I gotta go." Jessica tapped the end call icon and tucked the phone in her back pocket. "What's so important it can't wait?"

"The day of the avalanche, I saw Roy near the admin building around five in the morning, carrying a duffle bag and his backpack."

Jessica rolled her eyes. "Really." She leaned casually against the wall, blocking him from going further into her ground-floor suite. "What were you doing there?"

"I was on my way home from a party, but that's not the point. I've been thinking a lot about Roy. I think he stole the money."

"You and the cops. How could he? He had no access to the finance center or the safe."

"He could with your help."

Jessica clenched her fists at her sides. Didn't she have one friend left? One person who cared about what she was going through? Instead of being a friend, Aiden was hassling her about the money. "That's bullshit."

"I'm just sayin' ski patrol found part of his backpack, but no one's mentioned the duffle bag yet. So where's the money?"

"You think I have it?"

"Yeah. Remember the night I called you when you were in the finance center after hours?"

Jessica had been so angry with Roy and Helen after following him to her place. How dare he go to her in the middle of the night? Jessica had snuck into the finance center after hours, looking for ways to find fault with Helen's work and maybe give her a helping hand at getting fired. She'd used a flashlight instead of turning on the lights, and Aiden had seen the flickering beam from his office in the mountain ops building.

Aiden brought Jessica back to the present by shaking her shoulder. "Are you going to answer me or just stand there staring off into space? I said, I've been thinking about the night you were in the finance center after hours."

"What about it?"

"I think you were preparing for the theft."

"I think you're an idiot."

"I'm not an idiot. Why were you searching the center with a flashlight?"

"I told you the light was burnt out, and I needed a file."

"Sure it was. If you don't have the money, then who does?"

Jessica pressed her hand onto his chest and pushed him backward. An idea was forming, and she needed time to think. "I want you to go."

He leaned forward until their noses were almost touching. "If you don't want me to tell the cops what I know, I want in on the money."

Jessica shoved hard, and Aiden stepped backward. "Get out."

* * *

The following morning, four days after the horrid avalanche, Jessica entered Turner's reception area. His assistant, Gertrude Anderson, barely glanced at her. The fluorescent lights were too bright for the early hour and gave a bluish tint to Gertrude's skin.

"You can sit there." Gertrude nodded at the chair nearest Turner's office door.

Jessica waited, watching Gertrude hunch over her keyboard, resisting the urge to wave away the scent of her noxious perfume. How could this woman represent the president's office with her fifties hairstyle, her frumpy clothes, and the constant frown she'd perfected? She didn't exactly have the youthful, energetic image the marketing department tried to promote for the resort. If Jessica were the president, she'd hire a different assistant.

Making her wait after asking her to come in at seven in the morning was a nasty move. Twenty minutes passed, and Jessica broke the silence. "Any idea what he wants to see me about?"

While her fingers moved furiously across the keyboard, Gertrude shook her head.

Jessica waited another ten minutes, tapping her fingernails on the armrest and watching the clock round the bottom of the circle past seven thirty. Turner had never kept her waiting for so long before. He prided himself on being efficient and not wasting time, his or anyone else's. When he finally opened the door, her bottom remained epoxied to the chair.

"Come in." Turner walked to the table in the center of his office, placed a white, eight-and-a-half-by-eleven envelope on the surface and waited for her to follow.

She released her grip from the armrest and dragged her feet into his office.

"I'm disappointed in you."

Disappointment she could take.

"I understand how upsetting it is to lose a good friend and how that might cloud your judgment."

Jessica relaxed her shoulders, and the tension in her back subsided.

"Because you're the finance center manager, I'm holding you responsible for the theft."

She opened her mouth to protest, but Turner held up his hand.

"I'm not saying you stole the money. I'm saying you didn't have the right processes in place to prevent a theft. You left the combination to the safe the same for a month. You lost your key and didn't have the lock changed. You can't ignore company policy and expect no repercussions."

"I've updated the training manual, and I'm going to put the clerks through a new course on the process." As long as Turner didn't check the truth in her statement, and if she still had a job at the end of the meeting, she could churn out a new manual in an evening.

"That's great, and I'm sure we'll be able to use it. However, I need to think about what's best for thc company, and right now I don't think that's you."

"I'm not what's best for the company?" Jessica dug her fingernails into her palm. "Are you firing me?"

"Don't be obtuse. That is exactly what I'm doing."

Jessica tried holding his gaze, but his eyes sliced through her like the edge of a ski through soft snow. "You have no grounds to fire me. I've done nothing wrong."

"You have. I checked with our employment lawyer, and because you lost your key, didn't have the lock changed and didn't report the incident, I do have grounds. Gertrude is cleaning out your office now."

Jessica's pulse quickened, and a headache pounded at her temples. "She knew before I came in here you were going to fire me. That bitch just sat and typed. She never said a word."

"Careful with your language. Her job is to do as I ask."

Jessica crossed her arms and dug her heels into the carpet. “I won’t go.”

“You have no choice. We no longer have a constructive working relationship.”

“What if I take the polygraph?”

“It’s too late for that. You can take it if you like, but it won’t change anything.”

“Has Kalin approved this?”

“This is not about her.” Turner handed Jessica the envelope. “Your termination papers are in here. You’re being let go with cause.”

Jessica eyed him for a moment. She thought about the idea Aiden had planted in her head. Time to get busy. With rent due February 1st, she needed money. She’d lose her free ski pass and have to buy another. Her overdue car loan hovered in the periphery, waiting for payment. “You’ll be hearing from my lawyer.”

She snatched the envelope and stormed out.

CHAPTER THIRTEEN

Shortly before eight a.m., Kalin leaned her snowshoes against the wall outside her office. She slid her key into the lock and felt a hand press on the small of her back. She stumbled through the door and twisted violently to face her attacker.

Chica growled, and the hair along her spine bristled.

"If that mutt bites me, I'll have her put down."

"Easy, Chica." Kalin rested her hand on Chica's head, and the dog settled.

Jessica's face flushed, and she wiped an eye with the back of her hand. "How could you let Turner fire me?"

Kalin waited until her pulse returned to normal. "Can you calm down and have a seat?"

"I don't want to sit. I want answers."

"I'm happy to talk to you but only if you settle down. Please have a seat." Kalin waited for Jessica to take the guest chair, then sat opposite her. Sometimes she missed her old boss who didn't overstep his boundaries. A year-round employee should not have been fired without her approval and her making sure the labor laws were being followed. Turner was out of control. What was he doing firing Jessica? And who was going to fill the manager role now? Maybe the job at White Peaks was what she needed.

"What happened to your chin?" Jessica asked.

Kalin put her hand over her stitches. She'd tried to hide the bruise making its way up her cheek with makeup but had failed. "Nothing."

Jessica seemed like the type who would sue the resort if she thought she had cause. Taking the blame for Turner's mistakes was not on Kalin's agenda, but she wouldn't let Jessica know she'd been unaware of the firing. "Can you tell me what happened?"

Kalin listened to Jessica's version of her meeting with Turner. A control freak was an understatement when it came to him. He hadn't even let Jessica's boss fire her. "I'm sorry that happened to you."

"What are you going to do about it?"

"There's not much I can do. You've received a letter of termination. That's pretty final. If you'd like to clean out your office, I'm happy to help you."

"You mean you'll supervise, so I don't steal anything. Gertrude's already guarding the door."

Instead of reacting to the anger in Jessica's voice, Kalin stilled her body. She placed her hands in her lap and crossed her legs at her ankles. "I didn't say that. We have a process to follow, that's all."

"How can you do this to me after what's happened this week? You're Roy's sister. He loved me."

Kalin stretched forward and put her hand on Jessica's wrist. "I know he did. If you hadn't lost your keys and not changed the lock, I might have been able to help."

Jessica snapped her hand away from Kalin. "Why are you even working?"

"I miss Roy, too, but I have to do my job. I don't think about him as much if I'm busy."

"And now I have nothing to do but think about him."

"I'm truly sorry about that." Kalin's cell rang. White Peaks was calling. "Can I meet you in your office in a minute?"

Jessica stood and, without a word, left Kalin alone.

* * *

Kalin disconnected the call. Jessica was a hard person to like, but Kalin felt sorry for her. She rubbed Chica's head in an effort to calm herself before heading to Jessica's office.

Footsteps ghosted on the carpet outside her office as if someone was timidly approaching her door.

Ben poked his head around the frame. "Can we talk?"

Chica burst from her place at Kalin's feet and pranced in front of Ben. He kneeled and was rewarded with a lick on his nose.

Kalin swiveled her chair to face him but said nothing.

"Are you okay?" he asked.

She pinched her lips between her teeth. Her body betrayed her. The ache for his arms around her made it hard to breathe. She steeled herself against succumbing. "I'm fine."

Ben softly closed the door. "You went to bed without talking to me last night."

"I know."

"Can you at least tell me if your chin is okay?"

"It's fine."

"Did you get stitches?"

"Four."

Ben's fingers lighted on her chin and gently moved her head backward. He studied the wound. "We're going to have matching scars. That must mean something."

She yearned for a kiss, but how could she betray Roy that way? Ben had called off the search, and Roy's body wouldn't be found.

"I talked to Oliver about the snowmobile. It'll be covered by insurance."

"That's nice."

"Kalin, please. I'm sorry about Roy. I know this is hard for you. It's hard for me, too. I can't lose you over this."

Tears formed in her eyes.

Ben placed his forehead on the top of her head and wrapped his fingers around her hair. "I love you. We need to figure this out."

Reaching behind her head, she removed Ben's hand from her hair. She rolled her chair backward and stood. "I need time. That's all."

"Time for what?"

"I don't know. Just time."

"That makes no sense."

"I know. Roy's only been gone four days. I have to get my head around losing him so soon after he came back in my life." Hurt radiated from Ben's eyes. She'd cut right to his heart, and she knew it. Roy being caught in an avalanche was Roy's fault, but Ben would forever live with the search and rescue failure.

Ben stepped backward and leaned against the door. They were at opposite ends of her office, as far apart as they could be and still be in the same room. Chica picked up on the tension and paced between them, wagging her tail.

"Do you still love me?" he asked.

"I'm angry. I'm terrified about how Roy died. Don't make this into something more than it is."

"Fine. I'll give you time." Ben opened the door and left.

Kalin's knees buckled, and she dropped to the carpet. Chica trotted to her and licked her cheeks. She wrapped her arms around Chica's shoulders, buried her fingers in silky fur and held firm. She stayed there until the shaking stopped.

* * *

On her way to the finance center, Helen smiled at the thought of her two-minute meeting with Turner and Duncan Bosey, the ever-quiet director of finance. Being promoted was beyond her expectations.

She passed Jessica's office and cringed. Kalin hovered beside her, supervising her while she cleaned out her office. Jessica had a nasty streak and feeling sorry for her was not easy.

Although short on time, the aroma of freshly brewed coffee enticed her into the staff kitchen. She poured herself a cup with double cream and double sugar. A co-worker had left a box of doughnuts on the counter. She chose one covered with chocolate and rainbow sprinkles, grabbed a napkin, glanced around to see if anyone would notice and piled on a second doughnut. Fully supplied, she rushed to the finance center.

Constables Miller and Wagner entered behind her and closed the door.

"Good morning," Miller said.

Helen's stupid cheeks stung with heat, and Miller hadn't even asked a question yet. Why had two of them come? "I'm supposed to leave the door open. Sometimes employees need change for the registers."

"They'll have to wait. I have a few more questions," Miller said.

Helen bit the corner of her lip. She placed her coffee and doughnuts on her desk. If she got this over with, she could stop stressing.

Miller rolled the spare chair close to Helen. He placed his RCMP cap on her desk and removed a pen and notebook from his breast pocket. His partner stood with her back to the door.

"I've been trying to contact you. Where were you the last couple of days?" Miller asked.

"I'm not really sure what you want from me. I've already told you everything I know," Helen said.

"Please answer the question."

"I went to Calgary."

Miller scribbled in his notebook and turned his ocean-blue eyes back to her. "What for?"

"To visit my parents."

Wagner shifted but held her position at the door. Had something Helen said interested the female officer?

Miller glanced at Wagner but focused right back on Helen. “Odd time to leave work, right after a theft. Surely you knew I’d want to speak with you again. I told you we needed to get your fingerprints. Is there any reason you’ve avoided having that done?”

Helen smoothed her dress over her thighs and straightened her belt. “I went to visit my parents. I haven’t seen them since last summer, and with everything going on, I needed them.”

Miller held his pen ready. “Please give me the names and contact information for both your parents.”

“If you don’t mind my asking, what for?”

“I’m wondering why you went to see them when you obviously should be here.”

“But I already told you why.”

“So you did.” Miller wrote her parents names and phone numbers as she dictated them.

“That dress you’re wearing looks new, as do the boots. Did you do some shopping while you were in Calgary?”

She fidgeted with her bracelet, clicking the gold clasp open and closed. She bought the dress, thinking the sleek shape made her look trendier and Roy would like it. The new dress was her way of being positive about seeing Roy alive again. “I…yes.”

“You seem to be taking the theft personally. Is there anything you’d like to tell me?”

“It is personal. I was the last person on duty before the theft. I took the call and didn’t check it was real. I found the empty safe. I feel terrible,” Helen said in a voice just above a whisper.

Both of them turned toward the door when a knock interrupted them. Helen stood.

Miller shook his head. “They’ll have to wait. What’s your relationship with Roy McCann?”

Helen returned to her seat. Snow whipped by the finance center window in swaths thick enough to create a screen and added to the snow already dropped in the last twenty-four hours. The wind more than anything had forced the rescue team to call off the search. Roy lay somewhere on the frozen terrain, but the safety of the rescuers remained the priority. He’d been missing for too long. Even if the avalanche hadn’t killed him, he would have died from hypothermia by now, and she ached for him.

She wished she’d told Roy she loved him. He dated Jessica and didn’t feel the same way about her, but at least he would have known. Now she had to mourn in silence.

“Helen?”

“Yes?”

"Your relationship with Roy?"

During her lunch hour on the day before the theft, she'd attended her first snowboarding lesson. Roy had given her lessons as a Christmas present. Having never snowboarded or downhill skied, she'd hid the coupon in her desk and waited until the last moment to redeem it. She hadn't expected a gift and hadn't bought anything for him. Did Jessica know about Roy's gift? Maybe that's why she'd been hostile in the week leading up to the theft.

To Helen's amazement, she loved the lessons. She wasn't an adventurous athlete, but the experience of being on the hill with others who were new to snowboarding was exhilarating. When the weather cleared, she'd go again. "We're friends."

"Good friends?"

"I think so." The sting in her cheeks meant her face had turned red again. "Not romantic friends. I don't want to give you the wrong idea. We just hung out once in a while."

"Did you give Roy the combination to the safe?"

"You think Roy stole the money? He wouldn't do that."

"Did you give him the combination?"

"I didn't." With Miller staring at her as if she'd helped the thief, she couldn't hold his gaze. She darted her eyes to the window and back to him. "I'd lose my job if I did."

Miller had a talent for keeping his expression unreadable, and Helen fidgeted with her bracelet again but couldn't outlast his silence. "I didn't tell anyone the safe combination. Roy could be dead, and you're here thinking he took the money. That's cruel."

"Did you leave the combination written down anywhere he might have seen it?"

Keeping her eyes lowered, she shook her head in response.

"Jessica Scott suggested I talk to you about Roy. Why do you think she would say that?"

"I don't know. Jessica doesn't like me. She seemed jealous Roy and I were friends. Especially lately. I used to spend more time with Roy, but then he started dating her. I think he was getting tired of her, and we began hanging out again. Maybe she told Roy the combination and wants you to think I did."

"Meaning you think it's possible Roy took the money."

A second knock interrupted them, but this time Helen didn't move. "You're twisting what I'm saying."

"Do you know if Roy had money problems?"

"If he did, he never talked to me about it."

"Was he acting differently before the avalanche?"

Helen thought for a moment before answering. “He was moody. He didn’t used to be like that, but it could’ve been because of Jessica. I don’t really know.”

“Fair enough. Let’s talk about the phone call from the bank.”

“I don’t know what to tell you that I haven’t already.”

“It didn’t occur to you the bank closed at noon on Saturdays?”

“I never…I mean, I was busy. I didn’t think about it.”

“Did you take the money? Now is the time to admit it before this goes too far.”

“I swear I didn’t.” Helen cleared her throat and said with confidence, “I’ll take the polygraph. It doesn’t matter what Jessica wants anymore.”

“Why is that?”

“Paul Turner let her go this morning. She’s no longer my boss. So…”

Miller leaned toward her. “How do you know this?”

“I was promoted to manager of the finance center.”

“Interesting motive.”

CHAPTER FOURTEEN

While Jessica packed her office, Kalin used the time to regroup from the devastating conversation with Ben.

"I need to come back for my skis and boots," Jessica said.

"Sure. I'll put them in my office for you. Are both sets yours?"

"No. The blue ones are Simon Crane's."

"He'll have to come and get them. Do you want me to call or would you rather?"

"I'll call."

Jessica placed the last of her possessions in a box, and Kalin escorted her to the bottom of the stairs leading to the exterior of the administration building. Even with Jessica carrying personal items from her office, Kalin picked up her pace to match Jessica's as she pounded down the steps.

Jessica jolted to a stop on the landing and twisted to face Kalin. "Will you give me a reference?"

Kalin pushed the outer door open, using both hands against the force of the wind. "I would, but I don't think Turner's going to approve. If you were let go without cause, I'd be happy to."

"But I was good at my job."

Kalin squinted against the snow pelting her face. "I know you were. If someone calls and asks if we'd hire you back, I have to say no. I don't think that will help you."

"You can't give out details about me."

"And I won't, but I am allowed to answer if we would hire you again."

Jessica shifted the box from one hip to the other. “This really sucks.”

“Are you going to be okay?”

“Do you actually care?”

Kalin held the door open with her shoulder. She blew warm breath onto her bare palms and rubbed them together. “I do. If I could help you, I would.”

Jessica frowned and nodded once. “Sure.” She kicked snow out of her way and jogged toward the path leading to the parking lot.

Kalin shuffled back inside. Stress, grief, whatever, depleted her energy, and the walk back to her office seemed to double in length. Her gut clenched every time she thought about Roy buried and alone. And thinking of Roy made her think of her late husband.

She closed her office door and slipped the photo from underneath the shelf on her wall. A decisive man without fear, Jack had taken one look at Kalin and told her she would become his wife. Kalin laughed and told him to do his best.

After Jack died, she looked at the photo every day and told him she missed him. She’d kept up the ritual until she’d gotten serious with Ben. Out of respect for him, she no longer talked to Jack each day, but she couldn’t bring herself to throw out the photo.

She sat and swiveled her seat, taking in her surroundings. Duct tape held the arm of her chair together, and the carpet was worn through to the floor in several places. At the northern latitude, the building had been designed to let in maximum light and compensate for the short days, but the oppressive atmosphere beat the design. Was critiquing her work environment a way of looking for reasons to accept the job at White Peaks?

A staccato rap announced Turner. Her boss wore a striped button-down shirt hanging loosely over ironed khaki pants. He got straight to work, no preamble, no concern for her. “You understand why the search was called off?”

“I do. My mom’s having a hard time, but I’m trying to get her to understand, too.” Kalin held her breath for a few seconds. “I spoke with Jessica. It would have been better if you’d involved me in her termination. Gavin Reed kept me in the loop on all employee issues.”

“I’m not Reed.”

You certainly aren’t. “I understand, but it’s easier for me to ensure we’re compliant with the labor laws if I know before someone is fired.”

“Jessica Scott broke policy by losing her office keys and not having the lock changed.”

“Do you think she stole the money?”

"I don't know. I fired her because she didn't follow a security policy. We need to talk about Roy. You know he's a suspect."

"I spoke with Constable Miller about him. I don't believe he stole the money."

"Normally, I'd want you to lead an investigation into the theft, but considering your brother is the prime suspect, I don't think that's a good idea."

Turner's words drove Kalin to the opposite of what he asked. Her brother would never steal and certainly not such a large sum of money. "I don't believe—"

"He's the obvious suspect. I'll take care of the investigation until Fred returns from vacation. There's one other thing. I've promoted Helen to take over Jessica's role."

"But—"

"We need someone in place right away."

"I'm not saying Helen is the wrong person, but usually I would be involved in any organizational decisions, especially with a promotion to a managerial position. Until the theft is solved, maybe we should operate without a manager."

"She's already in place." Turner handed Kalin a letter. "The details of the promotion are here. I need you to process it effective today."

"Anything else?" Kalin tried to keep the coldness out of her voice but failed. She suspected Turner would push her out of the way until he found out who stole the money. But what if guilt lay with Helen and she was now the manager? Kalin didn't think Turner had made the best decision, but she'd lost the power to influence him.

The flop of Turner dropping a copy of *The Holden Press* drew her eyes to the surface of her desk. "Any idea how the newspaper found out about the theft?"

Kalin picked up the paper, keeping her head lowered, hoping Turner wouldn't smell the sweat rings seeping into her armpits. The byline belonged to Charlotte Summers.

Avalanche at Stone Mountain

Thirty-year-old Roy McCann remains missing in the Dragon's Bowl at Stone Mountain Resort.

McCann, one of the ski patrol's newest recruits, was lost in the early morning avalanche. So far only some of his ski gear has been found. Search and Rescue stated they have stopped the search until the weather improves. The search will resume when it is safe for the rescue team, but SAR is not hopeful about finding him alive.

The resort's president, Paul Turner, confirmed a theft occurred at the resort. At this time, he is unwilling to release details, but one has to question if the theft and avalanche are related.

"This says you told the reporter," Kalin said.

"She asked me if the theft and the avalanche were related, and I told her the theft details were confidential. I guess that was her way of confirming a rumor."

"I'm not sure what you want me to do with this."

"Find out who told her about the theft before she came to visit me. Then fire the person." Turner snatched the newspaper from Kalin and left her office.

She couldn't worry about Charlotte's article. Charlotte would never tell anyone she leaked the information. Kalin's mom was her priority, and she dialed.

"Any news?" her mom asked straight away.

Kalin could imagine her mom shrunken by sadness and wished she did have news. "No, I'm just checking in."

"If only there was something we could do."

"Oh, Mom. You know he won't be found alive. All we can hope for is to find his body and bury him properly." Kalin didn't know how to help her mom through this, but she did know she couldn't tell her about the theft and Roy being a suspect. What a way to break her heart.

"I know…It's just…I want him back."

"Me, too," Kalin said and decided to hell with Turner's wishes. If she couldn't have Roy back, she would prove his innocence.

The locksmith's office. That's where she needed to go. A quick check with Ben, and she'd head to the lower village.

She donned her jacket as she jogged across the path to the mountain ops building and waited while the administration assistant opened his top desk drawer and gave a locker combination to a liftie.

"Ben around?" Kalin asked.

"He's with the grooming team."

* * *

Kalin slogged toward the locksmith's office. She squinted against the blowing snow and tucked her hands in her pockets. She hunched forward and leaned into the wind. Why had she been so hard on Ben? He'd had no choice but to call off the search. Except Roy was still out there, and they'd left him alone.

Turner had told her not to investigate, but he hadn't told her not to work on better security for the finance center. If he found out what she was about to do, she'd use security as an issue and pretend she hadn't understood his orders.

Located in the basement of the same building that housed the front desk, the locksmith office contained a key-grinding machine. The keys to the hotel rooms were created using a card system, but the keys to the resort's offices and conference rooms hadn't been upgraded and still used metal keys.

She checked the time. Almost five. Hoping to catch Brightman before he left his office, she picked up her pace.

A crusty man in his mid to late fifties, Ted Brightman had a full head of frizzy hair, thick arms and an unfriendly demeanor. He didn't get up from the grinding machine when Kalin entered his workshop, and the screeching made her teeth hurt. Did he even notice the slight odor of burnt metal anymore?

As soon as he stopped the grinding machine, she got right to the point. "Who has a key to the finance center?"

Brightman stared at her in his usual rude fashion.

"I know you've updated the key recording process since the McKenzie murder, so I'd like to know who has a key." Before Kalin forced Brightman to update the process, he hadn't kept track of keys. Since then, Fred had installed a recording system, and the information existed on some hard drive.

Slowly Brightman stood, looking as if the effort hurt his knees, and limped toward his desk. He turned on the computer. "I'm not too fast with this thing."

Kalin followed him and waited.

"Hovering won't make me any faster."

He clicked on an icon on the desktop and pointed. "Jessica Scott, Eric Wilson, Helen Armstrong, Fred Morgan, Paul Turner, you and the rest of the directors."

"That's not right. I don't have a key."

"You have a master."

"I do."

"The master opens every hard lock on the resort."

Kalin re-read the names. Fred was in Hawaii, so that removed him from the suspect list. Turner and the other directors just joined the team of possible thieves. Again with the keys. "I'd like you to change the lock on the finance center door again. This time, don't give access to master keys. There's no reason to."

"That's difficult."

"Not my concern. Just get it done."

Kalin hurried back to the dark administration building, went directly to the finance center and tried her master key. She unlocked and locked the door, testing to make sure the room was secure. She didn't know Turner well, and if she was truthful, she didn't like him. She hoped her decision to call Miller instead of Turner had nothing to do with her feelings toward her boss and everything to do with furthering the investigation. Without hesitating, she dialed.

CHAPTER FIFTEEN

Ben slumped on the living room couch. Seven p.m. Was Kalin working late just to avoid him? If he'd done something, anything, differently, would Roy be alive? If only he'd gotten out of bed early on the day of the avalanche, he might have been with Roy and been able to save him or at least persuaded him not to go. Roy's dangerous habit of night skiing had gotten him killed.

Helping Kalin get closure without a body had to be his priority now. Somehow he had to make her understand his decision.

A low whine prodded him to pay attention to his world. Chica thumped her tail against the hardwood floor and gazed at Ben. He pushed himself off the couch, and she ran to the mudroom.

Ben chuckled. "I get it. You're hungry." He opened the bottom cupboard and grabbed the kibble.

While Chica gobbled her food, Ben jogged down the stairs to the ground-floor guest room and looked at Roy's things. He'd been sleeping in Ben and Kalin's guest bedroom for a month, and the shared accommodations had been getting a bit annoying. He'd wanted Roy to move out, but not the way he did.

Ben carried Roy's suitcase into the garage and stuffed it into a cubbyhole. He returned to the guest room and looked for Roy's army-green duffle bag. He checked the front hall, the back closet and the shelves in the garage but found nothing. Maybe when Roy left on the morning of the avalanche, he'd been in the process of moving out and taken the bag with him. After the tense conversation they'd had about why Roy should leave, he wouldn't be surprised if Roy had taken off without telling them.

When he returned to the living room, he found Chica with her nose pressed against the sliding glass door. He picked up her leash, and she pranced in circles. He grabbed his headlamp and secured the straps over his toque.

Ben walked Chica, thinking about the night before Roy died and how he'd left things in such a mess with his brother-in-law. He would never have a chance to fix that, but he did have the chance to recover with Kalin.

He reached Jessica's place and plodded through knee-deep snow to her door. He lifted the bird-shaped knocker and tapped the tail against a cast-iron base. He waited a minute, and getting no response from within, gave up.

He trudged along Black Bear drive until he reached the mountain ops building. Snowflakes drifted to the ground, but the ease in snowfall had come too late to help Roy. Tomorrow he'd order the team to check the surrounding terrain and determine if the slopes were stable enough to resume the search.

Considering the lateness of the hour, the light inside the building surprised him. Ben quietly opened the door and poked in his head.

Someone lay on one of the gurneys.

Chica burst past him and barked at the person, wagging her tail furiously. Jessica rolled to her side and sat, but stayed wrapped in a blanket. "What do you want?"

Ben stepped around the puddles created by the snow falling off Chica. "Are you okay?"

"I'm fine."

"Then why are you lying on a gurney?"

"It's stupid."

"What is?"

"Roy used to sleep here sometimes. I just wanted…I don't know what I wanted, but I had to get out of my house."

Jessica's hoarse voice and slow speech reminded Ben she'd cared for Roy. That little fact was easy to forget when Roy had been so difficult. Ben didn't know Jessica well but understood she was hurting. "Do you think Roy might have come here the night before the avalanche?"

"Maybe."

With the room almost empty, Ben smelled antiseptic cleaners from the treatment station and wool from the blankets stored on the shelf beside him, making him glad the employees change room and lockers were a floor below them and couldn't add to the odors. "Was he going to move in with you?"

"Not that I know of. Why?"

"I can't find his duffle bag. I think Kalin might want the contents. He left our place before dawn, but I don't know where he went."

"He didn't come to my house." Jessica swallowed hard. "He could have gone to Helen's. He went there sometimes when he'd had too much to drink. You could ask her."

"Oh."

"Yeah. Oh. It's not what you're thinking. They were friends. Roy would never be interested in someone like her."

Someone like her. What did that mean? Ben didn't ask.

Jessica slumped against the wall and tightened the blanket. "I can't believe this happened."

"Neither can we. Kalin's taking it pretty hard. Did you know Roy planned on skiing early that day?"

"No. And no, I don't think he stole the money, so don't start with that shit."

"I didn't say that. Kalin doesn't believe he did either. I'm only looking to get his things together. Kalin needs some closure and without…Well, you know. I want to help her if I can."

"You mean you want her to forgive you for calling off the search."

* * *

Just because Ben had been kind and walked Jessica home didn't mean she owed him anything. And he didn't need to know her real reason for being in the clinic.

She turned the deadbolt and phoned Aiden. As lift manager, Aiden had worked closely with Roy, but that didn't mean she trusted him. She just couldn't come up with anyone else to turn to. "I've been thinking about what you said the other day about Roy being near the finance center on the morning of the theft. Maybe you're on to something."

"Are you telling me you didn't take the money and he did?" Aiden asked.

If Aiden hadn't seen Roy with the duffle bag and hadn't seen her in the finance center at night using a flashlight, she wouldn't involve him in her plan. "You jerk. Of course I didn't."

"You have to admit, you must be high on the suspect list. Talk about suspicious. The money gets stolen, then your boyfriend disappears."

Jessica plopped on her couch and rested her feet on the coffee table. "I didn't take the money, but what if Roy had help from someone else in the finance center?"

"Who?"

"Helen. Always Helen this and Helen that just because she doted on him like a lovesick puppy. They hung around together a lot."

"Yeah, I can tell you weren't fond of that." Aiden snickered. "Is that why you set up Helen? Just sayin'."

"What are you talking about?"

"You could take the money and get back at Helen in one go. The night I caught you in the finance center after hours, it seemed odd you were using a flashlight. I don't believe your story of the burnt-out light bulb."

Even though Aiden couldn't see her, Jessica rolled her eyes. "Shut up. You don't seem too upset Roy died."

"It wasn't like we were friends anymore. It's sad, but not my problem. Anyway, you think he stole the money?"

Jessica walked to the kitchen and stared at the contents in her refrigerator. Who was she kidding? She couldn't eat. The depth with which she missed Roy surprised her, but she had to take care of herself. If she couldn't have him, she could at least find what he'd stolen. She set her phone on the counter and hit the speaker icon.

"Did you hear what I asked?"

"Yeah. I guess it's possible. Ben was just here. He was looking for Roy's duffle bag. I bet he thinks that's where the money is. He made up some story about getting stuff together for Kalin, but I don't believe him."

"If Roy stole the money, any idea where he'd hide it?"

"If Helen was in on it, then maybe at her place. It's also possible Kalin was his partner."

"The duffle could have been buried with Roy on the mountain."

"I can't see him carrying it up there," Jessica said.

"There is another possibility no one's talking about."

Jessica picked up a beer, then replaced the bottle on the fridge shelf with a clang. "And what is that?"

"Maybe Roy set the scene to look like he died in the avalanche and then took off with the money."

The stench of sour milk wafted in her direction, and Jessica slammed the refrigerator door. "You're an idiot. There's no way he would do that to me."

"You sure about that?"

She stared at her blurred reflection in the stainless steel appliance. She was sick of being a shoe wipe for Stone Mountain. If she found the money and didn't tell anyone, Turner and the cops would ultimately blame Roy. He was dead, so it's not like the betrayal would cause him any pain.

"Yes, I'm sure. Look, the money has to be somewhere, and I don't see why I should help the resort find it, but that doesn't mean I'm against looking for it on our own. You're not going to change your mind and tell the police what you saw on the night of the theft?"

"As long as you don't tell Ben. You seem to like him."

Who didn't like Ben?

CHAPTER SIXTEEN

"Let's snowshoe to work this morning," Ben said.

Kalin pressed her head into her pillow and debated whether to pretend she was sleeping or not. Why couldn't Ben just give her time to heal? The avalanche happened on Monday, and it was only Friday. Two days since Ben called off the search. Two days of anger filling her heart and clawing at her insides.

"I know you're awake. I can tell from your breathing." Ben massaged her back between her shoulder blades. "Come on. You have to talk to me sometime."

She curled into a ball, pulling her knees to her chest. Her flannel pajamas, the ones Ben made fun of, provided a soft barrier, a way to distance herself from him. "Sure."

"That was enthusiastic."

Kalin tossed the quilt to the side and stepped onto the plush carpet. She loved the texture on her bare feet. Without turning on the light or opening her eyes, she stumbled to the shower.

She got dressed in thermal underwear, ski pants and a sweater she could wear at work, and met Ben in the kitchen. He'd fried bacon and eggs, her favorite, and set orange juice on the table. She gave him points for trying.

Half an hour later, Kalin strode beside Ben, her snowshoes sinking in the deep snow. The blades on the bottom, meant to grip icy ground, wouldn't be needed. With each step, snow flew up the back of her legs and bounced off her ski pants.

Chica trotted behind them, smart enough to travel on the path flattened by their snowshoes, stopping occasionally to sniff at something.

Two beams of light from their headlamps bounced along in front of them, lighting the way.

"Kalin, we have to get past this."

"I know. I'm just so angry."

"At me?"

"No. At Roy, but I don't want to blame him."

"So you're not mad at me. Just not speaking to me."

Kalin stomped along without answering. Why was it so hard to articulate her feelings? She trusted Ben. He loved her, and yet, she couldn't express herself well.

"Your silence is kinda what I mean by not speaking to me."

In the darkness, she smiled, knowing Ben couldn't see her face. "This is hard for me."

"I can tell."

"Don't tease me right now. I can't take it."

"Sorry."

"I understand why you called off the search. I really do. I know it was the right thing to do. Roy being left alone to die is too horrible to think about, even though I know that's what happened."

"Maybe he was hit so fast, he didn't know he would die."

"I hope that's how it happened. The alternative is unbearable."

"We'll check the terrain today. If it's still not stable, it should be within the next couple of days. As soon as it's safe, I'll get the team out there."

"Okay."

Ben reached for Kalin's hand and pulled her to a stop. He drew her to him and hugged her. "I love you," he whispered.

She rested her head on his shoulder and let herself relax. Enough was enough. Time to forgive and let go. "I love you right back."

They cut to the path that ran along the bottom of a black diamond ski run. The steep terrain was one of Kalin's favorite runs. "Where's Chica?"

"She's back there somewhere. She'll—" The rumble of snow cascading down the slope drowned out Ben's words.

"Run," he shouted.

Without hesitating, she pumped her legs hard. She sensed Ben at her side, matching her stride for stride. Snow dragged over the back of her snowshoes, and she tripped.

Ben grabbed her jacket and yanked her upright.

They kept running and reached the safety of the thick forest. The mounds of snow descending pounded across the path where they'd hiked only seconds before.

Kalin scanned the area with the lamp but found nothing in the darkness. "Where's Chica? I can't see her."

"Chica, come," Ben shouted.

Nothing.

"Oh, Ben. Not Chica."

The slide stopped, and an evil silence fell around them.

Kalin's pulse throbbed in her throat and an ache pressed behind her eyes. "Chica!"

The soft padding of her paws on snow reached their ears before the sight of their dog.

"She must have run backward and waited on the other side. Smart dog," Ben said.

Chica ran to Kalin just as Kalin sank to her knees. Her wet tongue froze her cheeks, but she didn't care. She wrapped her arms around Chica's back and held her until her breathing returned to an acceptable speed.

"The groomers were supposed to groom that run last night," Ben said. "It shouldn't have been left with so much loose snow."

"Did you tell anyone we were hiking to work this morning?"

"Oliver. We're going to snowshoe across some of the higher terrain later today. We're taking Aiden with us."

"You don't think—"

"Man, you're suspicious. That was an accident."

"I guess this means you won't be starting search and rescue again today."

* * *

With Chica clipped to her leash, Kalin hustled toward the security office. Five days after the avalanche and the theft, Fred Morgan, the security manager, had arrived back at the resort from his brother's wedding in Hawaii. Turner would talk to him soon, and she'd better beat her boss to him, otherwise Fred might not keep her informed.

Her cell rang. A Calgary number she didn't recognize. "Kalin Thompson."

"Gavin Reed here."

She hadn't spoken to Reed since he'd left the resort in shame last spring. He'd been her previous boss and the president of Stone Mountain. After reporting to Turner for the last six months, she realized Reed had been the better boss. He'd been tough but fair.

"I thought you were a Timlin now."

"I kept my surname, but yes, I did marry Ben. Thanks for the reference."

"I'm glad I got your voicemail, or I might have called Turner to talk with him. Did you get an offer?"

"I did. I haven't decided yet what I'm going to do. They gave me a couple of weeks to decide because of the avalanche and theft. They understand I can't really commit yet."

"How's Turner taking the news?"

"I haven't told him. He doesn't need to know unless I accept the job."

"Hmm. I remember you like to keep secrets."

"I don't."

Reed laughed. "I'm kidding. But you might tell him before he finds out from someone else. If you go, what's Ben going to do there?"

"Ski patrol. Although the timing's bad. He was promoted to manager here."

"Good for Ben. Let me know if he needs a reference."

"Thanks." She still had to let Ben know she'd been offered the job. It was too soon to think about a reference for him. "How's Melanie? Do you know what's happening yet?"

"She's fine, considering. She was sentenced to two years less a day. I guess we couldn't expect any less for an arson charge. Ian's racing this weekend in Lake Placid."

Kalin guessed Reed wasn't comfortable talking about his daughter and what happened, so he'd changed the subject to his son. Kalin had done her best to help Melanie by being a character reference, and Reed had been grateful. "I know. Nora told me she was heading there to watch him."

"Have you seen Ethan lately?"

Ethan was Reed's grandson, born only eight months previously to Nora and Ian. "I have. He's as cute as can be. I hope Ian does well in the World Cup race."

When she hung up she found herself wishing Reed was still at Stone Mountain. She also wished Nora wasn't traveling and was here to help her get through this mess.

After the previous security office had burnt to rubble in the big fire, Fred and his team used an office in the upper village during the rebuild process, but now they were back in the lower village, enjoying new office space.

Kalin entered the room filled with new-carpet smell. The all-familiar BOLO list hung on one wall. Turner probably wanted Kalin and Ben's name on that list now.

Fred entered from his private office located in the corner of the room, shut the door, said hello to Kalin and pet Chica on her head.

"How was the wedding?" she asked.

Fred ushered Kalin into the small conference room, offering her a place to sit. "Great. I'm really sorry about Roy."

Kalin's throat tightened. More time needed to pass before she could talk about Roy without choking up. "Thanks."

"How's Ben doing?"

"Being in charge of search and rescue has been tough on him. I know he had to call off the search when he did, but he's second-guessing himself. I don't think he'd do that if Roy wasn't my brother."

"I can imagine. Any news on a second search?"

"Not today. Ben will evaluate the conditions again tomorrow."

"What happened to your chin?"

"I hit it on a snowmobile windshield. It's fine." As soon as her stitches were removed and people couldn't see the injury, the topic would be dead. Explaining she'd been an idiot wasn't a conversation welcome in her world. She hung her jacket behind the door and sat in the offered chair. Chica curled up on the floor and rested her jaw on Kalin's foot. "We need to talk about the theft investigation."

Keeping his eyes lowered, Fred doodled in his notebook, his pen scratching across the paper. The notebook usually kept important investigation information, but today's squiggles told her it was a prop to avoid looking at her. She said, "Don't tell me."

"I met with Turner this morning."

"And he asked you to keep me out of things?"

"He did. I'm sorry, Kalin. This is awkward, but I understand where he's coming from."

They both turned their heads toward the door when a knock interrupted them. Constable Miller entered. "We've one polygraph to repeat and then we're done."

Kalin stood and glanced between Fred and Miller. Chica wagged her tail and approached Miller for the required pet on her head.

"I didn't see you," Miller said to Kalin.

"I feel like the proverbial third wheel," Kalin said. "Any chance I can know the results and who has to repeat the test?"

"Sorry." Miller tucked his RCMP cap underneath his arm. "Don't take it personally."

"No, it's not personal. Not at all. Just because my boss has convinced everyone I'm a thief or my brother's a thief, and I can't be trusted to work on this. No, that's not personal."

Fred blushed and stared at his feet. Kalin had never seen him look so awkward, and she almost smiled at him.

"I'd like permission to search your home," Miller said.

Kalin took a deep breath. She couldn't see any reason to forbid the RCMP from going through her house, except the invasion of privacy, but looking guiltier wouldn't prove Roy's innocence, so she said, "Fine, do what you need."

"Thanks. I'll send some officers over this afternoon." Miller moved out of Kalin's way, giving her space to reach the door. "I need to bring Fred up to speed and then get back to Holden."

At least Miller had the grace to look apologetic as he ushered her out the door.

* * *

Minutes after Constable Wagner and the rest of the RCMP officers left his home, Ben put on his work jacket, gloves and boots. He flicked on the outdoor lights and stepped off the back porch. He grabbed the splitting axe, placed a log flat on the ground and swung. Hard. The wood split, and he picked up another log.

Chica ran to the edge of the stone wall and peed. She seemed content as long as she had someone, anyone really, to hang with. Earlier, she'd followed the RCMP officers from room to room while they searched the house. Constable Wagner had shown up without Miller. She was far less talkative and less friendly than him. All business, but polite. Maybe Miller knew Kalin too well to be allowed to search their home.

Both Turner and the cops spent more time searching for the missing money than for Roy's body. If the next attempt at finding Roy failed, Ben planned to search the mountain in the spring and find him, no matter how gruesome his remains might be. He owed Kalin that much.

He'd talked with the grooming manager about the small avalanche that crossed the snowshoe trail. The man had said he missed the instructions to groom the run. Ben remembered Oliver updating the whiteboard, but somehow the instructions were erased. He hadn't told Kalin that tidbit of information. She'd get all excited that someone had set them up. But there's no way they could have timed an avalanche for the exact moment Ben and Kalin were on the path. Unless—

Chica barked, ran to the front deck and wagged her tail. Ben followed to find out what she'd barked at.

Aiden Price smiled up at Ben from the driveway and dangled a six-pack in front of him.

Jessica stood beside him, just inside the dome of lights, and tucked her hands in her armpits. "We saw Kalin at work and thought you might need some company tonight. We heard the cops were here."

Juicy news spread like the common cold in the close quarters of the isolated resort. Ben waved for Aiden and Jessica to come up the side steps. He knew Jessica better than the lift manager. The question was why were they there together?

Ben led them to the backyard and pulled another log from the woodpile, a pile he'd created when the construction workers knocked down trees to clear the lot for their house.

"How are you holding up?" Jessica asked.

After only a couple of minutes of not working, the sweat soaking his back chilled Ben. "I'm okay. Mind if I keep splitting logs? I have to get this done."

Jessica sat on top of the hot tub lid and let her feet dangle. "What did the police want?"

Aiden placed the beer beside her but remained standing.

Ben released the axe.

Thwack.

The log cracked and flew in two pieces, one landing in the shadows, the other near Aiden's foot, who took a step closer to Jessica. "They asked if they could search our place."

"Did they have a warrant?" Jessica asked.

"We've got nothing to hide."

Aiden and Jessica exchanged a quick glance. "Did they say what they were looking for?" Jessica asked.

"They didn't say much while they were here." Ben didn't intend to talk badly about Roy. The cops suspected he stole the money, but Ben wouldn't contribute to the rumors. For Kalin's sake, he hoped they were wrong.

"Are you a suspect?" Aiden asked.

Ben rubbed the scar underneath his chin and thought about Aiden's question. The RCMP hadn't accused him of anything, and when they'd interviewed him, they'd only asked questions about Roy. "Hardly."

Chica nudged Jessica's knee, and Jessica shoved her away. "Did they say anything about Roy?"

"Only what I already told you. Why are you so interested?" Ben asked.

Jessica crossed her spindly legs and hugged herself tighter. "They've been hassling me, like I helped Roy steal the money."

Ben lifted the axe.

Crack.

More wood for the fireplace. "They can't be sure Roy's the thief. He's just a suspect because he disappeared."

"Did Roy leave anything here?" Jessica asked.

"No." Ben scratched Chica's ear, and she rewarded him with a tail wag. "Why?"

"He had photos of us that I'd like," she said. "I thought maybe he'd left his camera here."

"Sorry. Can't help. The cops took that with them." Ben contemplated the untouched six-pack resting on the hot tub. If he was going to drink, it would be with friends. "Thanks for the beer, but I'm exhausted, and I still need to walk Chica."

He let the axe hang loose beside his leg and waited for Aiden and Jessica to go. He hadn't mentioned Roy's suitcase stored in the garage. It didn't matter. The RCMP had searched the contents and hadn't found anything interesting enough to take with them. Besides, he didn't feel like helping Aiden and Jessica.

CHAPTER SEVENTEEN

"I've been phoning you all morning," Kalin's mom said. "Where have you been?"

"Meeting with my boss." How could Kalin tell her mom about the search underway for Roy's body? Seven days of snow piling on top of him dampened Ben's optimism. She'd met Ben in the mountain ops building before he left for the Dragon's Bowl and stayed while search and rescue reviewed the plan.

Best to wait until the search ended before telling her mom. She didn't want to think of her mom curled on her couch, waiting for news of Roy and the search. She'd had enough heartache.

"We need to talk," her mom said.

Kalin exited the mountain ops building and tromped down the steps to the snow covered path. The warble in her mom's voice told her something bad happened. "What's wrong?"

"Constable Miller called. He asked questions about Roy."

Kalin rubbed the back of her neck as if that would fend off the impending ache in her shoulder muscles. She should have figured Miller would call her mom. "What kind of questions?"

"He wanted to know if Roy had money troubles. And whether I knew if Roy had more than one bank account. What's going on?"

As she headed toward the Alpine Tracks lift station, the cold stung Kalin's bare forehead, but she ignored the pain and kept walking. "Did he say anything else?"

"I asked about the investigation into the avalanche, and he said he didn't have any new information. Why would he want to know about Roy's money situation?"

Kalin stood to the side of the lift maze. Skiers and snowboarders queued in front of the chairs, ready to head up the slopes. She hadn't skied since Roy disappeared, fear prevented her, but as a director she needed to be visible on the hill. "I wasn't going to mention anything, but there was a theft here the night before Roy died."

"You didn't think that was worth mentioning?"

"I didn't want you to worry."

"Why are the police asking about Roy?"

Kalin glanced around the area before answering. Frost tendrils spread across the metal rods that held each chair to the cable. White lights hung around the lift operator's shack, and the festive image brought thoughts of Christmas and family holidays. The image didn't match the anxiety inside her. "I guess it looks suspicious the money was stolen the night before Roy went missing."

"They think Roy's the thief? You can't be serious. He wouldn't steal anything."

"I know, but I can understand the cops have to look at all possibilities." Kalin described the theft to her mom, making the event sound unimportant.

"Miller asked about Jack, too."

"What?"

"He wanted to know how Jack's accident affected Roy. Then he asked what I thought about Roy being interviewed more than once about the hit-and-run."

"Why would he ask that?" Kalin whispered. She hadn't meant to, but her voice betrayed her. Roy interviewed more than once. About Jack's accident. What did that mean?

"I don't know what he was getting at."

"Don't worry. Miller likes to be thorough when he's investigating. He's just poking around."

"Are you sure?"

"I am." *Not.* Jack's case was unsolved, but why dredge it up again? Why not let him rest in peace?

"There's something else I want to ask you. But don't get mad," her mom said.

Kalin gripped her phone tighter.

"What's Ben doing about finding Roy?"

"Mom, you know he can't do any more than he already has. The failed search is killing him." Her words were true, but Kalin still treated

Ben as if she was mad at him. He needed to know she loved him and he'd made the right decision. The frightening experience with the mini avalanche helped, but she couldn't bring herself to let him close yet. The hurt pressured her insides and filled her. There wasn't room for Ben right now.

"You should use your position to prove Roy is innocent."

"I can't believe you said that. What happened to 'don't become obsessed with this like I was with Jack'?"

Before Jack died, Kalin spent Sunday mornings with him. He'd pull her into his arms, knowing they didn't have to get out of bed. She'd never again slept in on a Sunday. If she wasn't working, she rolled out of bed and asked Ben to go snowshoeing, hiking or skiing, whatever the season demanded. Drastic loss required drastic change.

"That was different. Jack's death was unsolved, but at least we got to bury him. Roy's reputation is at stake. Jack's wasn't."

Her mom was right. Time to refresh her memory. Kalin finished the call and headed for the HR file room. She pulled the files for Eric Wilson, Jessica Scott, Simon Crane and Helen Armstrong. All of the finance center staff.

* * *

Just as Kalin opened Helen's HR file and placed the folder flat on top of a metal file cabinet, the hairs on the back of her neck tingled.

"We've got a problem," Helen said.

How long had Helen been standing in the doorway?

"What's up?" Kalin closed Helen's file, piled it on top of the other files she'd pulled and gave Helen her attention. If Helen had tried to set up Roy, Kalin would make sure she failed. Maybe Kalin had it wrong. What if Helen set up Jessica? Then the manager's job opened up for her.

Kalin believed Jessica was one of the top suspects, except it didn't make sense Jessica would draw attention to herself by losing her key and not reporting it if she was going to rob the finance center. Unless she wanted Turner to think someone stole her key. Then she'd been fired. The whole situation confused her. Whom could she trust?

Helen interlocked her fingers and rested her hands on the front of her skirt. "I haven't dealt with staff issues before and was hoping you could help me with something."

"I'd be happy to."

Helen wore a blue skirt, high on her waist and held in place by a wide belt, topped with a short cream jacket. Kalin had only seen her in passing on her first day of her promotion, and since then she'd updated her hairstyle from tied tightly behind her head to loosely framing her face. The expensive-looking blonde highlights added a level of softness to her chestnut hair, and the trace of eye shadow feathered on her eyelids complemented her brown eyes. She seemed too timid to rob the finance center, but who knew.

Kalin glanced at her own jeans and wool sweater and had a sudden longing for something more elegant to wear.

"Simon Crane was caught using the Internet during his night shift."

"Why's that a problem?" Kalin asked. The night auditor worked from midnight into the early morning. He organized the resort's daily receipts, preparing them for the finance center to reconcile the following day. He used to report to Jessica, so now he would fall under Helen's responsibility.

"It's the sites he's looking at. They're pornographic. He left one of the sites up on the computer screen. The employee working the next shift saw the image. She's upset and scared to work alone with him."

"How often has he been accessing the sites?"

"The IT department gave me data from the past week. He's been logging on every night. The scary part is the photos are of girls wearing uniforms that look similar to the front desk uniforms. Could you come with me to talk to him? I'm friends with his wife."

"And that makes this awkward for you. Of course I'll come." Simon would know how much money the resort made every night. Clearly, his ethics weren't the greatest, leaving nothing to stop him from being a thief, too. She'd thought he was a little too perfect when she met him. "Does he have access to the safe?"

Helen pinched her bottom lip between her teeth. "He shouldn't."

"Could he have gotten the combination somehow?"

"I don't know, but I doubt it."

"Does he ever go to the finance center?"

Helen stopped fidgeting and clasped her hands. "Every morning he brings the previous night's receipts to me or whoever is on shift. Sometimes he hangs around to chat."

"So he could have seen the combination?"

"I guess, but he doesn't have a key."

Kalin checked the time. It wasn't quite late enough for Simon to have gotten much sleep following his shift, but after what he'd done, she didn't care. "Okay, call him and ask him to come in. We'll meet him in his office."

* * *

"You look like crap. What's wrong with you?" Aiden asked.

Jessica stood in line at the Mountainside Café at the base of the Alpine Tracks ski run. It wasn't even ten in the morning, and she needed a caffeine boost.

She glared at Aiden. He was such an idiot. So she wore a wrinkled gray sweatshirt with the hood pulled over her head. Her pants hung loosely from her hips, and she hadn't bothered to lace up her hiking boots. Who cared? "I lost Roy. My friends all think I helped steal the money and are avoiding me. I don't have a job. Turner promoted Helen. Like she's capable. She could hardly function as a clerk. If he thinks she'll do better than I—"

"It's got nothing to do with you anymore. I heard the real estate office needs people. You could work for them again." Aiden peeled the plastic lid off his cup and added a second pack of sugar to his coffee. He reached the outer door to the café, and instead of leaving, he turned and offered to buy Jessica a tea.

"You should really talk to the real estate guys." His eyes raked down her body. "But not in those clothes."

"I guess I have to. I don't have much money saved." Jessica accepted a chai tea from the barista. "And piss off about my clothes."

Ignoring her snap, Aiden dropped a couple of Toonies on the counter and ushered her away from the till to a secluded seat in the corner.

The radio clipped to the outside pocket of Aiden's lift uniform squawked. An operator at one of the lifts needed a break. Aiden hit the transmit button. "I'll be there in ten." He focused back on Jessica. "How much space do you think the missing money would take up?"

"I don't know."

"Sure you do. How big's the safe? You must have seen the money stacked. Could the bills fit in Roy's backpack?"

The café's window overlooked the base of the ski hill. For early January, the resort was unusually quiet, meaning low revenue. She gave herself a mental kick. It wasn't her problem anymore. "It's hard to say, but the money was in small bills. And it depends on what else was in the pack. Did the duffle bag look heavy when you saw him?"

"Yeah. So let's assume that's where the money was. Would he have taken both bags up the hill?"

"You're assuming he took the money."

"Of course he did. Why else did he trek up the mountain? Anyway, if the bills didn't all fit in his pack, maybe he stashed the rest somewhere."

"He liked to ski at dawn. Everyone knows that." Jessica lifted her cup and inhaled the scent of cinnamon. The heat penetrating the cup warmed her hands. "Ben doesn't seem to have anything of Roy's, and the police would have found the money when they searched the house if that's where Roy hid it."

"I bet the cops suspect Roy had all the money in his backpack. They have no way of knowing about the duffle bag." Aiden pointed at Jessica with his coffee. "You know Roy. Would he have split the money up and hid it in different places?"

"How could I know that? I never thought he'd steal in the first place. When Roy left the admin building, where'd he go?"

"Into mountain ops."

"Why didn't you wait until he came out and follow him?"

"I didn't know he'd robbed the finance center. I thought, as usual, he was too drunk to walk home and planned on crashing on a gurney. If I'd known what he'd done, I wouldn't have left him there."

"Could the duffle bag be somewhere in mountain ops?"

Aiden sipped his coffee and looked at Jessica over the steam. "That's dumb. How could the money be there and no one's found it?"

CHAPTER EIGHTEEN

Kalin sat beside Helen in the night auditor's office. Large by resort standards, the office's windows filled two of the walls, and a pale blue carpet stretched luxuriously across the room. The bright light highlighted the dark circles under Helen's eyes. Between the theft and the promotion, she had a lot to stress about. "Let's see what you have."

Helen handed Kalin the reports provided by IT. She turned to the computer and showed Kalin the site the night auditor had left on the screen.

Kalin's scalp prickled, and she moved her gaze toward a poster of Stone Mountain. "That girl looks sixteen. Is there more?"

"You need to see more? I think this is enough."

"You're right. I'm wondering how much of this stuff he was looking at. I can understand why the staff wants us to deal with this, and I certainly have no issue firing him today."

They waited for Simon. Kalin took in the high performance skis leaning against the wall. A set of touring skis rested beside his downhill skis. A water stain underneath the ends of the skis indicated Simon left wet skis there to dry. "That's a bit sloppy."

Helen glanced at the skis. "He used to store those in Jessica's office because hers was closer to the hill."

"I know. He moved them the same day Jessica was fired."

Simon arrived and slouched low in his chair, his posture indicating defeat before the conversation even started. He'd tucked his white dress shirt into neatly pressed Chinos. Not one blond hair stuck out of place, but Kalin could smell him from across the room. An odor of sweat oozed from his pores as if he were already stressed about the meeting. She wrinkled her nose and tried not to breathe deeply.

Helen looked the night auditor directly in the eyes, and Kalin was impressed by her demeanor. "It has come to our attention that you've been accessing the Internet during your night shift," Helen said.

"Damn it," Simon whispered, dropping his chin to his chest.

"Accessing the Internet for personal use is against company policy. If you weren't accessing pornographic sites, we might be able to let you off with a written warning, however, the sites you were looking at are forbidden by our business code of conduct," Helen said, sounding like she read from a script. "We're going to let you go. We have paperwork for you to sign, then we're done here." She passed several sheets to Simon.

He left the papers resting untouched on the desk. "Isn't there anything I can do?"

Helen's face was a ceramic mask. "I'm sorry, but no."

Simon gave Helen a smile that would've been hard for most women to resist. "Please. You know me. I need this job."

Helen shook her head, but the mask remained in place. "This is about breaking company policy and which sites in particular you were accessing, not about whether you need this job." She slid the list of sites across the desk closer to Simon.

"What am I going to tell Natalie?"

"Who's Natalie?" Kalin asked.

"My wife." Simon remained motionless, staring at the papers. "Helen?"

"I don't know."

"You're friends with her. You know how she'll take this."

"She won't hear anything from us," Helen said.

"If Jessica were here, she wouldn't fire me."

"I don't think that's true," Kalin said. "She'd follow policy."

"You don't know her. She's loyal to her friends." He lifted his eyes to Helen. "Unlike you."

Helen started to speak, but Kalin interrupted her. "Simon, there's no reason to take this out on Helen. The incident was reported to her, and she came to me for advice."

"You're one to make accusations. It's your brother who ripped off the resort."

Other than a slight heat low on Kalin's neck, she managed not to react. "That's not what we're here to discuss."

"It's too coincidental that he disappeared after the theft. He's probably spending the money right now."

Obviously Simon had lashed out at her for being fired, and Kalin gave him a moment to compose himself. Still, the idea made her nauseated. She would not believe Roy stole the money, pretended to die, then took off. He wouldn't do that. Not to her. Not to her mom.

Instead of calming down, Simon gave one more poke at Kalin. "Read the radio reports from the day your brother disappeared. Even ski patrol thinks he was up to something. You'll see what I mean."

Kalin took a deep breath. "This conversation has gone off track. The issue today is your termination. It's time for you to leave."

"Maybe you and Roy stole the money together."

"Taking your anger out on me is not going to help. We need you to leave, or we'll have security escort you out."

"Be careful what you do here. Stone Mountain is a small resort, and Holden's a small town." On his way out the door, Simon turned back. He looked as if he might say something and then changed his mind. They watched him stalk along the hallway until they could no longer see him.

* * *

Kalin stomped the fifteen-minute trek back to her office. Firing Simon didn't rank on her list of fun things to do, even if he deserved to be terminated. And no matter what her intentions were, she couldn't stop Simon's comment about Roy taking off with the money from niggling at her.

Not paying attention, she caught her heel on a rock, tripped and scraped her palms on the sand and dirt used to de-ice the roads. She pushed herself upright and wiped grit from her hands. Her palms stung. Her eyes teared. Taking a ragged breath, she kicked the offending rock and continued toward her office.

By the time she arrived at the administration building, she stopped feeling sorry for herself and refocused on work. She strode toward the IT department, intent on asking for information about everything Simon had been doing on his computer for the last month.

Muffled voices drifted from the office. She poked her head around the edge of the doorframe. Constable Miller was talking to Cameron Denham. She stood in the doorway, waiting to be acknowledged.

Cameron had been working in the IT department for twenty-plus years. He'd graduated from the University of British Columbia with a degree in computer science at a time when punch cards were still used. He'd been through several financial crises at the resort and was skilled at saving a dollar. He'd pieced together both the phone and computer systems with parts purchased on eBay or anywhere else he could get a deal. He wasn't up on the latest technologies, but he was the only one around who understood the systems completely.

Cameron was in the middle of an explanation of telephone technology. "Both calls came through the internal exchange, but the problem is our technology is old. We have a list of all calls made to the front desk, but we don't know where the calls were transferred to."

Miller wrote in his notebook. "So you can't confirm Helen got a call?"

Cameron shook his head. "I can tell you we didn't get a call from any bank. I checked the numbers received at the main exchange that afternoon and none of them belonged to a bank."

"I'll need the numbers." Miller lifted his head from his notebook and spotted her. "Kalin?"

"Sorry to interrupt. Can I talk with you privately?" Kalin asked.

Miller removed his cap and tucked it under his arm. "Sure."

They moved to a conference room on the opposite side of the hallway. The pine table shone from a recent polishing, and the chairs had been placed straight against the table's edge. The room overlooked the ski hill, the Alpine Tracks lift station and part of the hotel across the lane.

Both Kalin and Miller remained standing. Kalin rubbed her raw palms together and composed herself. She noted Miller examining her, probably taking stock. Miller could star in a calendar for police officers, similar to the kind used for hot firefighters, although Kalin suspected he was unaware of how his looks affected women.

"Are you ever going to tell me about your chin?"

"I drove a snowmobile too fast and hit the windshield, but that's not what I want to talk to you about. Something happened today I think might be related to the theft."

Instead of answering, Miller chuckled.

Kalin turned to see what he'd laughed at. One of the hotel guests hadn't closed the curtain and unknowingly showed off his butt. "Eww. I didn't need to see that."

"Me neither." Miller angled his body, so he wasn't looking out the window. "So what do you have?"

The conversation was the first relaxed moment they'd had together since the theft and the avalanche, and maybe that meant Miller didn't really suspect her. "Helen and I fired the night auditor, Simon Crane, this morning. He used the Internet to access porn sites. The photos were of young girls."

"Okay. I'll take a report and check if this falls under the child pornography laws."

Getting suspicion off Roy and onto someone else was a priority for Kalin, and she planned to use every opportunity to make that happen. "That would be great, but I'm not explaining this well. Simon brings receipts to the finance center every morning, usually at the same time the safe is being opened. He knows the exact amount of money kept in the safe each night. I'm not saying he stole the money, but I thought you should know he could have seen the combination."

Miller made a note in his black book. "Anything else?"

"I got the feeling he's friends with Jessica Scott. He said he wouldn't have been fired if she was still his boss."

"You're not supposed to be working on this."

"I'm not. Firing Simon had nothing to do with the theft, and I don't think Turner wants me to hide information from you. He just doesn't want me investigating."

"How's Ben doing?"

"What do you mean?"

"With calling off the search."

"He's okay. I know he feels horrible, and he's dealing with it, but they're out searching again today." Kalin resisted the temptation to call Ben. He'd call if he had any new information. If only they could find Roy, then her mom could have a real funeral instead of a memorial service. Turner wouldn't allow resources to be allocated for an endless number of searches. If nothing happened today, the searches were probably over.

"My mom said you called her."

"I did."

"Any reason you were asking about Jack?"

"Look at the time. I've got to go."

"Ha ha. I should've known you wouldn't answer me."

* * *

"I need to see what Simon Crane has been working on for the last month on his computer. I'd like access to everything he did." Kalin hovered in the IT office. Following up on what she'd overheard was a priority.

"Can I ask why?" Cameron said.

Kalin stalled, giving herself time to decide how much she could tell him without breaking privacy laws.

Cameron hit the restart button on a server tucked in the corner of his office. "I can't give you information without a good reason. I've already provided Helen with the list of sites he'd been looking at."

"I have reason, but please understand this is a confidential conversation." Kalin gave him a brief description of her meeting with Simon. "Constable Miller will investigate whether his actions fall under child pornography laws. I need to make sure he has all the relevant information."

"Did you know Simon worked in IT in Calgary before he was the night auditor?"

"No, but that would explain how he bypassed the firewall to access porn sites. Listen, I heard the end of your conversation with Miller. Could you give me the phone numbers you mentioned?"

"Why not? I seem to be giving you everything else."

Kalin smiled at his sense of humor.

She returned to her office and opened her email. Cameron had sent her the information she'd requested in record time. Here was a man who understood priorities. He'd given her access to Simon's hard drive along with the full list of Internet sites he'd searched over the last month. Gotta love a good IT department. She couldn't imagine the same freedom to access information in her government job. The paperwork alone would have stopped her from making such a request.

Kalin scanned Simon's email, found a few non-work related messages, but nothing of interest. She checked his folders and read the titles of files. She opened a folder called *Front Desk.* Inside the folder, she discovered two more folders. One called HD1 and the other HD2.

Curious, she double clicked on HD1. The files pertained to financial information about the resort. One spreadsheet contained a list of all fulltime employees, their years of service, salary and a calculation of termination packages. *What the heck?*

Why would Simon have this and whom did HD1 and HD2 belong to? She backed up a level in the folders and studied the rest of the contents. HD1 belonged to James Turner. She clicked over to HD2. As far as she could tell, it belonged to the director of finance. So how had Simon copied these to his computer? And more importantly, why?

In the finance director's folder, she discovered a financial evaluation of the resort, a list of assets and debt, and a five-year projection of income.

Kalin leaned back in her chair and let her thoughts wander. She knew what this type of information was used for, but what should she do about it? Who to tell about the copied hard drives? Turner? Did she trust him? Constable Miller? Would that constitute releasing the company's private information? She'd signed a confidentiality agreement when she was promoted to director.

Turner calculating termination packages without her input made her nervous, but she couldn't deal with him now. She needed to prove Roy's innocence first. The phone numbers calling the front desk on the day before the theft gave her a starting point.

She clicked on her Internet browser and opened the reverse white pages for Canada. She searched for the first number Cameron had given her.

Holden Laundromat.

Kalin called the director of lodging. "Do we clean our linens or do we outsource that?"

"Outsource," the director said.

"Do you know to where?"

"Of course. Holden Laundromat."

Kalin hung up. That call made sense. After researching the rest of the numbers, only one more interested her. The number was listed under Stone Mountain Employee Housing.

Kalin bee lined to Monica Bellman's desk. As the HR manager, Monica was also responsible for employee housing. When Kalin first came to Stone Mountain, Monica had applied for the HR manager job, but Kalin took the position and Monica resented her. When her previous boss promoted Kalin to director, Kalin promoted Monica to manager, and their relationship improved.

"Is there still a communal phone in the staff lounge area?"

"Yes. Why?"

"So if a call came to the resort from Stone Mountain Employee Housing, then it came from there?"

"Yeah."

Of all the finance center staff, only one lived in housing provided by the resort. "Does Eric Wilson live in that building?"

Monica drew a quick breath. "He does. You don't think—"

"I'm only speculating. Please don't say anything about this." Kalin called Miller, got his voicemail and left the information.

She returned to her office and retrieved Eric's employment file she'd taken earlier in the day. The folder was thin, but she read the contents, hoping she might find something useful. His job application for a seasonal clerk in the finance center provided nothing interesting. She read Eric's criminal record check he'd brought from Australia. The paper looked photocopied and could be a forgery. She called Miller and left a second message.

Just as she hit disconnect, her cell rang, and Ben's name appeared on the screen.

Neither Ben nor Kalin said anything. Kalin's heart pinched. The news was bad. She pushed the HR folders to the side and held her breath.

Finally Kalin broke the silence. “You didn’t find him.”

“I’m sorry. There’s too much snow.”

Kalin squished her eyes tight. “Thank you for trying. I know this is hard for you, too.”

CHAPTER NINETEEN

For the second time in her life, Helen sat in the interrogation room at the Holden RCMP headquarters. Holden was eighteen kilometers from the resort, but in winter conditions, the drive could take up to an hour to cover the twelve-hundred-meter drop in altitude. She'd left her place early and ended up waiting half an hour in an empty room before anyone spoke with her, giving her an agonizingly long time to wonder if they knew she lied during the first polygraph. What other reason could they have for asking her to take the test again?

As the finance center clerk on duty both the night before the theft and the morning after, of course, she'd be a prime suspect. Her ex-boss, Jessica, certainly thought she stole the money.

When Helen finished the second test, she waited another ten minutes. The police wouldn't tell her why they wanted her to re-answer their questions. Miller only said the polygraph specialist found some discrepancies in the first test. This time, a woman asked the questions, and she'd been tough.

Sweat trickled down Helen's spine, and she shifted in the chair, unsticking her shirt from her back. She didn't know where to look. She guessed people were watching her through the mirror on the wall, and wished they'd hurry up. Did Turner know about her failing the polygraph, and would he change his mind about promoting her?

When the door finally opened, Constable Miller entered. He sat across from her and placed a folder on the table. "We have some issues with the way you answered a few questions."

Helen swallowed over the lump in her throat. The first time she met Constable Miller, she'd liked his friendly face, but now he looked stern. Still, he wasn't as intimidating as the woman who had just interrogated her.

Miller drew his chair closer to the table, and the legs squeaked over the linoleum floor. "You lied during the questioning. Do you want to tell me why?"

"I don't know what you mean. Where am I failing?"

"It's not about passing or failing. You registered high around certain questions."

"Am I in trouble?"

"You could be if you don't tell the truth."

Not knowing who was behind the mirror unnerved Helen, so she focused on Miller. "It's about the combination, isn't it?"

Miller smiled, not with his mouth, but with his eyes. "If it has to do with Roy McCann, you should tell us. You can't hurt him now, and it's only going to be worse for you if you try to protect him."

"Roy was my friend. I don't believe he stole the money."

"I understand. Sometimes people we care about do terrible things."

"What will happen if I lied during the test?"

"That depends on what you tell me, but you won't be punished for the lie itself. Now's the time to talk to me."

Helen glanced in the direction of the one-way mirror. "I did write down the combination, and it's possible Roy saw it."

"Can you elaborate?"

She thought back to the night Roy had come knocking on her door. "I just got back from cross-country skiing and was planning on going to bed, when Roy showed up."

"Did he come by often?"

"Not really. I could tell by the way he called me through the door that he was drunk. I wasn't even sure if I should let him in. It was so late, and if anyone saw him…"

"Why would that be a problem?"

"He dated Jessica, my boss."

"So you let him in?"

"I did. He could barely walk. I knew he wouldn't make it home, so I helped him get to my bed and I left him there passed out face down on my comforter."

"And?"

"My friend Natalie lent me a paperback, and Roy fell face down on it. I tried to get it but couldn't."

"And that's relevant how?"

"As I leaned over him, I noticed my day timer on my bedside table."

"You seem to be getting off course here."

"I'm embarrassed. I wrote the combination in the back of my day timer. I shouldn't have done that."

"When was that?"

Even though Helen couldn't see the people on the other side of the glass, she knew they were there and guessed they all leaned forward to hear her answer. "Early December."

"Was it the same combination as on the day of the theft?"

"Yes," Helen whispered.

"What makes you think Roy saw the combination?"

"In the morning, when I went to look for him, I found my day timer open. I'm neat and organized and would never have left it that way."

"How would Roy know where to look?"

Helen could feel heat in her face and wished her cheeks wouldn't turn blotchy. "I did something stupid. He was complaining about Jessica's temper, and I was being supportive. I told him how she snapped at me when I forgot the combination and that I'd written it in my day timer, so I wouldn't have to ask her for it again." Helen's shoulders slumped. She'd been gullible. She guessed Roy gave her the snowboarding lessons as a way to make up for what he'd done. She'd thought Roy liked her. Maybe he wasn't even drunk that night. Maybe it was her fault the money was stolen.

"Do you have the day timer with you?"

Helen pulled it from her purse and handed it to Miller. "Do you have to tell Paul Turner about this?"

* * *

Minutes before the chairlifts opened at nine, Kalin made a quick stop in her office and picked up her skis. She couldn't help Roy, but she could save his reputation. She'd shifted focus to two other people for the finance center theft. Her confidence she'd prove his innocence was growing. All she had to do was keep the pressure on.

Getting on the hill. Sounded easy, but her entire body tensed. She hadn't quit cycling because Jack died while riding, so she shouldn't quit skiing because an avalanche killed Roy.

She'd had every variation of nightmares, Roy dying a different way each time, but she needed to get on the slopes and make a move to get her life under control. Eight days had passed since the avalanche. Surely she could work up the courage to get on the mountain.

She couldn't face skiing her first run alone. She'd asked Ben to take her during one of his shifts. Besides, skiing with Ben would give her a chance to talk to him about the job offer at White Peaks. She'd put off the conversation long enough. Maybe they could talk rationally about the future if they were distracted by skiing. Ben might not go on the defensive immediately if he was trying to help her get over her newfound fear of skiing.

She clomped to the chairlift with her skis balanced over her shoulder, her fingers holding the tips. Blue sky stretched from peak to peak, letting the sun bring some warmth to the air. She reached the lift, and Ben skied in from the side. She fell in behind the last person in the lineup.

Ben chuckled and shook his head. "This way." He nodded toward the front of the line. "I'm on duty. We don't need to wait. Let's hit the summit."

She had to admit, even though she missed the city a little, skiing on duty was a great job perk, but she didn't like cutting in line in front of other staff. Ben was right though. He was on duty, and he needed to get up the hill quicker than the other skiers.

Simon Crane stood in line and glared at Kalin. Why had he been looking at the resort's finances? Too bad she didn't have a reason to question him.

The chair swung behind Ben and Kalin and scooped them off the ground. Ben didn't lower the safety bar, and Kalin followed his lead, letting her skis dangle above the snowy expanse.

The trees grew sparser as they ascended on the third chairlift, but the scent of pine still filled the air.

"You sure this isn't too soon?" Ben asked.

"I can't avoid skiing forever. After yesterday…" Heat stung her face. She'd been about to say failure. "After not finding Roy, I need to move on." Ben wouldn't be able to see her expression underneath her goggles and the neck tube pulled over her nose.

The chair lurched into the disembarkation station. They dismounted and skirted to the side of the lift shack.

"We'll be here a minute. Do you want to kick off your skis and help me check the sled?"

"Okay." Kalin stood with her knees buckled, easing the pressure on her toes and shins. Now was the time to mention White Peaks. They could talk while he readied the sled, and he'd be distracted.

The radio clipped to Ben's chest pocket squawked. The patroller on dispatch duty broadcast there was an accident in the Dragon's Bowl.

Kalin grabbed his wrist. "I can't ski there."

"You'll be fine. I'll take the sled. All you need to do is follow me."

Ben hooked the sled to his waist, snapped into his bindings and took off, leaving Kalin to follow or not.

You promised not to ski in the backcountry. Even though her mom wasn't there, her voice was clear. Kalin swallowed hard, mentally kicked herself and chased Ben.

Shoving the White Peaks discussion to the back of her mind, she flexed and compressed her legs over the soft moguls and turned her skis around any trees blocking her way. After the twenty-centimeter snowfall the night before, the branches hung full and heavy, and snow thudded to the ground as she skied close by. She managed to keep up with Ben and was not far behind him when they reached the edge of the Bowl.

He skied as if a sled wasn't attached to his hips and launched into the run without hesitating. Kalin jumped over the edge, not thinking about where she was going, and pressed herself to ski faster. They arrived at the accident scene within seconds of each other, but Kalin's breathing came in short, rapid bursts, and Ben wasn't breathing hard at all.

Two patrollers stood waist deep in a tree well beside an injured boy. The boy had fallen into the well and hit the tree head first. The skid line across the top of his helmet meant the helmet had prevented the boy from being scalped. The patrollers hadn't attempted to move him yet.

"Hey buddy, what's your name?" Ben asked.

"Dawson."

Ben balanced himself beside the boy. "Can you tell me where it hurts?"

"My face."

"How old are you?"

"Ten." His neck tube muffled his tiny voice.

Ben gently shifted the tube below the boy's chin and inspected his face. He squeezed Dawson's gloved hand, slipped two fingers underneath his sleeve and checked his pulse. He cut the goggle strap, releasing the seal around the eyes, and a pool of blood mixed with tears spilled across the boy's face.

Kalin looked away.

"Dawson, buddy. You okay?" a voice boomed from below. A man climbed toward the accident scene, clearly out of breath. Kalin guessed he'd skied ahead of the boy, then climbed the slope when the boy hadn't followed.

"Daddy." Dawson shifted his head in the direction of his dad, and Ben placed his hand on Dawson's forehead to keep his neck still.

The patrollers took fifteen minutes to get Dawson out of the tree well and packed into the sled.

After they'd stabilized Dawson, Ben turned to the patroller beside him and said, "Can you take him in the sled?"

Ben and Kalin watched the group snowplow down the run.

"Did you give the father Dawson's snowboard to make him feel like he was helping?"

Ben nodded.

"That's smart."

Standing on an angled slope in the Dragon's Bowl, Kalin looked at her feet. Was she standing on Roy? She shifted to the left a foot, then shifted back. No matter where she stood, he could be beneath her.

As if reading her mind, Ben said, "This is where the avalanche happened. See the terrain on the side of the run, how the trees have been wiped out?"

Kalin stared at the debris of trees, willing the mountain to produce Roy. A metallic-yellow object lodged on a broken branch caught her eye. "What's that?"

Ben sidestepped to the object and plucked a boot buckle from the branch. He opened his pack, pulled out a hazard line and tied the orange plastic strip around what was left of the tree.

"What are you doing?"

"Marking the spot," Ben said.

"I can see that, but why?"

"This could be Roy's buckle. It'll give us a starting point to search after the snow melts in the spring."

"Do we have to wait that long?"

"Twenty more centimeters of snow fell last night. You know we've been getting dumps like that regularly since the avalanche, and each snowfall makes it less likely we'll find him. Until the snow starts to melt, we…I can't justify taking the team away from the resort when there's no chance we'll find him."

Even though she didn't want to, Kalin believed Ben. Her eyes followed the destruction farther up the mountain. She pointed to a spot where the trees stood strong and healthy. "What's over the precipice?"

"The slide started there."

"Let's climb up."

Ben studied the terrain for a moment and finally nodded. "Okay."

They sidestepped their way, taking a few breaks when their legs tired, and after twenty minutes, reached the area.

"Why would the avalanche start here?" Kalin asked.

Ben surveyed the area and shook his head. "I can't answer that. There are too many possibilities."

"I don't understand. There's no overhanging ledge, no snow piled high above here, so what would trigger this spot to let go?"

* * *

Later that afternoon, Kalin entered the real estate office located in the center of Stone Mountain's upper village just as Simon Crane was leaving. He scowled at her but didn't say anything. Would the night auditor hold a grudge for being fired or would he realize she'd had no other move? *The former.*

Books and contracts littered the desktop. Downhill and touring skis leaned against the wall, and two pairs of ski boots rested askew on the floor.

"What do you want?" Jessica asked.

Jessica seemed upset, but Kalin didn't think it was because she was there. She turned and glanced back in the direction of Simon. "Do you have time for coffee? I thought we could talk about Roy."

Jessica's collarbones protruded above the neckline on her low-cut sweater. A slight blush shone through her translucent skin, and like most people working at the mountain in winter, she had a case of hat head. Kalin had the urge to find her a brush. Despite the hair, Jessica could be a runway model with her chiseled bone structure and long features. She was exactly Roy's type, and for the first time, Kalin noticed Jessica's resemblance to Roy's ex-fiancée, Patricia.

Kalin and Jessica strolled to the Mountainside Café and ordered a mochaccino for Kalin and a chai tea for Jessica. They grabbed a table for two tucked in the corner. The rustic café, with its hardwood floor, maple chairs and tables, and mustard walls exuded a welcoming atmosphere. The aroma of coffee reminded Kalin of Roy's addiction to the brew.

"I don't know if you heard about yesterday's search, but SAR didn't find Roy."

"I know. Ben called me."

"I wish…"

"Me, too," Jessica said.

"I'm glad you got a job so quickly," Kalin said instead of asking about Simon and why he'd been in Jessica's office. She couldn't break HR confidentiality and talk about him or why he'd been fired.

A slow smile crossed Jessica's face. "It would've been better if you'd helped me keep my job. Turner was way out of line."

Kalin stirred her mochaccino, clinking the spoon on the inside edges of the cup and avoiding eye contact with Jessica. Turner had been right to fire her. "I don't have a lot of influence with him yet. He's not as easy to work with as Reed was. Did the cops give you a hard time about the theft?"

"What a bunch of jerks. They treated me like I was the thief. Talk about disrespect. I worked hard at that job."

"I'm sorry you were badly treated. How are you doing? I mean about Roy."

"Not great. I miss him."

"I do, too."

"We had a fight, and he wasn't talking to me. That makes it worse," Jessica said.

Roy hadn't said anything to Kalin about fighting with Jessica, but she guessed that's why he'd moved in with her and Ben instead of Jessica. Jessica wasn't the only one who'd fought with Roy. Kalin had kicked Roy out the night before the avalanche. His fighting with Jessica made her feel even worse. "What about?"

"Nothing. It was stupid."

"Can you tell me? It might help."

"I thought he was cheating on me with Helen."

"Helen?"

"I know. I never should have fought with him about her. If he was going to stray, he wouldn't cheat with a loser like her."

Jessica, Simon, Helen and Roy all linked together in this mess. What did the connections mean? Kalin sipped her mochaccino and waited for Jessica to say more.

"The worst part of the whole thing is that everyone in admin got focused on the theft and didn't care about what Roy's accident meant to me."

"Why do you think he went up the mountain?" Kalin could see the question upset Jessica, and maybe she shouldn't have asked her about the avalanche so abruptly, but she couldn't help herself.

"How can I possibly know? All I do know is it made the cops think he took the money with my help."

Not intimidated by Jessica's raised voice, Kalin pressured for more. "He really didn't say anything about going skiing early?"

Jessica stiffened and pushed her cup toward the center of the table. "No. Is there any reason you're asking about this?"

"I'm trying to understand what happened."

"Don't tell me you think I stole the money."

"It's not that. I want to clear Roy's name." Kalin had never been friends with Jessica, but she'd made an effort for Roy's sake. Jessica had always been polite with her. Now the underlying hostility in Jessica's demeanor was probably because Kalin hadn't stopped Turner from firing her. Unless Jessica took the money and hoped to blame Roy.

"Did you ever go out on touring skis with Roy?"

Jessica smiled as if she were remembering a happier time. "Early in the season, before the lifts were open, Roy and I went every chance we got. If I couldn't go, he sometimes went with Aiden. Roy loved being up on the mountain at night. I guess he liked the adrenaline rush."

"Did he go with Aiden often?"

"Not as much as he would've liked. Aiden had to get to work by seven thirty and didn't like being tired. Roy never cared."

"Roy's downhill skis are still at my place. Only his touring skis are missing, so he must have used them. Any idea how long it would've taken him to get to the Dragon's Bowl?"

"We never skied that high together. We mostly stayed on the lower mountain. What are you getting at?"

"I'm just trying to figure out the timing of the theft and the avalanche."

"So you do suspect Roy?"

"I'm trying to prove he's innocent." Kalin placed her cup on the table hard enough to slosh the liquid over the edge.

* * *

Turner didn't know how his life could get much worse. Someone stole one hundred thousand dollars, and the amount would come right off the company's bottom line. The insurance policy had a deductible of two hundred thousand. The cheaper policy that saved money when they purchased the bloody thing was now going to cost them.

An avalanche killed an employee, search and rescue hadn't found his body and the director of security couldn't investigate the theft because the guy in the avalanche was her brother. The resort couldn't afford another scandal. Not after what happened last year.

Gertrude hovered in his doorway, and her perfume wafted toward him. Someone should tell the woman the scent was overdone.

"You're scheduled to meet Oliver at eleven thirty for an update."

"Fine. Until then, I don't want to be interrupted." He shut the door quietly this time, leaned back and drummed his head several times against the wall.

Fifteen minutes later, Gertrude entered without knocking.

"I told you not to interrupt me."

Hovering at the entrance to his office, Gertrude fussed with the buttons on her flower print dress. "I'm sorry, but Constable Miller is here to see you. I thought you'd want to speak with him."

Miller moved around Gertrude's heavy frame and into Turner's office. "Is this a bad time?"

"No, it's as good as any. What have you found out?"

"I thought you'd like to know we finished the polygraph tests."

"And?"

"None of the tests implicated anyone." Miller shrugged. "One employee had to take the polygraph twice but was cleared."

"Who?"

"I can't divulge that."

Turner grunted. "I don't understand. Why two tests?"

"The first was inconclusive. We thought the person was trying to trick the test."

"Trick the test?"

"Anyone can read about polygraphs on the Internet. They learn if they pinch in their butt cheeks or bite the inside of their lip when they're answering truthfully, the monitor will show a spike on the graph. If they lie, a similar spike occurs, making the results difficult to analyze."

"How can you be sure the second results are correct?"

"We're sure."

Turner clenched his jaw and said nothing.

Miller stood with his hands hanging at his sides, his equipment belt forcing his left arm farther away from his body than his right. "I'm not going to justify our methods, Mr. Turner."

The formality of Miller's answer made Turner change tactics. "Did Jessica Scott take the test?"

"She refused. She said since you fired her, she was under no obligation."

"So you have no idea who did this?"

"I didn't say that. I said the polygraphs didn't implicate anyone."

Gertrude interrupted again.

"What?" Turner asked.

"Your wife's on the phone. She says it's urgent."

Behind his back, his left hand gripped his right wrist, pinching the skin. He needed a drink, and he needed it now. "Tell her I'm busy. I'll call her later."

Gertrude shut the door, and Turner circled back to Miller. "What is it with you? It doesn't seem like you're trying very hard to solve this crime."

Miller straightened. "I'm here out of courtesy. Technically, I don't have to share any information with you. I thought it would be helpful for us to talk about the investigation. I'm sorry to have bothered you." Miller started toward the door.

"No. Wait. You're right. It's frustrating not knowing who did this."

"I understand," Miller said on his way out the door.

Turner cursed.

"Your wife," Gertrude said.

As if he didn't have enough to worry about without Gertrude nagging him. He kicked the door shut with a thud and tapped on his wife's name.

Before he had a chance to speak, Crystal said, "Warren's sick."

"I don't mean to be cold, but you know I have a lot going on right now. Is he more than his usual sick?" Turner listened to her cry. "I'm sorry. What can I do?"

"His doctor says he needs to go to Calgary. I need you to come home."

"You know I can't. You'll have to take him."

The sigh through the phone had the same impact as a slap on his face.

"What am I going to pay the hotel and gas bills with?"

Turner slowed his speech and said, "Use the Visa."

"It's maxed out. All the cards are at their limit, and we only have fifty in cash in the account."

"Can the trip wait till Friday?"

"No. It can't."

Now was not a good time to talk about their expenses that weren't related to Warren, but the time was never right, so Turner said, "We should put the house on the market. It's too big for us anyway."

"I don't want—"

"I know, but we need to be realistic. Our mortgage payments are killing us." *And soon, I won't have a job.* Turner waited while Crystal sobbed. Finally he said, "Okay, I'll put some money in the account. Use cash."

"Where are you going to get money from?"

"I'll figure it out." Turner opened his desk drawer, slid his hand behind the file and pulled out his silver flask.

CHAPTER TWENTY

Wednesday morning, Kalin cross-country skied along a path with Chica running by her side. She'd downhill skied the day before with Ben, and today she found sitting at home doing nothing was not a solution to grief, so she'd geared up and hit the Nordic trails behind her house.

Muffled from within her pocket, Kalin's cell rang. She snowplowed to a stop, pulled off her glove with her teeth and answered.

"I was just thinking about you," Kalin said to her mom.

"What are you doing? Your breathing sounds funny."

"I'm cross-country skiing with Chica."

"Alone?"

Kalin surveyed the endless terrain around her. No matter how long she ended up working there, she didn't think she'd ever get over the beauty of Stone Mountain. "No. I'm with Chica."

To stop her mom from lecturing her about being in the backcountry by herself, she said, "I met with Roy's girlfriend yesterday. I think she's pretty sad."

"I wish I'd had a chance to meet her. Have you heard anything more about the theft?"

"Jessica's a suspect, too."

"You mean along with Roy?"

"Yes." Kalin transferred her cell to her left hand and tucked her right hand into her pocket. "Did the RCMP call you again?"

"Constable Miller called. He asked if I'd received the package the resort sent me with Roy's things."

Kalin skied forward a few feet to a sunny spot on the trail. She tilted her head toward the sky and let the sun warm her cheeks. "Have you?"

"No. He wants me to call him when it arrives and let him know what's in it."

"Can you let me know, too?"

"Of course, but this means they think Roy stole the money."

"Not necessarily. There're other suspects, too. Things are a bit tense, but I'm going to prove Roy's innocent. I don't want this hanging over him. Or me for that matter."

Chica jumped over a mound of snow at the edge of the groomed trail and ran through the trees, barking at something. What was she chasing? It had better be a squirrel or a rabbit and not a larger animal.

"Hang on a sec." Kalin moved the phone away from her face. "Chica, come."

Chica obeyed and trotted back to Kalin. "Sorry about that. Chica likes to stray once in a while."

"Maybe you should let this go. You made yourself miserable after Jack died, looking for answers when none existed. Don't do that with Roy."

"It's not the same thing. And why are you changing your mind again? Last time we talked, you wanted me to prove Roy's innocence."

"This whole thing is making me crazy, and I'm worried about you. You spent all that time trying to find out who killed Jack and discovered nothing. Don't put yourself through that again. We have to accept Roy's gone. The RCMP will find out who stole the money."

"I won't obsess." Chica meandered away from Kalin but not far enough for her to be concerned. "My boss is letting me in on what's happening with the investigation. Don't worry. I won't get into any trouble." She hated lying to her mom, but she couldn't explain that her boss had told her not to investigate, and she was going against his direct order.

"The reason I called is we're having a small memorial for Roy this Saturday. Can you fly home?"

Holding a memorial meant her mom had accepted that Roy was dead. "I wish I could, but there's too much going on here."

"Please. Just for one day. I'll pay for the flight."

"I'll try. Let me call you back later."

Kalin disconnected, knowing she would spend more time searching for answers than her mom would approve of. Every time she thought about Roy, she believed she owed him.

Pain and sorrow were unique to each person. No matter how connected Kalin was to other people, the depth of her loss was her own.

How could she be lonely when she was married to Ben, and she had friends, good friends, and her mom was on the other end of the phone?

She couldn't talk to Ben or her mom about Jack. The burden wasn't something a second husband should have to carry, and her mom would just worry about her. Now she couldn't talk to Roy either. He'd been close with Jack, too. Since moving to Stone Mountain, she'd been able to wake up without a grinding headache. She slept a full eight hours most nights. Most days the flashback to the police at her door remained at bay.

Now with Roy and the avalanche, Jack had returned with a vengeance. Like he was trying to tell her something. She laughed at herself. *Really. Listening to ghosts now.*

Maybe if the Ottawa police had found out who'd killed Jack, she wouldn't be obsessed with him now. Kalin figured a drunk driver had hit him and been too cowardly to stop. The police said he'd died instantly, but what if they were wrong?

She called Chica back to her side and pushed forward with her ski poles.

* * *

Kalin skate-skied across the flats, reached a steep descent and tucked her elbows to her sides. While she sailed down the hill, her phone rang again. At the bottom, she stopped abruptly, and Chica bumped into the back of her legs. Kalin fell face forward, landed in soft snow with a thump and rolled onto her back. Chica bounded on her chest and licked her cheek.

"Get off me, you silly mutt."

With her rump in the air, Chica wagged her tail and continued to lick. Kalin had already missed the call, so she played with Chica for a moment.

"Alright, enough. Get your dog breath away from my face." She nudged Chica aside, sat and pulled her cell from her pocket.

"I know it's your day off, but can you come in?" Helen asked Kalin. After Helen explained the problem, Kalin called Fred and requested he join her in Helen's office. Violence at work was always a worry, especially when emotions ran high.

She rubbed Chica's head. "Too bad I didn't answer the call at the top of the hill."

Chica ran around her in circles.

"You don't care, do you?" Not wanting to make Helen wait too long, she ascended as quickly as her muscles would let her.

Kalin and Fred arrived at Helen's office at the same time.

"You out skiing?" Fred asked.

She wore her cross-country ski pants and jacket. She'd left her toque on, thinking her hair would be matted to her head with sweat. Not a good look for the office. At least Fred looked professional in his security uniform. "I didn't have time to change. Give me a sec to drop Chica in my office. Then let's get in there. I'm sure Helen's had enough by now."

They found Helen face to face with a thirty-something woman. The woman stopped yelling mid-sentence and swung around toward Kalin.

"This is Natalie Crane," Helen said.

"You." Natalie pointed at Kalin. "This is all your fault."

Fred positioned himself in front of Kalin. "You need to step back and settle down."

Natalie flared her nostrils at Fred but relented. Her hair was pulled back into an elegant roll behind her head. Her makeup, expertly applied, accentuated her blue eyes, but she couldn't compete with Simon in the looks department.

"Have we met before?" Kalin asked.

"I know who you are. You fired Simon. I want to know what you have against my husband. What did he ever do to you?" Spittle sprayed from her mouth and landed in a glob on her chin, marring her flawless complexion.

Kalin watched the spittle drip. Instead of passing Natalie a tissue, she ignored the drop. "He's done nothing to me. He lost his job because he broke company policy."

"He told me you hated him and fired him for no reason."

"Does that seem likely? The night auditor position is difficult to fill. Along with her regular job, Helen has to cover some of his shifts personally until we find a replacement. It could take months."

"Simon told me you're a fast talker. We're going to sue you if you don't give him his job back."

Without taking her eyes off Natalie, Kalin asked Helen, "Do you still have the Internet reports?"

"Yes."

"Natalie, if you sit calmly, I'll show you why we fired Simon," Kalin said.

Before she sat in the nearest chair, Natalie looked from Kalin to Helen. She balled her camel hair coat on top of her knees and clutched the material in her fists.

"I'm not sure this is a good idea," Helen said. "Natalie doesn't need to hear this from us."

"I know you're friends and don't want to hurt her, but I don't see what choice we have. Simon's not going to tell her the truth."

"I agree." Fred nodded at Kalin, giving his approval.

Natalie stood. "Simon doesn't lie."

"Please sit again," Kalin said. "Let me show you what we discovered." She handed Natalie the list. "These are sites Simon accessed during his night shift. He left the pages open on the computer, and the employee working the next morning found photos. As you can imagine, the sites disturbed her, and she made a formal complaint."

Natalie read the list, grimacing a couple of times before she finished. "This is so unlike Simon. He's not the type to look at porn, and this doesn't prove anything. Anyone could have looked at the sites."

"I'm afraid not," Kalin said. "The computer was logged on with Simon's password, and he worked the shift alone. No one else had access."

Natalie scratched the side of her neck until the skin turned red. "You could have had IT fake the list."

Thinking how upset Natalie must be, Kalin softened. "You don't really believe that."

"Can I have a copy of the list?"

Kalin shook her head. "These are our private documents."

Natalie held the pages toward Kalin, which fluttered in her shaking hands. "I have a right to take them."

"You don't," Kalin said. "They're company property."

Natalie placed a hand on Helen's wrist. "You don't understand. Simon's been depressed lately, since before you fired him, and this could push him over the edge. He can't take the loss. Surely you have some compassion for him."

"I wish I could help," Helen said.

"But how will Simon get another job?" Natalie tightened her grip on Helen, and Fred stepped closer to her. "Helen, we're friends. How can you do this to me?"

"I know this is hard, but there's nothing Helen or Kalin can do to change the situation," Fred said.

Kalin was impressed by the softness in his voice and the respectful way in which he spoke.

Natalie's back stiffened. "We're still going to sue you." She slapped the papers on the desk in front of Helen and rushed from the room.

"What do you think?" Helen asked Kalin.

"If I were her, I wouldn't believe us either."

* * *

Meeting with Natalie Crane reminded Kalin of what Simon said when she'd fired him. He'd mentioned she should check the radio reports from the day of the avalanche. Why hadn't she thought of that earlier?

The security reports might contain a link to the radio reports. Mostly she left the database for Fred, her security manager, to manage, and she didn't spend much time accessing the data. Maybe the time had arrived for her to become more involved with the information. Still wearing her cross-country ski clothing, she scooted her office chair close to her desk and turned on her computer.

Chica flopped and rested her chin on Kalin's foot.

Before she had a chance to open the software and start a search, the squeak of ski boots walking in the direction of her office announced a visitor.

Aiden Price interrupted her. "Got a minute?" He edged the door until it was ajar, keeping his hand on the doorknob. "I have a problem with a liftie. I think he's been smoking dope on his breaks and coming back to work stoned. I wanted to check with you before I fire him."

Chica thumped her tail but didn't get up from underneath Kalin's desk.

Kalin took in his bulky frame. Aiden wore his orange and yellow lift operator uniform. He kept his auburn hair in a Caesar-style cut, brushed forward to his temples, hiding a receding hairline. His nose was anything but a Caesar nose. It was flat and squished, more like a boxer's. She didn't want to be involved in a second firing in one day, but asked, "Do you have proof?"

Aiden sat, and his ski pants rustled against the worn fabric of the chair. Snow melted off his boots, leaving water stains on top of the many water stains that had soaked through the carpet over the years. "He smells like dope when he comes back to work."

"Could he be hanging around with people who are smoking up, and the smell clings to him?"

"I thought that, too, except last night on the staff bus to Holden, he told one of our crew chiefs he smoked a joint at lunch, then worked the rest of the afternoon. He laughed about it. The crew chief wrote a statement." Aiden passed a signed, handwritten note to Kalin.

She smirked and took the paper. She stopped smirking when she read the name of the employee. Greg Parker. "Not smart. How long has he worked here?"

"This is his second winter."

"I gather since he was on the bus to town, he lives in Holden and not in employee housing."

Aiden nodded.

"Then we don't need to involve Monica," Kalin said. "Write him up, bring him in and let him go. Whatever you do, don't let him near the lifts again. We can't have a stoned liftie on duty."

Kalin made a copy of the note and recorded the conversation in her notebook. "One more thing. I'd like to speak to him before he leaves. Can you ask him to come see me?"

"Sure, why?"

"I have something to ask him."

"Um…I haven't had a chance to say I'm sorry about your brother."

"Thanks."

"It must be hard having everyone talking about him."

The stoned liftie wasn't a complicated employee issue, so what did Aiden really want from her? "What do you mean?"

"Well, with the theft and all."

"Do you know something?"

"No, I only wanted to say I was sorry for what happened to him."

* * *

By five o'clock Greg Parker hadn't arrived in Kalin's office. She guessed he'd decided not to visit her as requested. After locking her door, she carried her cross-country skis to the ground floor of the administration building and headed toward the path leading home. The path meandered between the forest and the golf course, rising and falling with the terrain, and she loved the commute.

She unclipped Chica's leash, and Chica bounded ahead of her. Before crossing onto the deep snow, Kalin snapped her boots into the bindings. The lights from the resort illuminated the snow-covered surface until the first bend in the path. Kalin switched on her headlamp and was about to shove off.

"Hey, Kalin."

She turned to see Greg Parker tromping toward her. Her headlamp lit his face, and he shielded his eyes with one hand. He'd cut his hair and shaved since she'd last seen him, but somehow he still looked like the kind of guy who'd cause trouble. When she read his name on the note the crew chief wrote, she'd assumed he was the same Greg Parker Roy hung out with.

Kalin skate skied a few meters closer to the resort, back into the lights. She whistled for Chica to return to her side. "I have some questions for you."

"You know I've been fired. What else do you want?"

Another person stood off to the sides in the shadows of the trees. “Who’s that with you?”

“Just a friend. I’m in a hurry, so what’s up?”

“I want to talk to you about Roy.”

He shielded his eyes from the beam streaming from her headlamp. “I’m sorry he died.”

“Thank you.” Reaching to her forehead, she turned off the lamp, giving Greg a break from the light. “Do you have any idea why he went on the mountain so early?”

Greg used his middle finger to flip his bangs to the side of his head. “Why should I tell you anything?”

Kalin pretended she didn’t notice the gesture, although the way the light from the resort fell, the shadow made his finger look as if it belonged to a giant. She felt an unreasonable urge to giggle. Wind whistled between the lodgepole pines ubiquitous to the mountain, almost as if moaning a warning, and she turned serious. “Meaning you do know?”

“Nope. I hadn’t seen him for a few days.”

“I was hoping we could make a deal. I won’t report your drug activity to the police, and you talk to me about Roy.”

Greg scanned the area, avoiding eye contact with Kalin, and spit on the snow-covered path. “What do you want to know?”

Skiing home alone in the dark didn’t bother her. Being alone on an isolated path with a guy who exuded hostility did. She’d been trapped on this path before and didn’t intend to let that happen again. “I forgot my house key at work. Let’s head that way.”

“No.” Greg shook his head once. “I don’t plan on being here long.”

Kalin faced him squarely, standing with the front of her skis touching his toes, letting him know she wasn’t intimidated. “Okay. I know you hung out with Roy.”

“I did.”

“Did you consider him a friend?”

“You’re his sister. What’d he tell you?”

Greg lifted the sides of his lips, and Kalin interpreted the movement to be a smile. She waited.

“What do I care? We were more like business partners.”

“What type of partners?”

“I sold him things.”

Behaving like a teenager, Greg played twenty questions with her. His abrupt answers annoyed her but were better than nothing. She suspected he spoke in a curt manner to appear cool. “What things?”

“I’m not spelling it out for you.”

"Drugs?" After Jack died, Roy started using drugs in Ottawa until Patricia straightened him out. Then Kalin ruined things between them. She didn't know if Roy had gotten back into drugs while he was still living in Ottawa, mainly because she hadn't seen him after the disaster at his engagement party. She hated thinking about that night but couldn't help herself.

There must have been over a hundred friends and business associates gathered, all dressed for a formal garden party. When Roy was half an hour late, tensions began to rise. Kalin's stepdad ordered her to find him as if he was her responsibility. Before she had the chance, a delivery van pulled into the driveway in full view of the guests. Roy had sent flowers to Patricia's mother, apologizing for not coming, and Patricia was forced to tell her parents what had happened. Kalin, along with her mom and stepdad, were asked to leave. Her mom was hurt, her stepdad angry, and they both thought the disaster was Kalin's fault.

"I don't do drugs."

Kalin was willing to accept the lie if she could get Greg to tell her more. "Was Roy in trouble?"

"Not going there. I've told you all I'm going to. If you want to call the cops, that's up to you. I'm done here." Greg walked back toward the resort, leaving Kalin to decide whether to follow or head home. She turned on her headlamp and aimed the beam at Greg. The light hit him just as he joined Eric Wilson and headed back to the resort. Eric was the finance center clerk. She didn't know much about him except he came from Australia. Did this mean Roy and Eric had known each other?

She skied away from the resort, pumping her arms hard, and picked up speed.

CHAPTER TWENTY-ONE

Kalin snowshoed to work and simultaneously tapped the screen of her smart phone. She searched the security database for the date Roy disappeared. The sun had yet to rise over the peaks, and the screen glowed.

Considering what Simon said when she'd fired him, the radio transcripts might give her some insight. She scanned the database until she found a link to the incident reports. She clicked the link. Roy's name, written in crisp black letters, jumped off the screen.

Kalin's snowshoes crunched in the snow. Tapping on her phone and snowshoeing at the same time slowed her progress, but she was almost at the parking lot near her office.

She read an entry by one of the patrollers. Over the radio he'd said, "Figures it's Roy. It's always something with him."

Kalin inhaled sharply. How cruel.

Turner stepped from a dark corner of the administration building. "You're here early."

Surprised by the unexpected interruption, she dropped her phone into a snow pile. "Don't do that," she snapped, then remembered she was talking to her boss. "Sorry. You startled me."

Turner didn't make a motion to retrieve her phone or apologize for scaring her, so she bent her knees and stuck her hand in the cold snow. She checked the display, and the phone didn't seem to be damaged.

The way Turner snuck up on her in the dark gave her one more nudge in the direction of accepting the job at White Peaks. She just had to prove Roy's innocence first. And talk Ben into moving.

"Has the RCMP asked you for anything regarding the theft?"

"They asked for a copy of Roy's personnel file along with the files for everyone who had access to the safe combination and the office key."

"Anything else?"

"Just what you already know about Simon Crane. He's friends with Jessica Scott. So's Simon's wife, Natalie. Helen's also friends with her. Did you know that?"

"No, but I see where you're going with it. You know I don't want you involved in the investigation. You can relay information to me if you happen to stumble across something but don't go actively looking." Turner rubbed his hands together as if he was cold. "Simon's uncle called me. I know him from the Chamber of Commerce meetings. Are you sure you had just cause to fire Simon?"

"I am. What did you tell his uncle?"

"That I couldn't divulge private information, and he'd have to talk with Simon."

"I hope that goes okay."

"It didn't. Another of Simon's uncles owns the Laundromat in town. They're going to cancel our linen contract if we don't hire Simon back."

"Are you serious?"

"Very."

One by one, the lights in the administration building turned on. The glow flooded the area where she stood with Turner. He wasn't wearing a jacket, so had he come outside to catch her unawares? "Is there another company we can use?"

"There are companies in Calgary but none closer."

"How much time did they give us?"

"There's a one-month out clause in the contract. They've notified us they're going to cancel then."

"That's blackmail."

"It's a small town."

Kalin couldn't believe Turner would give in to blackmail. He liked being in control and holding the power. So submitting? Where was the alpha now? "What do you want me to do?"

"Let's give the lodging team a chance to find another provider. If they can't do that in a couple of weeks, we'll have to hire Simon back."

"We can't."

"There's no other choice. We can't run a lodging business with dirty sheets. And they know it."

The ethical action was to fire the Laundromat and report Simon's uncle to the RCMP, but she was quickly learning Turner didn't care about ethics. "Is there something I should know about Stone Mountain?"

"Like what?"

Now or never. Just ask. "Is the resort for sale?"

Turner stepped closer to Kalin. "Why would you ask that?"

"It's just a feeling I have."

"Well it's not," Turner said.

"But—"

Turner checked his watch. "I need to go. You won't mention this to anyone." He stepped backward and disappeared as abruptly as he'd arrived.

* * *

"I need to speak with you." Aiden wore his liftie uniform, and the Gortex material crackled from being outside and cold. A slight sheen of sweat covered his forehead.

Funny, Kalin had just been reading about him. She clicked the security database closed and twisted her monitor away from Aiden. She was going to find a quieter place to review the database entries since her office seemed to be open to anyone anytime. "Sure. Come on in. It's not like I was doing anything."

Aiden ignored her sarcastic answer. "One of our guest services attendants said a teacher reported a liftie having a fight with a student from the Holden high school."

Kalin didn't get Aiden's motive for involving her. He seemed to be finding excuses to spend time with her, but she would hear him out. Fighting on duty was a serious charge, and Aiden making a mistake in dealing with the situation would be a disaster. More negative media attention would anger Turner. "What happened?"

"The teacher said one of my lifties, Justin Bradley, shoved a student when he tried to get on the lift. Another student said she saw him do it."

Kalin scribbled notes. "Did anyone else witness the event?"

"I don't know."

"Was the teacher there?"

"I don't think so."

"What's your take? Is the behavior consistent with Justin's personality?"

"I don't know him well. He works hard and is friendly, but my only experience with him is on the job."

"Is there anything you do know that you'd like to share with me?" Kalin raised her hand to stop him from talking. "Don't answer that."

The situation seemed fairly clear, so Aiden's motive for involving Kalin again in the termination of a seasonal staff member was suspicious. She'd let the scene play out and see where Aiden led her. He was good friends with Jessica, so maybe he had access to the finance center, and she'd read in the radio reports that ski patrol couldn't find him on the morning of the avalanche. "We need to talk to Justin."

* * *

Aiden radioed the crew chief and instructed him to send Justin Bradley to Kalin's office.

Kalin cleared her desk of papers while they waited. "I understand you were late for work the day of the avalanche."

A flash of anger crossed Aiden's face. "Not by much. I'd been out late at a party."

"I'm thinking that's not a good example for you to be setting."

"Are you reprimanding me?"

"No, just filling time. So whose party were you at?"

"A friend's. What's with the questions?"

Before Kalin could answer, Justin arrived.

"This must be serious if you're both here." Justin flopped into a chair, relaxing against the backrest. He took off his toque and ran his hand through blond, curly hair. He had the same face tan all lifties acquired, white around his eyes and below his chin, but bronze everywhere else.

"How was your morning?" Kalin asked.

"Fun. Why?"

As Kalin waited for Aiden to question Justin, she studied the employee. He was slightly scruffy in appearance, with peach fuzz growing on his upper lip, more skin showing than strands of mustache, not enough to shave but enough to exude an image of a young man struggling to leave puberty but never quite getting there. When it became apparent Aiden was going to remain silent, Kalin spoke to Justin. "Did anything unusual happen during your shift this morning?"

Justin sat with his fingers tucked under his armpits and his thumbs pointing toward his shoulders. "Nope. There was a ton of new snow, and I had a snowball fight with some school kids."

He appeared too relaxed for someone in trouble. "Did you wear your name tag all morning? Or wear anyone else's?"

He tossed a smile in Aiden's direction. "I wore mine. Aiden doesn't allow us to wear someone else's."

"No one wore your name tag at any point? Maybe borrowed your jacket?"

"No." He shifted his gaze between Kalin and Aiden.

"So if someone referred to a lift operator named Justin that would have to be you?"

"Yeah, I guess."

"What time did you start work today?"

"Seven thirty." Without asking, Justin took a candy from the jar on the desk and popped it into his mouth. Cherry scent filled the room.

"What lift did you work on?"

"What's with all the questions?" Justin continued to suck on the candy, sliding it from one side of his mouth to the other. "Why don't you just tell me what's going on?"

"Did you get into a fight with one of the guests?"

"You're kidding, right?"

Kalin and Aiden waited.

"Nothing happened."

"This is serious. I don't think you fully understand what's going on. We've had a formal complaint against you," Kalin said.

"I'm telling you, nothing happened. I want to know exactly what was said about me."

Kalin glanced at Aiden, thinking he might step in and contribute. Apparently too much to hope for, so she said, "A kid from the high school said you shoved him when he tried to get on the lift."

"I didn't do that. I never would. I sometimes have to touch people to help them get on the rope tow. I can't believe this. Why aren't you worrying about something important instead of this crap?"

"This is important."

"More important than the theft? My roommate just got a new Go Pro and a top of the line smart phone. Said his dad sent it to him."

"Who's your roommate?"

"Eric Wilson."

One more tidbit for Constable Miller. One more piece of information to drive suspicion away from Roy. As a junior cash office clerk, Eric had keys and the combination. "That's very interesting, but here's how we're going to proceed. I'm suspending you from duty, with pay, until we sort this out. We can't take the risk of having you work when there's an outstanding charge against you. We're not saying you did this, only that we have a liability if you work the lifts. In the meantime, I suggest you be on your best behavior."

"When can I come back to work?"

"When we have this resolved. Give Aiden a call tomorrow, and we'll see." Kalin stood, indicating the meeting was over.

Justin faced Aiden. "This sucks. What am I supposed to tell people when they ask why I'm not at work?" He waited, and when neither

Aiden nor Kalin responded, he picked up his mitts and bolted from the room.

Aiden shut the door behind Justin.

"I have to tell you in this type of meeting you should be driving the conversation. I'm here for support and as a witness. I'm not here to do your job."

"Sorry. I wasn't sure what I was supposed to do. Let's talk to the other lifties who were working nearby. Maybe one of them saw something." Aiden radioed to set up appointments with the relevant lifties.

CHAPTER TWENTY-TWO

Jessica plunked her butt on a stool beside Simon at the bar of the Dragon's Bowl Hut. The hut overlooked the entry point into the Bowl, and she avoided glancing in that direction. Roy's last moments, his last time on his skis, the last time air caressed his face happened somewhere on that terrain, and she had no intention of ever skiing there again.

The bartender placed a hot chocolate in front of her on the wooden bar. The stone fireplace, the weathered log walls, and the chill that entered every time the door opened reminded her of Roy and made her wish he sat beside her instead of Simon.

"What the fuck am I supposed to tell my family?" Simon asked.

The flames in the hearth licked and snapped around the logs, and she drew her eyes away from the fire and back to Simon. "Huh?"

"My uncle asked why I was fired. Says he has a plan."

"I guess you can't go with the truth."

"Very funny. This job was supposed to prove I could support myself. That I'm not the loser in the family looking for handouts. Now I'll have to do whatever my uncle wants."

"Make something up that sounds legit, like you lost a key and didn't have the lock changed."

Simon sneered. "There's a slight problem. If my uncle thinks he can fight this, he'll sue Stone Mountain. Then he'll find out why I was really fired. I'm supposed to see him tonight. What am I going to say to get him to back off?"

"Tell him you have another job. That you hated this one. Whatever."

"If you got your job back, then you could hire me again."

"That's not going to happen."

"Take the polygraph, and Turner might relent. I can't imagine Helen's doing a stellar job."

"I can't. Turner's not going to hire me back if he finds out I stole from a previous employer."

"I'd forgotten about that little incident." Simon laughed. "I can see how the test would go. Have you ever stolen money? You say no. The buzzer goes off, and they know you lied."

"It was only a little petty cash, and I would've put it back." Jessica inhaled the heavenly smell of cocoa and took a deep sip. "How's Natalie taking the firing?"

"Are you trying to dim my sunlight? She's barely speaking to me, but she won't tell anyone why I got fired. It's too embarrassing for her. Any news on the theft?"

"Not really. Roy's still the main suspect."

"So they haven't found the money?"

"Why would you think there's money to be found? Everyone's saying Roy took it up the mountain." Could Simon know she was searching for the missing duffle bag and some of the money? Had Aiden blabbed? He was such an idiot.

Cold air shot through the room, and Jessica turned to see who'd entered. Speaking of the idiot. Aiden's jacket displayed his lift manager badge. What's to be so proud of? You'd think he was the president, the way he strutted around in his uniform.

Aiden sat beside Simon, tossed his gloves and toque into the metal basket underneath the bar stool, and said, "It's the two fired ones. Commiserating, are you?"

* * *

After Aiden left, Kalin sat alone. The quietness of the administration building settled around her. She worked until darkness fell. Ben would already be at fire practice, so she might as well get some work done instead of going home. Clicking on the security software icon, she settled in to read. Engrossed in reports, she was annoyed when some time later a noise distracted her. She shifted her gaze away from the computer, and the hair on the back of her neck stood on end.

Justin Bradley blocked the entrance to her office, placing his hands on either side of the doorframe. "When can I start working again?"

Something about his stillness and his deadened eyes caused her skin to prickle. "It's too soon. Call Aiden tomorrow, and he can give you an update…if he has one." Kalin stood and faced him.

"You can't prove anything. It's the kid's word against mine. I treated him like I would any other skier. Here, let me show you. Pretend you're getting on the rope tow." Justin reached around her, placed his palms on her back and pushed her forward. "There, you see. It's impossible to help someone without touching them."

Kalin stepped back, leaning into her desk. She slid her hand across the surface, searching for her cell.

"What's the diff from me telling everyone you harassed me? I could say anything about being alone here with you at night, and everyone would suspect you. Then you'd see how it feels to be accused of something you didn't do."

"Do you think it's smart to be threatening me right now? You should leave before you say or do anything to make your situation worse," Kalin said in a loud voice. "If you go now, I'll forget that you were here."

"Now you know how it feels. Don't make a big deal about it."

"Fine."

Justin gave a tight nod and plucked his toque off the chair. "Fine."

Tension drained from her neck when the outer door of the administration building slammed shut. Blood pulsed to her forehead. A headache worked its way up the base of her neck, nudging her to swallow two ibuprofen.

Ben worried too much when he thought she was in danger, so she snatched the phone, and instead of calling him, she called security and asked for a ride home.

* * *

Jessica grabbed a couple of beers from her fridge and returned to the living room. She glanced at her bedroom. Compassion kept her from curling underneath her blanket, from trying to drop into oblivion. Simon looked forlorn, and she wasn't callous enough to send him away.

She handed Simon a beer and sat in the chair closest to the fireplace. Since Roy's death, she couldn't seem to sleep in her own bed, and she was starting to hate the couch.

Simon gulped his beer, wiped his mouth on the back of his hand and sagged into the chair opposite Jessica. "What a shitty week."

"I thought you were meeting your uncle tonight."

"I told him I'm sick. I can't deal with him right now."

Jessica had listened to Simon's problems for years, and this was the first time he seemed deeply upset by them. He was the type of guy who liked to look as if things were hard on him, made him seem tougher somehow, and he bragged about difficulties. She never believed he was genuinely upset when he complained, but something looked different now. Shadows filled the space underneath his eyes as if he hadn't slept well, and his usually perfect hair shined with grease.

"Are you hungry?" Jessica asked.

"No, the beer's fine."

"So what happened? You seemed okay when we were skiing."

Simon stood and walked to the hearth. He picked up the fireplace poker and examined the charred end.

Jessica waited for him to speak.

"Natalie left me."

"No way. Because of why you were fired?"

"That and a bunch of other reasons. I always thought I'd be the one to leave her, not the other way around."

His comment made Jessica question whether Simon was upset that they split or that Natalie gave the final blow. "I'm sorry. I thought you two were a good match."

Simon released the poker, and it clanged against the stones surrounding the fireplace. "Don't bullshit me. You always wondered why I married her."

"I did not. I thought you married her because you loved her. Why else—"

"Why else what?" Simon flopped into the couch, spilling beer on his shirt. He didn't wipe the spot.

Simon ignoring a stain on his clothes worried Jessica. She suspected he was more upset by Natalie leaving than he was admitting. "Nothing."

"You were going to say why else would I marry someone so ugly."

"I was not." But she was. She didn't like the thought and hated to think of herself as shallow.

"So what's the latest on the theft?"

The theft always came up in conversation. Couldn't she have one friend who didn't talk about the stupid finance center? To postpone answering, she grabbed the fireplace poker and moved a log, causing sparks to disperse and land on the tile in front of the hearth. To avoid burning her socks, she took a step back. "I don't know. It's not like I'm in the loop."

"What does Aiden think?"

"I haven't talked to him."

"Really. I've seen you two hanging around a lot."

"I need friends right now."

Simon swigged what remained of his beer and plunked the bottle on the table. Without asking, he walked to the kitchen and helped himself to another. "Tell me about it. Have you seen Kalin much?"

"I try not to. She reminds me of Roy."

"Doesn't she tell you what's happening in the investigation?"

"I think she's doing her best to prove Roy's innocence, and I kind of hope she succeeds."

"Why would you care?" Simon asked.

"Other than the obvious reason that I want Roy's name cleared? If it's hanging out there he might be guilty, people will always suspect I helped him."

"Did he call you on the morning of the avalanche?"

"That's an odd question. Why would he?"

"I thought he might have told you he was heading up the mountain."

"All I know is Kalin and Ben kicked him out. My best guess is he was going to crash at mountain ops."

Simon chuckled. "You wouldn't have him over since he stayed the night at Helen's."

"Don't be mean. Are you going to stay in your condo?"

"I was hoping I could sleep on your pullout for a while."

CHAPTER TWENTY-THREE

Kalin entered the women's washroom and checked all three stalls. All empty. She'd been trying without success to finish reading the security reports during the day. Someone always interrupted her right when she opened the database. So there she was, sneaking into the can, hiding on the toilet.

She sat on the lid, pulled earbuds from her pocket, stuffed one into her ear and plugged the cable into her phone.

The mountain ops team recorded all radio traffic at the resort. The recordings were overwritten monthly unless something major happened, then security would transcribe the traffic for use in case of a lawsuit.

Kalin played the recordings from the day of the avalanche. Some of the chatter was difficult to listen to. The panic in the voices, the fear, the frustration all tore at her.

A series of words rose through her earbuds.

There are tracks directly above where the slide started.

She hit pause. The words floated in front of Kalin. They supported what she'd seen with Ben in the Dragon's Bowl. The kaleidoscope of images mixed together, but one thought came through.

She restarted the recording. Ben's voice filled her head. *How close?*

A female voice. *Close enough that the avalanche could have been started by a person.*

Ben's voice again. *Roy?*

The female voice. *We've no way of knowing.*

Why wasn't anyone looking for a second person who'd been up the mountain? Ben said the guest who'd heard the avalanche thought he saw two people climbing the slope.

A shadow crossed the crack between the door and the stall. She tapped her phone, flushed the toilet and opened the door, half expecting Justin Bradley, but instead found Helen leaning on the counter, watching her.

"You look like you're about to go skiing," Helen said. "Do you have a minute?"

Kalin had forgotten she wore her ski attire, but getting dressed was a good excuse for taking so long. "Sure. I'm going for a few runs, but I have time."

Helen shuffled her feet on the chipped tile. "Have the RCMP talked to you about me?"

Kalin moved to the sink and washed her hands. "No. Why would they?"

"I did something stupid. I told them about it when I had to redo the polygraph test. I asked them not to tell Turner, and I don't know if they did or not."

So that's who took the test twice. Kalin reached behind Helen and pulled a paper towel from the dispenser. "What did you tell them?"

"You know Roy and I were friends, right?"

"Sure. What does this have to do with the theft?"

"It was a chance to spend time with him. I was so happy when he came over that I wasn't paying attention. I hadn't expected him to stay the night."

Kalin stopped wiping her hands on the paper towel, giving Helen her full attention. "You and Roy?"

"It's not what you think. He was drunk and needed a place to crash. I think I might have shown Roy the combination to the safe by accident."

A crack formed in Kalin's heart. Every time the evidence steered elsewhere, it turned around and came right back at Roy. "Are you saying Roy took the money?"

"I think so. I can't stand not knowing if I'm going to lose my job over this. Can you discreetly find out if Turner knows?"

Focus on Helen. Don't think about Roy. "From what I know of Turner, I think he would have talked with you by now if he knew."

"You're saying I have to wait and see. I don't know if I can stand the pressure."

"You could tell Turner yourself. It won't sound as bad if he hears it from you."

"What should I do?"

"I bet the police only inform Turner if it ends up meaning something."

"I guess," Helen said. "Simon called me this morning."

Kalin tried to stay with the change in conversation, but all she could think was Roy stole the money. Her brother was a thief. Who really cared about Simon? "What'd he want?"

"He asked if there was any way he could have his job back. He said he's desperate for money. His wife kicked him out, and he can't afford another place until he has enough for a damage deposit. I felt bad telling him he couldn't come back until I remembered the porn."

"I'm sorry he's bothering you."

Helen left Kalin alone. Alone to think about Roy. She soaked a paper towel with cold water and pressed it against her face. Her eyes stung. *How could he?*

* * *

Kalin walked from the cafeteria to her office, warming her hands on a take-out coffee. Nine p.m. was fast approaching, but after skiing for part of the afternoon, she thought she should catch up on a few things.

Ben was on a backcountry night hike with his buddies, and she couldn't sit at home thinking about Roy being the thief. How could she keep working here after that knowledge spread? Would Turner think she helped Roy? How was she going to tell her mom?

Ben seemed to be avoiding her, and she let him because she couldn't face talking yet. They needed to discuss White Peaks and come to an agreement that made them both happy. Maybe Roy's guilt made the decision for her. And with Turner hiding financial information about the resort, would she be pushed out anyway?

Aiden exited the mountain ops building, jogged down the steps and headed in her direction.

She stopped at the path leading to the administration building entrance and waited for him to catch up.

"I saw you heading to your office. Maybe, if you're not busy, do you want to go for a beer?"

Kalin held up the coffee she'd bought. "Now?"

"If you're not busy."

Had Aiden been waiting for her? The lifts closed hours ago, so what other reason did he have to be in the mountain ops building so late in the evening? She tilted her head to one side and said, "Sure. Why not?"

She drank the last of the coffee and tossed the cup into the bear-proof garbage can. They strolled to the bar, and she told him about her encounter with Justin the previous night. The list of people who disliked her grew every day. It might be because of her job and the way she disciplined employees, or possibly that small-town living made it hard not to get involved in other people's messes. Would she ever get used to living in an environment where every move she made was judged by someone?

Since the lineup into the bar wouldn't start until eleven, they were able to find a table near the fireplace. Antique skis and boots mixed among sepia photographs of skiers decorated the walls. They ordered two pints of Kokanee and waited for the beer.

"What are you thinking about?" Aiden asked. "You seem a bit distracted."

"Oh, I was wondering if Justin's guilty."

"I think so, but without proof, there's not much we can do. We can't suspend him forever."

"I think if you let him come back to work, and we're still not sure, you could assign him to a chairlift instead of having him work the rope tow in the beginner area."

"Any news on the theft?" Aiden asked.

"Not really. Since Roy's a suspect, and I'm his sister, I don't get a lot of info from Turner."

"It must be hard that Roy was living with you when it happened."

"It's hard no matter where he was living."

"What are you going to do with his stuff?"

"I don't know."

"You could make some money selling his ski gear. He had high-end equipment."

"I can't believe you said that. I don't need to make money from him. Besides, I don't know where all of his things are. He tended to keep his belongings scattered."

"Sorry. That was insensitive."

Kalin's gaze shifted to the other side of the room. "Look behind you."

Justin staggered away from the bar, sloshing his beer over the top of his glass and onto a nearby patron. He swore and tried to swallow his beer in one go, spilling most of the liquid down his chest.

The bartender hustled over and asked Justin to leave. Apparently, he wanted to stay. The bartender grabbed his arm and angled him toward the door. He swung his fist at the bartender, missed and fell. Two security guards arrived, wearing black jackets, black gloves and black expressions.

Justin refused to move. The guards each grabbed one of his arms, but he lashed out, broke free and lunged at the bartender, biting his arm.

The bartender slapped Justin's face with his free hand. One guard twisted Justin's arm behind his back. The other lifted him by his shirt collar and belt, leaving his feet dangling in the air. Justin had no choice but to relax his clenched jaw and let go of the bartender's arm. Security escorted him through the bar and tossed him outside.

Kalin took a sip of beer and studied the group as they left. Simon Crane held the door open for them, and once they were outside, he entered the bar and headed toward Kalin. "Wow, that was weird."

"I'm surprised he'd do that when he's suspended. I'll talk to him tomorrow."

Simon scooted around Aiden and slammed his palms on the table. "I didn't do anything wrong."

Kalin scraped her chair backward and stood. "This is not the place."

"I want you to clear my reputation."

Silence lowered over the room, and Kalin didn't have to look around to know all eyes were on her. "I understand, but really, we've been through everything with you. We had cause."

Simon's chest heaved, and he leaned forward, placing his face inches from Kalin's. "You're ruining my life. What did I ever do to you?"

Aiden stood and squeezed himself between Simon and Kalin, forcing Simon to step backward. "Simon, dude. Don't do this here."

Simon held Aiden's gaze and after a tension-filled moment, picked up peanuts from a bowl on the neighboring table and threw a handful at Kalin. He swiveled and left without saying more.

* * *

After stopping at the resort's only convenience store, Kalin carried two bags of groceries. Her arms ached, and she was relieved she was almost home. As she walked in front of her neighbor's driveway, she spotted a moose standing in the shadows.

The immense creature studied her, then stepped behind a tree as if it could hide. Positioned with its head behind the tree trunk, its nose protruded from one side, and its body from the neck back protruded from the other. The moose stood still. Kalin smiled to herself. Was the creature actually hiding?

When she turned up her driveway, the motion sensor should have detected her and switched on the light at the front of her house as it had the night before. Without the light, her night vision was clear, and she could see the moose in her neighbor's front yard.

Clutching her bags tighter to her chest, she continued toward the house. She stepped on broken glass, hearing the pieces crunch as her foot hit the ground.

The moose stood rigid and alert, staring at Kalin. After a moment, it turned and moseyed away.

Kalin struggled to get her keys out of her pocket, took a step toward her front porch and froze.

Justin Bradley stepped out from the shadows at the side of her house.

She kept her distance. “What are you doing here?”

“I want to talk to you.”

“I was in the bar when you got kicked out. I don’t think you want any more trouble tonight.”

“I just want to talk,” Justin said in slurred speech.

“Aiden is working on it. I told you to get updates from him, not me. He’s your boss.”

“Why can’t you just tell him what to do?”

Kalin fumbled with her keys, trying to place one between her middle and index finger, but the keys slipped from her hand and plopped into the snow.

Justin stumbled forward. “Let me help.”

“No, I’m fine.” Kalin stooped, reaching for the keys, but the grocery bags blocked her way, and even in his drunken state, Justin snagged them first.

“We’d better get your food inside,” he said.

“Really, I’m fine. I’ve got it.”

He lurched toward her, his alcohol-filled breath assaulted her nostrils, and he wrestled a bag from her arm. Before she could stop him, he walked to her door with her keys and a grocery bag.

Kalin removed her cell from her pocket.

“You don’t need to call anyone.” Justin opened the door, leaving the key in the lock, and motioned for her to go inside. “I only want to set the record straight. We’ll put the groceries away. By the time we’re done, I’ll have said what I came to say, and I’ll go. I promise.” Justin reached inside and turned on the hall light.

“I want you to go now. Speak to Aiden tomorrow, and you can say whatever it is you need to say.”

Kalin tapped her phone and called security.

“I should have known you’d be too stuck up to talk to someone like me.”

“I want you to leave.”

“Fine. Have it your way.” Justin weaved toward her, shoved the grocery bag into her free arm and stumbled down the driveway.

CHAPTER TWENTY-FOUR

Before dawn on Friday morning, Kalin woke from a deep sleep with an ache in her jaw, telling her she'd spent at least part of the night grinding her teeth. She'd dreamt about Jack again, only this time Roy had been in the dream, too. Probably because she was flying home later in the day for Roy's memorial.

She rolled over, caressed Ben's pillow and instead found Chica's furry head. Ben had gone to work at five to assist with avalanche forecasting for the day. He'd resisted leaving her after the scene with Justin the night before, but since Roy's death, Ben had been diligent about making sure his team was on top of forecasting. She admired his desire to keep everyone safe. She eased Chica to the side, pressed her nose into Ben's pillow and inhaled his scent.

If Roy stole the money, did he trigger the avalanche? What if he had a partner and things went bad on the mountain? Jessica spent time on touring skis with him. She could have gone with him, but would she have left him to die?

The effort Aiden made to spend time with her, always asking about the theft, and being late for work that day made him a good suspect. She couldn't imagine Helen trekking up the mountain. As far as she knew Helen didn't even ski.

Kalin rolled out of bed and walked to the picture window framing the forest behind her house. She hauled on the string, and the heavy wooden blinds clacked to the top.

In the shadows at the edge of the forest, Kalin spotted movement. Something leaped behind the firewood stacked at the edge of the forest.

In a flash, a cougar raced from behind the wood to the neighboring trees and vanished.

Kalin phoned security. "There's a cougar in my backyard."

"Hang on. I have to pull over. I can't hear you."

Background music switched off.

"What's up?" Fred asked.

"There was a cougar behind the firewood in my backyard."

"I'll be right over. Don't go outside. It's weird it's so close to your house. The animal could be sick."

Kalin shifted away from the window, hiding behind the wall. She peeked occasionally but didn't see the large feline again. She changed from flannel pajamas into a T-shirt, an aqua Stone Mountain hoodie and black slim-fitting jeans. Underneath she wore high-tech thermal underwear.

"You okay?" Fred asked when he arrived.

"Yup. The question is…are you?"

Fred looked sheepish. "I wasn't quick enough last night and took a hit." He touched the purple bruise that surrounded his eye and seeped onto his cheek. "I didn't see it coming, and I should have."

"Someone hit you?"

"During a bar fight. It's nothing, just embarrassing."

Kalin smiled at his humility. "It'll fade quickly. I don't remember seeing you."

"What do you mean?"

Kalin took Fred's jacket and hung it on the hook by the door. She avoided looking at the bench Roy carved. "When security evicted Justin Bradley from the bar."

"I wasn't there. I got hit later, at closing time."

"He came here last night."

"Who?"

"Justin."

"Why would he come here?"

"We suspended him indefinitely this week, and he asked what the status was."

"He came here at night? I'll speak to him."

"I wish you wouldn't. That'll only make my life more difficult. I can't appear afraid of the employees. I'll let you know if he bothers me again."

"You sure?"

"Yeah. Come on, I'll show you where I saw the cougar."

They entered Kalin and Ben's bedroom, and she pointed. "I saw it run to the neighbor's yard." She told Fred about the cougar being near the hot tub a couple of weeks ago and killing a rabbit.

Fred nodded. "We'll look, but to be honest, if we can't find it, there's not much we can do." He noted the time, date and location of the cougar in his black spiral notebook. He stuffed it in his shirt pocket and headed for the bedroom door.

"So how's the investigation going?"

Fred cleared his throat. "You know I can't talk about it."

"Can you at least tell me if the RCMP suspect someone other than Roy?"

"You know Miller. He casts a wide net."

"That's hardly an answer. Are they searching for the second person who went up the mountain?"

Fred lifted one eyebrow. "What second person?"

Kalin bit the inside of her cheek. She'd assumed Fred would have read the security reports and talked with Ben about the avalanche.

"Do you know something?"

"Please don't tell Turner, but I read the security reports." She explained what she'd found, along with what she'd seen when skiing in the Dragon's Bowl with Ben. "I think the RCMP should be following that up."

"You know you're supposed to stay out of this."

"I do, but he was my brother."

"I'll talk with Miller." Fred spotted her packed suitcase. "You going somewhere?"

"My mom's having a memorial for Roy in Ottawa. I'll be back the day after tomorrow."

When they reached the front hall, Fred sat on the bench carved by Roy and put on his winter boots.

Kalin took Fred's security jacket off a hook and passed it to him. "What happens if you find the cougar?"

"I'll call the conservation officer. He'll trap it and let it go on the next mountain ridge, far enough away that it shouldn't come back."

* * *

Kalin had spent the afternoon at Roy's memorial service in Ottawa. Being back in her mom and stepdad's home swamped her with memories.

She dragged her feet along the shag carpet toward Roy's bedroom. She placed her hand on the knob and rested her forehead on the door. How could she be this tired? She nodded to herself once and entered his bedroom, the one their mom still kept for Roy even though he hadn't lived at home for years.

She picked up a trophy he'd gotten when he was twelve for some bike race he'd won. She carried it to his bed and sat with her knees curled into her chest and her arms wrapped around her shins.

Her mom put her hand on Kalin's knee. "You okay?"

"I am. Just sad."

"What did you think of the memorial?"

"It was lovely. I'm glad so many of his friends came." Who probably wouldn't have if they'd known Roy was a criminal.

"And your friends, too."

"Can you believe the Ottawa bike club attended, even the people who hadn't ridden with Roy?" Kalin asked.

"That was nice."

"Do you remember the last time Roy rode with them?"

Her mom joined her, sitting on the other side of Roy's bed. "Not really. It's been too long."

"I remember. Jack and I went to watch. Jack died two days later and everything changed."

Her mom reached over and caressed Kalin's cheek. "You need to let him go."

"Speaking of that. Let's clear out this room. You could use the space for an office."

"I'm not ready."

"Yes, you are. Roy hasn't slept here for a few years. Let's do this together. It'll be good for us. We both need to move forward."

Her mom shook her head and played with the top button of her sweater. After a moment, she said, "Okay. I'll get some bins from the garage."

Kalin started with the dresser drawers and smiled at the amount of clothes stored there. Clothes that would no longer fit Roy. What was her mom thinking, keeping these? She'd use one bin for donations.

Her mom returned with two plastic bins and a garbage bag. She also carried a small cardboard box. "This is what Stone Mountain sent."

Kalin reached for the box and placed it on the bed. She lifted the lid. So little. Roy's kayak helmet. She ran her fingers along the stickers, stickers representing various places he'd gone white-water kayaking. Where was his kayak?

Underneath the helmet, she found a watch engraved with Roy's name and the date of Kalin and Jack's wedding. The watch was a present to Roy for being Jack's best man.

"Can I keep this?"

Her mom fingered the gold band. "Of course."

Kalin emptied three drawers while she tried not to notice her mom wince every time Kalin placed an article in a bin. "They'll go to a good cause."

Her mom held a sweater tight to her chest. "I know."

Kalin moved to the wooden trunk pressed against the far wall. She lifted the lid and stared at Roy's bike gear. His helmet, his riding gloves, his jerseys and a repair kit. "When did Roy put this stuff here?"

"I don't remember."

Amongst his jerseys, Kalin found a bag that had belonged to her. Jack's personal effects had been returned to her after he died, and she'd asked Roy to dispose of the bag. So why had Roy kept this?

Her fingers trembled, and she slid the zipper. A piece of cloth stuck between the teeth. She picked it free with her fingernail, glanced over her shoulder at her mom and undid the zipper. She ran her hand over the crack in Jack's helmet, pictured his blond hair curling underneath the lip and closed her eyes tight.

His wallet, watch and phone rested below on the bottom of the bag. Hiding her find from her mom, she placed the helmet and empty wallet in the garbage bag. Did Roy forget to deal with this for Kalin, or had he been too angry about Patricia to care about helping her?

She turned to the closet. Stuffed animals from her childhood were lined up and facing her. Clothes that she hadn't taken to Stone Mountain hung from the rack. Her beautiful suits with matching pumps. Should she take them with her or donate them along with Roy's things?

Her mom handed Kalin a photo album. "This we'll keep."

She flipped the pages. The photos of her and Roy started from when they were tots and went to their early teens. When Roy still idolized his big sister. Kalin's anger at Roy for stealing the money grew. She needed something to remind her of better times. She'd held her breath through most of the memorial, hoping a call wouldn't come through to her mom telling her Roy was the thief. How could he do this to them? "Can I keep this, too?"

"You can take anything you want."

"Dinner's ready," Kalin's stepdad shouted from the kitchen.

CHAPTER TWENTY-FIVE

Kalin returned to Stone Mountain from Ottawa and didn't waste time getting to her office. After perusing the album she'd taken on the plane ride home, she was greedy for more.

She opened the HR Facebook page and scrolled through the posts, searching for pictures of Roy and was soon rewarded. One photo showed Ben and Roy ascending the Alpine Tracks chair lift. Seeing Roy smile lightened her heart.

For a while after Jack died, Roy stopped smiling, but Kalin didn't believe his death would cause Roy to be unhappy for so long. Something else must have been going on in Roy's life, and she wished she'd paid more attention instead of leaving Ottawa and ignoring the issue. Jack and Roy had been close. They'd spent hours cycling together, and Roy had been shaken to the core by Jack's death. But still, the length of time Roy grieved seemed out of perspective.

Jack's funeral had been the hardest part for Kalin to endure during the week following the hit-and-run.

His mahogany coffin had dropped slowly into the freshly dug hole. The smell of earth would forever be a sad memory for Kalin. The gears whined, and she glared at the crane operator. She was astounded he hadn't had the hoist working perfectly for lowering the coffin, her husband's coffin.

She held a tissue to her mouth and suppressed a sob. How could this be the end? She leaned into Roy and grabbed his hand, needing to hold on or she would collapse. Her hand slipped along the sweat on Roy's palm. She could feel him shaking and checked if he was crying. He wasn't. His whole body shook with…what? She stared at him.

"What?" Roy whispered.

"Why are you shaking?"

"I don't know." He shook his head. "Are you okay?"

"No."

Kalin roused herself back to the present. After the funeral, the pain changed into a persistent dull ache and nightly dreams. Not all the dreams were nightmares. Sometimes she dreamt Jack was still alive. She could smell him, feel his skin, but then she woke, and the instant she realized he was gone was worse than any nightmare.

Tragedy had shattered Kalin's life before Roy died. It was up to her to choose how to deal with Roy's death now. She would not start feeling sorry for herself again.

Assuming the post dates were close to the date the photos had actually been shot, she found several pictures of Roy and Aiden taken in December.

In one, the men were sitting in the resort bar, grinning, arms draped across each other's shoulders, lifting their beers in salute to the photographer. Aiden wore his ever-present lift manager uniform. Roy was skinnier than when she'd left Ottawa, and despite the grin, he looked worn out. She hadn't noticed in person, but she should have.

Jessica told her Aiden sometimes went out on touring skis with her and Roy. Aiden could have been in on the theft with Roy. Kalin refused to believe Roy came up with the idea on his own. Someone talked him into stealing the money.

She found photos of Jessica and Simon, Eric Wilson and Simon, Helen and Jessica and many other combinations of the people in Jessica's department. She studied the photos, looking for a pattern.

When she didn't find the magic clue, she went back to the photo of Roy and Ben and hit full screen. Something about the photo caught her attention, demanding she examine it more carefully. Roy's ski boots were visible, and the buckles were yellow. The buckle she'd found when on the mountain with Ben had also been yellow. She'd have to tell Ben the buckle was definitely a starting point for the next search.

Aiden stepped into her office. "What's that?"

"Just looking at photos of Roy." Kalin pointed to her computer screen. "There seem to be a lot of the two of you together. I didn't know you were close friends with him."

"We weren't really. Monica snaps pictures of people anywhere at anytime. That's all."

"You two seemed chummy."

"They're just photos."

"But were you friends?"

Aiden sighed. "He's your brother. I don't want to say anything bad. We started out being friends. We just didn't stay friends. Turns out we didn't have much in common."

Kalin couldn't say why, but she thought Aiden had lied.

"Have you seen all the cards on Roy's locker?" Aiden asked.

"A few."

"There's a lot. I could collect them for you at the end of the season."

"Sure. That would be nice." Roy's locker. Maybe he'd left a clue inside. She'd check that out later.

"I came by to see if you were free for lunch. It's warm and sunny, and I thought we could take advantage of the weather and eat at the barbecue on the deck."

"I have too much to do, but thanks for asking." Kalin was surprised by the sour look on Aiden's face when she said no. What was with his current effort to be friends with her?

* * *

A few minutes after seven p.m., Kalin stood alone in front of the mountain ops building. The unpredictable mountain weather had reared over the peaks in a sudden storm. Wind whipped against her cheeks with an intensity that stung her skin. The swirling snow could have been a family of ghosts dancing around her. *Don't think. Just go inside.*

She let her flashlight guide her to the mountain ops assistant's desk. She'd seen the assistant give out locker combinations to staff and knew the list was in his top drawer. She slid the drawer open and ran her finger down the names until she found Roy's.

After unlocking the basement door, she crept down the unlit stairs using her hands to guide her toward Roy's locker. She couldn't let Turner or Ben know what she was up to, but she needed to see for herself what was in Roy's locker. She planned to meet Ben in fifteen minutes, so she had to be quick.

Deep in the basement, wearing black on black, she was invisible. A few more steps and the flashlight beam couldn't be seen from the top of the stairs or from the outer door. She scanned the beam across the wall in search of a light switch. Finding it, she flicked it twice, hearing a distinctive click each time, but the room remained dark.

She inched her way to Roy's locker. Condolence cards Aiden had mentioned filled the surface. The ski patrol team decided to keep Roy's locker untouched until the end of the season as a tribute to Roy. She gently pressed her fingers against one of the cards. She flipped the top and read the sentiment. She hadn't realized people liked him so much. Most of the cards were from the ski patrol team. There was a lovely note from Helen but none from Jessica.

Kalin pulled a scrap of paper from her front pocket and entered his combination. She dropped the lock, and the sharp crack of metal hitting the concrete floor reverberated across the room. She froze, checking for any signs someone was coming to investigate. Hearing nothing, she steadied herself and swung open the metal door.

She didn't know what she expected but hoped she'd find anything to link someone else to Roy. The RCMP might have missed something if they didn't know about the second person.

Only Roy's ski patrol jacket hung on a silver hook. Kalin rummaged through the pockets, found a set of keys and tucked them in her own pocket. She took out safety manuals and books, putting them aside to check later. He'd taped a safety guide for white-water kayaking on the inside of the locker.

Somewhere above her, a door creaked. She snapped off the flashlight and crouched in the deepest corner of the locker bay.

"Who's in here?"

Kalin's pulse quickened. She knew Justin Bradley's voice well enough to recognize it. A seasonal liftie on suspension couldn't possibly have a legitimate reason for being there after working hours.

"I know someone's in here. I saw a light."

She remained motionless. To her ears, her breathing sounded as loud as the storm outside. The light from his flashlight approached, and she closed her eyes, placing her head on her knees. Her face was the only part of her not covered in black. He had guts coming in here at night. If caught, he would only get into more trouble.

Justin stopped at Roy's open locker. "Huh."

Without looking away from her knees, she couldn't see what he was doing. Only by the sound of his feet shuffling, did she know he was still near. After an agonizing minute, his footsteps faded.

The seconds ticked by on her phone display, and when she clocked five minutes, she rose. She shut the locker door, and fumbling in the dark, managed to put on the lock. She gathered the books and tiptoed toward the exit, stopping every few steps to listen for Justin.

She eased the outer door ajar, peeked outside, and when she didn't see anyone, slipped through the narrow opening. Thick storm clouds blocked out all but a sliver of moonlight. Snow swept across the parking lot, blurring everything more than a few meters away, and even though she couldn't see them, she could feel the looming mountains pressing down, giving her a sense of irrelevance.

Justin stepped out from behind the corner of the building. "I knew someone was in there. I'm not surprised it's you sneaking around in the dark. What are you up to?"

"None of your business." Before Kalin could rush past him, he grabbed her arm, and she dropped the books from Roy's locker. An envelope slid from between the pages and landed at her feet.

"What's this? Stealing things?"

"Let go of me. These are for work." Kalin wrenched her arm free and picked up the books, slipping the envelope back between the pages.

"You liar. You took those from McCann's locker. I saw the open door."

"I don't know what you're talking about. Get out of my way."

"Why are you looking in a dead guy's locker?" Justin clutched Kalin's shoulder and shoved her backward.

She stumbled and fell, dropping the books a second time.

CHAPTER TWENTY-SIX

"What's going on?" Ben asked.

The wall of snow blurred Kalin's view of Ben, but she didn't care. He was here, and she'd be safe.

Justin clenched his fists by his sides. "Get lost, dude."

At five-foot-nine, Ben was no match for Justin in height, but he had more strength in his muscles. He stepped between Justin and Kalin, flexing his bulk. "Are you all right?" he asked her.

She picked up the books and shook snow off them. "I'm fine. Let's go."

Justin's body was primed for a fight. "I said get lost. This is none of your business."

"Move away from Kalin."

"Who the fuck are you?"

"Her husband."

Justin took two steps backward and pointed at Kalin. "I'm not finished with you."

"Yes, you are," Ben said. He turned toward Kalin. "Come on."

Justin swung, punching Ben in the back of his head, knocking him to the ground. A piece of ice slashed Ben's forehead, and blood dripped between his eyebrows. He launched into a standing position and threw a punch that glanced off Justin's chin. His second punch slammed into Justin's nose.

Justin teetered backward, leaving his neck exposed.

Ben thrust his hand directly into Justin's throat, catching him by surprise. The bony edge of his hand made contact, and Justin bent forward, gasping and coughing. While Justin was vulnerable, Ben kicked him hard on the side of his ankle and knocked him to the ground.

Kalin didn't waste time. "Let's go." She reached for Ben and pulled him with her. They left Justin moaning and holding his ankle between his hands.

When they reached their place, Ben trailed behind Kalin into the bathroom. Chica followed, wagging her tail, demanding attention.

"Here. Sit." She pointed at the toilet and Chica sat, making both Kalin and Ben laugh.

Kalin opened a drawer containing medical supplies, all labeled and standing side by side, and selected a bottle of disinfectant.

Ben watched her as she wiped his forehead. "You have amazing eyes." The absorbent pad caught the edge of the gash, and he winced.

"Sorry, did that hurt?"

Ben laughed, and his smile widened. "Not really."

"Tough guy. It's going to hurt later." Kalin grabbed a bottle of acetaminophen with codeine from the drawer. "Here, take two of these."

Ben accepted the pills along with the glass of water she offered him. "Are you going to tell me what you were doing?"

She tossed the pad into the garbage and rinsed her hands in scalding water. "Don't be mad."

With a gentle touch, she dabbed antibiotic cream on his forehead. "I don't think you need stitches, although what do I know." She rinsed her hands a second time. "I'm really glad you came by when you did. I'm not sure what I would have done."

"Flattery won't work."

She sat on the edge of the bathtub. "I wanted to check out Roy's locker."

"I could've done that for you. And why at night?"

"I didn't want Turner to know what I was doing. And I didn't want you to get in trouble with him."

"You're going to get yourself fired." Ben held eye contact with her for several seconds. "Or is that the idea, so you can take the job at White Peaks?"

"How can you say that?" Kalin left the bathroom and plopped on the living room couch.

Ben followed and took the chair across the room as far from her as possible. He tucked his fists underneath his armpits and leaned farther away from her. "Well?"

"I think Roy stole the money, but I don't think he did it alone. If someone triggered the avalanche and left him there, I won't let them get away with it. I can't live with this hanging over my head. It's got nothing to do with White Peaks."

"What makes you sure Roy's guilty?"

Kalin explained what she'd learned, and Ben moved to her side of the room, picked up her hand and kissed her palm. "I love you, you know. You don't have to go through this alone."

A lump filled her throat. "I know." She leaned her head against his chest. Ben had been extremely patient with her and not mentioned White Peaks for a while. He let her get on with her career without interfering. What had she done to deserve such a great guy? The truth was her only option now, and she hoped it didn't lead to a fight. "They offered me the job."

Kalin could tell Ben held his breath.

"I haven't accepted yet."

"But you might?"

"Only if it'll work for both of us. But I need to find out what happened to Roy first."

"Then let me help you. I'm on your side. I don't mind keeping secrets if it's for you."

Kalin tilted her head and placed a wet kiss on his lips.

When she finally let him go, Ben said, "Let's see what you found."

She gathered the collection of things she'd taken from Roy's locker and placed them on the pine coffee table. Fingering the envelope she'd found tucked between the pages of one of the books, she pulled out a printed email. She was invading Roy's privacy. What if she found something horrible? But what if she missed something important?

Taking a deep breath, she unfolded the email and pressed the paper across the table. A love note from Patricia, his ex-fiancée. He must have still been hurting over her, otherwise, why keep the email? And what did Patricia mean by Roy should forgive himself? Kalin regretted coming between Roy and his fiancée. She handed the email to Ben and noticed writing on the backside.

"What's on the back?"

Ben flipped the paper. "It's a list. Parker $150, Price $200, Wilson $175. Price could be Aiden, but who are the other two?"

"I'm pretty sure the first is Greg Parker. I think he sold drugs to Roy. Aiden fired him for smoking dope at work. The last one might be Eric Wilson, the finance center clerk from Australia. I saw him once with Parker."

"So did these guys owe Roy money, or did he owe them?"

* * *

Ben woke feeling nauseated. Sometime during the night his mouth had dehydrated, leaving his tongue furry. His eyelids stuck to his eyeballs, and he slowly pried them open. At thirty-one, he couldn't drink as much alcohol as when he was twenty. *Go figure.*

After the previous night's excitement, Kalin and Ben had opened a bottle of wine, lit a fire and spent the evening reconciling. He drank most of the wine, and they'd skipped dinner. Not a good combination. He lay in bed and kept his head still.

Why did Kalin have to get an offer from White Peaks? He loved her. Maybe he should be the supporting husband and put her career first, but he loved living in Stone Mountain, too. He'd been there so long, he couldn't remember what life was like before.

Being the guy from the Stone Age who put his career over his wife's wouldn't impress anyone. Quitting and starting over wasn't appealing. If there wasn't a ski patrol job for him at White Peaks, he didn't know what he'd do. The volunteer fire department had room for him, but only in a junior position.

Chica eyed him from her spot on the floor, her brown eyes turning up soulfully, her jaw resting on the bed and her tail wagging. He wanted nothing more than to sleep longer on his day off, but Kalin had already been at work for a couple of hours, and he shouldn't still be lying in bed.

"What are you looking at?" Ben rubbed Chica's head, and interpreting that as an invitation, she put her front paws on the bed. "Give me a minute, will you? I feel like crap."

Chica swung her tail harder, causing her rump to wiggle.

"Ever hear of a hangover? No? I guess not." Unable to resist her charm, he plodded to the back door and let her out. Without waiting, he grabbed a couple of ibuprofen and checked the cut on his forehead. Nothing to worry about, so he went back to bed. Chica expected attention every moment they were together, and most of the time he gave it to her, but today his soft mattress called him.

He could relate to Kalin's need to find out what happened to her brother. He agreed with her that Roy stole the money. If he had a choice, he'd drop the matter, but Kalin was determined to find out if someone else was involved. Ben didn't want her to put herself in danger again, and he didn't want Turner to fire her for ignoring his instructions to stay out of the investigation. Then she'd take the White Peaks job for sure.

Roy had been acting weird during the weeks preceding the avalanche. When Ben asked him if anything was wrong, Roy shrugged and said it was nothing he couldn't handle.

Ben thought back to the night before the avalanche. He'd stood in the front hall and glared at Roy.

Snow blew in around Roy and the security guard who stood beside him. The flakes glowed in the beam from the front hall light. Ben's body ached from the previous two days of avalanche training. He should be stretching his muscles and going to bed early instead of dealing with Roy and his issues.

Roy's head hung low, with his chin almost touching his chest. Ben suspected he hid a smile and didn't care they were upset. How could he be Kalin's brother? Miss Responsible related to Mister Irresponsible.

The security guard hung on to the back of Roy's jacket, keeping him from falling over. "Hi, Kalin. Sorry about this."

Kalin held onto Ben's elbow and frowned at her brother. "Don't worry. You need to do your job."

The guard nudged Roy further into the foyer. "He said he lives here now."

Ben motioned for Roy to come inside. "We'll take him from here."

The guard bit the corner of his lip. "Um."

Kalin smiled at him, and Ben admired she could be generous with her kindness when she was obviously furious with Roy. The poor guard brought his director's brother home drunk.

"What do you want me to put in the report?"

"Exactly what you normally would. I don't want any special treatment for him."

"Nice," Roy mumbled.

The guard nodded and backed out of the doorway, looking as if he couldn't wait to disappear. Ben didn't blame the guy.

"Why are you drinking so much?" Kalin asked.

"If only you knew." Roy put his hand on the wall, leaving a smear of dirt and wet snow. He must have fallen at some point. He used the wall as a brace as he lumbered toward his room.

"Stop," Ben said.

"I need to lie down."

"I recommended you for ski patrol. It's a hard day on the mountain tomorrow. Take it seriously if you want to keep the job."

"Christ. What am I? Twelve?"

"I'm not cutting you slack at work because we're related. We're leaving here at seven thirty. Be ready."

"Jack would never have treated me this way," Roy said.

At the mention of her deceased husband, Kalin breathed in sharply. Even for Roy, the comment was a low blow.

Kalin's lip curled. "Go to bed, Roy."

"Don't be so sensitive." Roy plodded along the hallway, occasionally using the wall for support. His boots left a trail of dirt on the slate tile. "Jack was more man than Ben will ever be."

"Pack your bags," Ben said. "You'll be moving out in the morning."

Chica's sassy bark returned Ben to the present. If he hadn't kicked Roy out, he wouldn't be lying in bed now worrying about Kalin.

The RCMP had searched through Roy's things, including the suitcase stored in the garage. Maybe they'd overlooked something, and it couldn't hurt to check. Ben stood and winced. Okay, maybe it could hurt. He sat on the edge of the bed, letting the pounding ease. Man, he really should cut back on the booze. He tried again, took his time standing, pulled jeans over his boxer shorts and headed toward the back door.

Chica followed him to the garage. The suitcase was tucked in the back behind other junk. He carried it from the garage to the guest bedroom, his head throbbing with every step. Chica stayed inches behind his legs, and when he put the suitcase on the floor and flipped the lid open, she stuck her nose in the clothes, wildly sniffing Roy's scent.

The RCMP had repacked the suitcase without folding the clothes, leaving them in a wrinkled clump. Ben removed the clothing and scoured the suitcase, but found nothing. He replaced the clothing, carefully folding each piece, checking every pocket, and discovered a key tucked inside the pouch of a gray hoodie. He knew instantly which lock the key was meant to open.

CHAPTER TWENTY-SEVEN

After the adventure the previous night with Justin Bradley, Kalin needed to settle down and focus on work. She sat at her desk and contemplated the summer plan. If she thought about something other than Roy and the theft, her brain might process in the background and figure out what was going on. She'd been tempted to stay in bed with Ben earlier but managed to resist since his snoring would have kept her awake.

Her cell rang, but she didn't recognize the number.

"It's Nora. You busy?"

"Not really. How's Ian doing skiing?"

"Great. Lake Placid is a blast."

"You sound excited. What's going on? Did Ian win a race?"

"Ian thought I should wait until I got home to tell you, but I just can't."

"Tell me what?"

"Ian proposed. We're getting married."

"Congratulations. I can't wait till you get home, so we can plan your wedding."

"Will you be my matron of honor?"

"You don't have to ask. Of course. I owe you that one." Nora had helped Kalin dress for her own wedding and stood by her side when she exchanged vows with Ben. She'd even helped Ben arrange getting Kalin's parents and Roy to attend. Ben had surprised Kalin with the ceremony, and Nora had kept it secret until the last moment.

She missed Nora and wished she'd come home soon. After giggling over the proposal with Nora, Kalin disconnected the call. *Now how am I supposed to concentrate?*

The resort needed summer employees for the restaurants, hotels, mountain bike park, retail shops, golf course, kayak rentals and guest services, and her HR team had the task of hiring the three-hundred-fifty people required to operate for the summer season. The quality of employees hired could make or break a season, and Kalin's HR manager, Monica, liked her involvement in the process.

If she was going to help Monica when she presented the plan to Turner, she'd better review the requirements. The number of employees would be greater than the previous summer since the fire damage had been repaired and the resort would be back up to full staff again. On the white board hanging on her office wall, she wrote a heading across the top for each department, the approximate start dates down the side and the number of people needed in the intersecting boxes.

"Hello?"

Kalin put down the marker and glanced into the reception area. A woman, somewhere between twenty-five and thirty held the hand of a little girl. The girl wore baggy blue pants a size too big for her and worn at the knees. A stain, which might have been mustard, marred her worn ski jacket. Her faux fur-lined hood drooped on her shoulders, framing uncombed dark brown hair. The woman looked at Tessa with a quizzical expression.

Tessa sat at the reception desk, her head down, ignoring the woman. Even with her cochlear implant, sometimes she missed hearing things. She must have seen Kalin walk to the reception desk, and she stopped what she was doing.

"Oh sorry," she said to the woman. "I didn't hear you come in."

"I'm looking for Aiden Price. Do you know where I can find him?" The woman was twenty pounds overweight, a little over five feet tall, with emerald eyes that glistened.

"I'm not sure if he's working today," Kalin said. "If he is, he'll be on the mountain."

"I need to talk to him." Dark circles under the woman's eyes blended into slush-colored cheeks. She looked as if she needed sleep.

"If you want, I can call him," Kalin said.

"Would you mind? Tell him his wife and daughter are here."

* * *

"Your wife and daughter are looking for you," Kalin said to Aiden. She tucked her cell phone tight against her ear and continued walking.

"They'd like you to meet them in the cafeteria. I gave them lunch vouchers."

"Adrienne's here? Do you know what she wants? What did she say?" His questions came in rapid succession.

"So it's true. You're married, and you have a daughter."

"She's my ex-wife."

Kalin entered the cafeteria kitchen through the back entrance. The aroma of a Bolognese sauce simmering on the commercial-grade stove top made her stomach growl, and she decided pasta for lunch.

Something was strange about Aiden. Kalin stood at the edge of the kitchen and watched the woman and child. Since Kalin had secrets, she couldn't criticize him for having his own. She was snooping, and she didn't like the trait, but curiosity won over ethics.

Five minutes later, Aiden shuffled in, looking like a man walking to the edge of a cliff. Scowling, he said something to Adrienne but never looked at the child.

Adrienne spoke.

Aiden shook his head and scurried away.

Kalin waited until he was out of sight before she approached.

"Hi again." Adrienne rubbed the girl's back, pulling her close for a quick hug.

"Is everything okay?" Kalin asked.

"We're all right. I don't know why I keep expecting Aiden to change. Even if he doesn't want to see us, I thought he'd at least help us out with some money."

Kalin hadn't expected such a revealing answer from a woman she didn't know. "Can I do anything?"

"I hate to ask, but we need a place to stay tonight."

"I can reserve a room for you," Kalin offered.

"Sweet, except I can't really afford one."

Adrienne's eyes pleaded, and Kalin understood how difficult it must be to have her daughter see her dependent on a stranger. "Don't worry about it. I can give you a complimentary night. We are in the lodging business, after all."

"If you want, you can wait here, and I'll get a room organized." Kalin made eye contact with the little girl. "What's your name?"

"Samantha."

"Well then, Samantha, did you happen to pack a bathing suit?"

Samantha shook her head.

"The outdoor pools are fun. I'll get you a couple of suits from lost and found, and you can go for a swim this afternoon." Kalin laughed at the look on Adrienne's face. "Don't worry. The pools are heated.

Samantha, if you'd like some dessert, there are lots of yummy things to eat."

Before Kalin was out of earshot, she overheard Samantha say, "She's nice, Mommy."

Kalin phoned Aiden, talking as she strode back to her office. "Adrienne said they needed a place to stay, and I thought I'd let you know they're spending the night here. I set them up with a poolside room."

"Now you're on a first-name basis with her?"

"Don't get mad at me. I'm letting you know they're staying tonight. What you do with that is up to you."

"You're not going to tell anyone about this, are you?"

"No. This is your business, not mine," she said.

"You don't know the whole story. It's not what it looks like."

"Like I said, this isn't my business. I'm busy today. I gotta go." She skirted the bottom of the Alpine Tracks run, passing a lift line that stretched beyond the end of the maze gates. Families talking, laughing and exuding happiness waited for the chair to take them to a higher altitude. So unlike Adrienne and Samantha.

Kalin spotted Justin Bradley working at the lift. Aiden had restarted Justin's three-month probationary period, allowed him back at work and warned him if another incident occurred, he'd be fired. Kalin was uncomfortable with him as an employee but had supported Aiden's decision.

* * *

Dark green lodgepole pines loomed over Kalin, creaking and moaning as each gust of wind twisted through their scraggy branches. As dusk settled, the trees began to fade into one another, and she could no longer make out detail in the underbrush. She walked in the center, not running, but moving fast enough to reach the road within a few minutes.

She was within five meters of a lone coyote, posed in silence at the edge of the path, before she noticed the animal and stopped. She sunk slightly in the soft snow. She yanked bear spray from her pocket, held the aerosol can at arm's length and pointed the nozzle at the coyote.

The coyote twitched its tapered ears and tilted its head to one side. A tree branch snapped, breaking the trance. The coyote flicked its eyes in the direction of the offending tree, then back at Kalin, and bolted into the forest, swishing the black tip of its tail. The stench of a wild animal, close to the scent of a dog but riper, lingered. She waited until the coyote disappeared, and alert to her surroundings, hiked toward home.

Before she reached the road, she heard the coyote yipping with its pack. The animals made unique sounds: one like a barking dog, another a crying child, the next a howling wolf. They looped around in front of her and were now between her and the road. Kalin couldn't tell how many of them blocked her way.

She turned around, walked back to the office and took the long way home. Along the road, she bumped into Jessica. Jessica rented a suite in a vacation home on Black Bear Drive ten houses farther along the road than Kalin and Ben's house.

"I was looking at employee photos and found some of Roy and Aiden. It looked like they were good friends for a while. I didn't know that," Kalin said.

Jessica stomped her feet, first one, then the other, and tucked her hands underneath her armpits. "I don't mean to be unfriendly, but I don't want to talk about Roy."

"You're good friends with Aiden. Do you know why he and Roy stopped being friends?"

"Simon Crane needs his job back. Can't you do something for him?"

The question came out of nowhere, somewhat like the speeding truck that swerved around the corner. Sidewalks were not part of the resort's design, and Kalin and Jessica were forced to move to the road's edge as the truck sped by. They were briefly illuminated by the headlights, then fell back into darkness. In that second, the anger in Jessica's face lit up, and Kalin backed away.

"I can't talk about that with you."

"Did you know Simon and his wife split? After you showed Natalie the Internet sites you accused him of looking at, she left him. You never should have shown her the list. They might still be together."

"I'm sorry to hear that, but maybe it's better she knows what Simon was doing. Relationships are hard. You should know that." Kalin was being blunt, cruel even, but she couldn't help herself. Jessica brought out nastiness in her, and the words were out of her mouth before she realized she didn't want to hurt her.

Jessica wrapped her arms tight around her chest. Even in a bulky ski jacket, she looked anorexic. "I don't know why you think I should talk to you. You called the cops on Simon, told them he might have access to the safe combination, and do you know what you caused? Do you?"

Kalin, stunned into silence by the viciousness in Jessica's voice, shook her head.

"They interrogated me again. They asked if I gave Simon my key to the finance center and then told the locksmith I'd lost it. If I didn't give it to Simon, did I give it to Roy? Did I leave the combination the same for a month on purpose? Did I fake Eric's criminal record check? I haven't done anything wrong. I was fired. My so-called friends won't be seen anywhere near me, and no one cares I lost Roy. What did I ever do to you except love him?"

Jessica took off, running away from Kalin, disappearing into the darkness.

* * *

Ben glanced at the time on his phone, and only ten seconds had passed since the last time he'd checked. Kalin had called when she left her office and should have reached home by now. He'd called her office and her cell, both times getting her voicemail. He paced around the living room, looking out one window, then the next. Chica joined him, playing follow the leader. He picked up a *Ski Canada* magazine, put it back down and turned on the TV.

When he heard the front door open, he ran down the stairs. He reached Kalin before she crossed the threshold. Chica scooted around him, bouncing at Kalin's feet.

"Where were you when I needed you?" she whispered into Chica's ear. In response, Chica licked her. Kalin didn't turn her head fast enough, and Chica landed a slobbery kiss on her lips.

"Lucky dog," Ben said.

"She's not the only lucky one." Kalin pressed her lips to Ben's, seductively kissing him. "I love you."

Hearing Kalin say the words was a salve to Ben's ego. Trying not to sound controlling, he asked, "What took you so long to get here?"

"I got half way on the trail and had to turn around and go the long route. A coyote pack blocked my way to the road, and I was too chicken to stay on the path."

"Why didn't you call me?" Ben was sure he sounded controlling but couldn't help himself.

Kalin gave him a full dimple smile. "Battery's dead."

"Are you all right?"

"I'm fine, just a little frazzled. I bumped into Jessica. She's pretty pissed at me." Kalin took off her ski jacket and handed it to Ben. Before sitting on the wooden bench that filled most of the front hall, she ran her fingers across the hand-carved backrest that peaked into a mountain range, making her think of Roy.

"What for?"

"She thinks it's my fault Simon's wife left him."

"Yeah, and the sun rose in the west this morning," Ben said.

Chica snatched one of Kalin's mitts and ran up the stairs and into the living room. Kalin chased her, but Chica kept out of reach.

Chica lay on her stomach, swishing her tail across the hardwood floor, looking at Kalin with mischievous eyes and clamping the mitt between her jaws. Kalin laughed at Chica's furry face. Chica lifted her ears and tilted her head to one side. Each held their place in the stand-off game.

"Come on. I'll show you what I found." Ben strode back down the stairs and toward the spare bedroom with Kalin and Chica trailing behind. Chica brought the mitt, carefully keeping her distance from Kalin.

As soon as Kalin saw Roy's clothes, she paled.

Ben gently touched her wrist. "I shouldn't have surprised you with this."

"I gave him that blue sweater one Christmas. I didn't know he still had it. He never wore it in front of me." She hugged the sweater to her chest. The wool matched the navy turtleneck sweater she wore.

"I was thinking about you and Roy this morning, and I remembered his suitcase stored in the garage. Out of curiosity, I opened it, not really thinking I'd find anything useful since the RCMP searched our place, but look what I found." He held up the key. "Tucked inside a pocket."

"Do you know what it's for?"

Ben nodded. "I think a storage locker. You know the self-storage place on the highway about a kilometer south of Holden. I used to have a locker before I met you, and my place was too small for my stuff."

Kalin absently picked up an avalanche training schedule and ran her finger across Roy's name.

"You look a bit pale. Let's go upstairs," Ben said.

Kalin sat at the pine table that served as both a kitchen and a dining room table. "Did Roy leave anything else here that we might have forgotten about?"

Ben poured her a glass of cold water. "Not that I can think of."

She swallowed a sip and set her glass on the table. "It wasn't your fault, you know. If you'd been with him, you might have died, too. You have to stop beating yourself up."

Sometimes Kalin's ability to know what he was thinking was eerie. "I wish I'd gotten out of bed that morning. Talked to him. If he'd left a few minutes later, maybe the avalanche would have missed him. It's weird how timing changes everything. I feel like I let him down."

Chica's nails clicked on the hardwood floor as she approached and dropped the mitt at Kalin's feet.

"Bad things happen all the time for no reason." She eyed Chica to see if she'd leave the mitt alone, then picked it up and wiped the slobber on her jeans.

Ben grabbed Chica by her ears and rubbed them. "Good girl." He looked at Kalin for a moment, and her face tightened.

"I just had a thought I'm not proud of," she said. "Do you think Roy dated Jessica because she ran the finance center?"

"I've been wondering about that, too," Ben said.

"I don't want to believe Roy was that calculating."

Chica bolted to the kitchen window, put both paws on the windowsill and barked.

Ben rose and looked outside. "Did you hear anything?"

Kalin remained at the table. "You don't think there's a cougar outside, do you?"

Chica growled. A deep in-the-throat rumble that exploded into a bark. The hair on her back bristled, creating a ridge from the base of her neck to the top of her tail.

Ben laid his hand on Chica's head to settle her. "I don't know."

"Maybe it's the same cougar that hid behind our woodpile the other day."

"It's weird, but right before Chica barked, I had the feeling we were being watched."

CHAPTER TWENTY-EIGHT

Ten after two in the morning.

Kalin rolled over and answered the phone before the ringing woke Ben. She stretched her right leg and rubbed her foot on Chica's silky fur. The dog's sides rose and fell with deep and steady breathing. She sat up in bed, trying not to disturb her sleeping husband or her sleeping dog.

"We've an inebriated guest who's refusing to go to his room," Fred, the security manager, said. "We found him sleeping in a stairwell in the Evergreen hotel. I'd like to call the RCMP and have him put in jail for the night."

The Evergreen was a premier property at the resort and not a place a guest should be passed out in a stairwell. Still groggy, she pushed herself up on her elbows, tugged the blanket from underneath Chica and wrapped it around her bare shoulders, leaving Ben with only the sheet.

Kalin tiptoed across the bedroom, eased the door shut and headed from their loft toward the kitchen. "Okay. Although, I'm not sure why you're calling me."

"I called front desk and asked for his room number. Turns out the guy's a director from head office. He's here to evaluate the new finance center procedures. The problem is he hit another guest. We've been trying to get him to his room, but every time we try, he takes a swing at one of us. I guess he couldn't find his key, and he broke the door to the Evergreen. Normally, the RCMP would arrest a guest for that behavior, but since he's a senior employee I want authorization from you."

"Do you want me to talk to him?" Kalin hadn't been told head office was sending an auditor to review procedures. Was Fred using this as a way of sharing information with her? Or maybe the auditor was there for something else.

"Sure. His name's Brian Sobey."

Kalin waited while muffled voices discussed something at Fred's end. Then a man said, "Hello."

"Mr. Sobey, my name is Kalin Thompson. I'm the on-duty manager tonight."

"What d'ya want?" Sobey's words slurred together into one long sound.

"I want you to go to your hotel room, but I hear you don't want to cooperate. So here's the deal. I'll give you a choice. You can let security escort you to your room, and you can stay there for the rest of the night," Kalin paused to give him a chance to understand, "or security will call the RCMP, you'll spend the night in the drunk tank, and I'll call head office in the morning and explain the situation." Kalin heard the cell phone hit something with a clunk.

"I guess I'll call the RCMP. It's not likely he'll cooperate now," Fred said.

Holding her phone to her ear, she meandered to the edge of the dark kitchen. She peeked outside. The weather had cleared, and moonlight reflected off the snow. "Go ahead. I'll talk to head office in the morning."

Kalin screamed.

Chica bolted down the stairs and to her side.

A man stared at her through the sliding glass door. He had a hood pulled over his head, covering most of his features. His hands were pressed against the glass, shielding both sides of his face. His breath fogged the window.

Chica bounded at the glass door. Her nails clattered and slipped on the window, but her teeth were bared at the intruder.

The man turned and ran before she could identify him.

"What's wrong?" Fred asked.

Kalin's heart pounded as if she'd skied a double black diamond run beyond her skill level and she'd been lucky to reach the bottom. "A man's peering in my kitchen window."

Ben ran into the kitchen and stopped inches behind Chica. He held the fireplace poker ready to swing. "What's going on?"

Fred asked, "Did you see who it was?"

"What happened?" Ben asked.

Kalin answered Fred. "No. He took off when I screamed." Her initial thought was Justin Bradley, except the man didn't move like him. Still, something was familiar.

"Should I send one of the guys over to check it out? I have to stay here until someone from the RCMP arrives."

Kalin pressed her trembling fingers into Chica's fur and took a couple of deep breaths. "No, Ben's here. We're fine."

She hung up and checked the windows, the back door that led to the hot tub and the front door. Every time she went near a window her pulse raced. She rechecked each lock, made a pot of tea and scrunched into the corner of the couch, pulling her knees to her chest. Chica jumped up beside her and gave her a look as if daring Kalin to push her off.

Ben joined them on the couch. "This is out of control."

* * *

"I think it's time we had another chat," Constable Miller said. "Your boss told me about the person looking in your window last night."

Kalin stopped in front of the administration building and unbuckled one snowshoe. "How did Turner know about that?"

"You'll have to ask him. But I think there's more going on here than you're telling me."

Turner could have read the security reports, or Fred could have reported to him. She checked the time on her phone. Miller was up at the resort before the work day had begun. "How come you're here so early?"

Miller gave her an easy smile and winked. "You know I can't reveal that."

"That's right. I forgot we're in secret spy mode."

"Can we go for a walk and talk?" He lifted his arm and pointed along the path leading to the lifts.

Kalin undid her second snowshoe and leaned the pair against the outside wall of the administration building. A low theft rate was one of the things she loved about small-town living. Her equipment would be there when she returned. "So what's up?"

"Any idea who was looking in your window last night?"

"Ben and I talked, but there are too many possibilities. The only reason I saw the person was because Fred had just called me about a security issue."

"Were you planning on reporting the incident?"

"Nothing happened."

"So that means no."

"You didn't come here to ask me about last night. Why don't you ask me whatever it is you want to know?"

"I've been hearing rumors about your relationship with Roy. Can you tell me about your past together?"

Miller had no need to know about her family history, still, she wanted him to find out what really happened to Roy and if he had an accomplice. "I helped Roy get his job, so we could be near each other. When I left Ottawa, we weren't exactly on speaking terms. Since Nora's son was just born and she took the summer off, he spent last summer working for Ben as a fly-fishing guide."

"And how were things going?"

"Fine."

"Except that you kicked him out the night before the theft."

"How do you know that?"

Miller straightened his back and held eye contact with Kalin.

"How I was getting along with Roy had nothing to do with the theft."

"It's my job to decide what's relevant, not yours."

Kalin laughed. "Do you know how many times I've heard you use that line?"

"If you weren't speaking to Roy when you left Ottawa, what happened to cause that?"

When Miller waited longer than Kalin could stand, she said, "So we are having a serious talk. Roy and I had a fight. I told him something about his fiancée that wasn't true, and they broke up."

"What did you tell him?"

"That she'd cheated on him. I thought she had, but found out too late maybe it wasn't true. I've felt terrible ever since."

Miller remained silent while they walked by several housekeeping staff on their way to work. When they were alone again, he continued with his questions. "Did you know Roy planned to steal the money? Is that why you kicked him out?"

"That was a bit direct. I don't believe Roy is the thief. I think it's convenient to blame him when he's not able to defend himself." Kalin wasn't sure why she lied. In the safety of Ben's arms, saying Roy was guilty was one thing. Telling Miller was another.

"The timing of his disappearance is suspicious. Did you help him steal the money?"

"That's crazy."

"Maybe you kicked him out, so we wouldn't think you were in on the theft with him. Is this something you planned together?"

Kalin's anger tightened in her chest. She resisted the urge to walk away from Miller. "I didn't do anything wrong and neither did Roy."

"Did you lend Roy your master key?"

"No, I…What are you talking about? Did you find an extra key?"

"Just wondering if Roy had access to yours."

Kalin had worked with the locksmith and Fred on a new key protocol when keys had been used to gain unauthorized access to a ski-tuning room. Miller had been involved in that investigation and had met the locksmith. He'd probably called Brightman after Kalin told him all the directors had a master key that opened the finance center.

"This is not the first time you and Roy have been investigated."

"I haven't—"

"Really. I know about your husband's unsolved death."

Her intake of cold air froze her lungs. She planted her boots in the snow but didn't say anything.

"Did you inherit much when your husband died?"

"We didn't have any money or life insurance."

"Did Roy gain anything from his death?"

"Of course not."

"You and Ben must owe quite a bit of money now."

The change of subject threw her off a bit. Miller wasn't holding back because they were friends. "We can afford the payments. Besides, one hundred grand barely covers a quarter of the house. It's not enough."

"It's enough to ease things a bit."

"What's wrong with you?"

* * *

Kalin flopped onto Roy's bed in the guest room. Resting her head on his pillow, she inhaled, searching for a lingering scent. How could she have lost him?

Miller's questions frightened her. She didn't understand the link back to Jack's death or why Miller had looked into her past. After Miller left her standing in the cold at the bottom of the lift station, she'd gone straight to the locksmith's.

"Other than the list you already gave me, are you sure no one else has a master key?" she asked.

"Positive," Brightman answered in his customary gruff voice.

"When was the latest key issued?"

Brightman checked his records. "I gave one to Oliver Ward when he was promoted to director of mountain ops."

"Why didn't you give him the key from the previous director?"

"It wasn't returned to me."

"So where is it?"

Brightman shrugged his shoulders.

Knowing Brightman shut down if he thought he was being criticized, Kalin hid her frustration. During the investigation into the death of a local ski hero, Kalin had discovered Brightman's atrocious record keeping and forced a new process in place.

She rolled over on Roy's bed, shoved her hand underneath his pillow and bunched it tighter. She felt a lump and pulled out Roy's wallet. Either he forgot it when he took off the morning of the avalanche or he was planning on coming back.

She put his wallet to her nose, breathing in the leather. After saving for several months, she'd given it to Roy for his twentieth birthday. It was the first expensive gift she'd ever given him, and she'd bought it at Roots, hoping he'd think it was cool.

She spread the contents of the wallet across his comforter, including a crumpled newspaper clipping she found stuffed into the billfold. Kalin didn't need to read the words to know what it said. The *Ottawa Citizen* published the article not long after Jack died. It was a summary of the accident, stating the hit-and-run driver hadn't been located and asking for information. The clipping was an odd thing for Roy to save.

She examined a small photo of Roy and Patricia standing at the side of the Rideau Canal getting ready to skate on Canada's second-longest outdoor rink. Had anyone called Patricia and told her about Roy? Even though she was no longer engaged to him, she had a right to know.

Roy's bank and credit card were in the pile. She ran her fingers across his name embossed on his bank card and blinked to clear her eyes. She believed he'd been planning to return to their place. Otherwise he would have taken his wallet. He wasn't on the run with the finance center money. Still, she asked herself if Roy took her keys without her noticing and copied the master. Maybe he stole the money, but at least he wasn't pretending to be dead.

The doorbell rang. On her way to the front hall, she dropped the bank card on the windowsill. She opened the door an inch. "Ben?"

"It's Aiden."

"What are you doing here so late?" Kalin looked down at her sweats and tank top. Good thing she wasn't wearing pajamas.

"Hi to you, too."

"Hi."

"Can I come in? I'd like to talk to you." When Kalin didn't move he added, "Please."

Letting politeness get the better of her, she relented and gestured to the stairs leading to the living room. After he passed by her, she nudged the door, pretending to close it, but left the bolt unlatched against the frame. Her intuition told her there was something off about Aiden. Maybe he was the one who'd been looking in her window.

When she reached the living room, Aiden gazed at her for a moment. "Are you okay?"

Kalin slid her hands into the pockets of her sweat pants and leaned against the wall beside the fireplace. "I'm just tired."

Aiden unzipped his ski jacket but didn't remove it. "I'm not the bad guy, you know. The scene with my ex-wife is complicated."

"You don't need to explain."

"Can we sit?"

"Okay." Kalin perched on the arm of a chair. Aiden brought a chill to the room, and she couldn't get settled.

He sat on the couch with his head lowered and his hands clasped between his knees. He stared at the ski socks covering his feet. "Samantha is not my daughter."

Kalin waited.

"Adrienne cheated on me. Samantha's not mine."

"How do you know for sure?"

"This is something I don't usually tell people, so please don't repeat it. I can't have kids. I should have told Adrienne before we got married, but I wasn't sure she'd marry me." He shrugged. "She thought she could get away with pretending Samantha was mine, and when she told me she was pregnant, I knew I couldn't be the father."

"That's a big secret to keep from your wife."

"I know. I was engaged. Before Adrienne. The woman dumped me because she wanted kids. I thought the second time, I'd tell Adrienne after we were married, and she wouldn't leave me. I never got around to it. The night she told me she was pregnant, she had this fancy dinner ready with candles and music. Like I'd be thrilled with the news. So I left her. What was I supposed to do?"

"Why are you telling me this?"

Aiden bit his bottom lip. "We have to work together, and I don't want you to hold this against me."

Kalin ignored the implication she would be influenced at work by a person's private life and decided she wasn't going to let him off easy. "If Samantha's not your child, what's Adrienne doing here?"

"She wants money. My parents don't know about Sam, and Adrienne is threatening to tell them she's mine. My parents are religious, and if they believe I had a child and left her, it would kill them. They're not happy we split. It's hard for them to understand it's better for some people to be apart."

Kalin fixed her gaze on Aiden. Was he telling the truth? How long had Adrienne been blackmailing him for? If he needed money badly enough, maybe he was Roy's buddy in crime. But then why would he tell her he had a motive? "Your parents really don't know about Samantha?"

"Adrienne hasn't seen my parents since I left her. I told them she cheated on me, so they wouldn't try to contact her. Right now, they think she's at fault. I want her out of my life."

"Why don't you tell your parents?"

"You don't understand what they're like. I can't."

"I'm supposed to meet Ben soon. I've got to go," Kalin said. She escorted Aiden downstairs to the front hall.

Aiden glanced through the open door to the guest bedroom where the contents of Roy's wallet were spread across her bed. "What's that?"

"Nothing. Just looking at Roy's things."

He entered the front hall. "You don't want to lose this." He picked up Roy's bank card off the windowsill and handed it to Kalin.

* * *

"What are you doing here?" Jessica glanced back into her house, then at Aiden. He stood on her front steps, looking down his nose at her. In typical ski resort fashion, he wore a ski jacket, a toque pulled over his ears and jeans. No liftie uniform in sight to boost his status. Who did he think cared if he was the lift manager?

"I have an idea about finding the money," Aiden said.

"Are you crazy coming here to talk about that? Simon's inside." Jessica slipped her bare feet into her winter boots, stepped outside and pulled the door closed. "What if he overhears us?"

"He's not going to, so stop worrying. Kalin has Roy's bank card."

Jessica shivered. She wore a long-sleeved T-shirt and jeans, and denim never kept the cold at bay. "That's quite the news flash."

"I think she's trying to find the money."

"You idiot. With Roy's bank card? You think Roy put stolen money into an account? The police would've checked his bank already. Besides, he didn't have time between the theft and the avalanche."

Using his teeth, Aiden ripped a thread of skin off the side of his thumbnail and spit. "Who says Roy died in the avalanche? Maybe he put the money in the bank later, and maybe the cops don't know about this account."

"That's a dumb idea. How would he deposit money if Kalin has the card? You can't really believe Roy staged the avalanche. There's no way he would just disappear." Why did her friends always think the worst? Roy would never hurt her in such a cruel manner. Would he? They'd had their problems. Maybe she'd completely misjudged him.

"If you don't believe that, how about Kalin thinks Roy stole the money and that's why she was going through his wallet tonight?"

"What a bunch of bullshit. Maybe she just misses Roy." *I miss him.*

"What if we steal the card from Kalin and try to get the money?"

"You really are an idiot." Jessica backed across the threshold. "I have to go."

"We still need to find Roy's duffle bag. There's a good chance some of the money's in it," Aiden yelled through the gap in the doorway.

Jessica clicked the deadbolt in place, muting his voice.

CHAPTER TWENTY-NINE

The sky, leaden with black clouds, promised another storm. Kalin tucked her hands into the sleeves of her ski jacket. “How many times have you done staff checks?” she asked Tessa.

Everyone in the HR department took a turn checking the employee housing units, and without a doubt, no one liked the role. Kalin and Tessa were searching for stolen housekeeping supplies, and the checks could get ugly. Instead of abandoning Tessa to deal with the difficult situation by herself, Kalin used the opportunity to spend time with her recruiting specialist.

“Only a few, and Monica always came along.” Tessa knocked on the door and waited a couple of seconds before punching the code to the combination lock. She opened the door and yelled, “Staff checks.”

Kalin and Tessa clomped single file up a narrow set of creaking stairs from the entryway to the common area. Three employees sat on the couches, each of them too lazy or uninterested to answer the door. The acrid stench of beer and stale cigarettes mixed with air freshener accosted her. Tessa dropped her hood and pulled her hair over her cochlear implant.

One woman leaned into the shoulder of another and whispered something.

“Is anyone upstairs?” Tessa asked in a harsh tone.

“Nope,” a young woman said from her place huddled into the twenty-year-old couch that was permanently imprinted by hundreds of bodies.

Tessa and Kalin ascended the second flight of stairs leading to the bedrooms. “What’s with the attitude?” Kalin asked.

“Didn’t you hear what that woman said?”

“She was whispering.”

“Sometimes I forget not everyone can read lips. She said, ‘That’s the bitch who has it in for Justin.’”

They entered the first bedroom without knocking.

Kalin wrinkled her nose at the odor emanating from the pile of sweaty ski clothing crumpled on the floor of the first bedroom they entered. The stale smell of human sweat was worse than the stink of beer and cigarettes. She slipped between the bunk beds and lifted one of the blankets.

“Hey,” a shout came from underneath.

Kalin dropped the blanket and jumped backward, stepping on Tessa’s foot.

Tessa’s eyes widened in surprise. “Ouch. What are you doing?”

Kalin laughed. “I’m sorry. I didn’t know anyone was in here,” she said to the woman in the bed. “Let’s check the other rooms first.” Kalin backed into the hallway, dragging Tessa with her. “They said no one was up here.”

“They probably didn’t know. Did you see the look on her face? I’ve never seen anyone sit up so fast.”

“Stop laughing,” Kalin said.

Tessa pulled Kalin by the arm. “You stop laughing. Come on. Let’s check the other room. We can come back to this one.”

This time, Kalin knocked before entering. She lifted the blanket on the nearest bed, checked the sheets and found a housekeeping code printed on the edge. “These are stolen.” She stripped the bed and handed the sheets and pillowcases to Tessa.

She checked the bed on the left, and sure enough, the sheets were stolen, too. She passed them to Tessa and pulled off a pillowcase.

While Tessa rolled the sheets into a bundle, Kalin lowered to her knees and searched underneath the bed. “This is disgusting. A rotten apple core is under here, and gross, a used condom.”

“What’s that?” Tessa pointed to the end of the bed.

Kalin picked up an empty baggie and sniffed the contents. She handed the baggie to Tessa. “Pot?”

“Maybe,” Tessa said. “I’m not an expert.”

“Whose bed is this?”

Tessa checked the staff-housing list. “Three guys share this room. Eric Wilson, Paul Atkins and Justin Bradley.”

* * *

Kalin entered the staff gym and found Ben doing bench presses. The head office decision makers had allocated space for the gym in the basement of the resort's oldest hotel. And old, not meaning cozy or quaint, but old meaning run down and in need of repair. The room was chosen because the gym was for employees, not guests, and expensive real estate would not be wasted on housing employee equipment.

She hovered at the edge of the gym, watching Ben. Droplets of sweat covered his forehead, and he grunted as he lifted the bar ninety degrees from his shoulders. Volunteer Fire Department, written in white letters on his midnight-blue T-shirt, stretched across his chest, showing off his muscles. When he noticed Kalin, he let the bar clang into the slots and grinned.

Fitness-conscious employees occupied the stationary bikes, treadmills, elliptical machines and free weights. Kalin weaved through the machines, nodding at various staff members. Years of water stains from the spring melt decorated the carpet. The hotel was at the lowest altitude in the resort, and the water found the path of least resistance through the basement.

Kalin crouched beside Ben and spoke quietly. "I did a staff housing check today, and just by chance, I ended up checking Justin Bradley and Eric Wilson's room. Justin's the liftie you had a fight with, and Eric's a seasonal finance center clerk."

Straddling the bench, Ben leaned close to Kalin. "And?"

"Don't you think it's odd that the finance center clerk is roommates with the employee I'm having issues with?" Kalin told Ben what the employee on the couch said about her.

"Not nice, but I imagine Justin's telling everyone his version of the story. It can't be flattering to you. What happens about the sheets?"

"Nothing. Too many staff steal them. If we fired everyone who'd stolen sheets, we wouldn't have very many employees left."

Ben wiped sweat off his forehead with the bottom edge of his T-shirt. "Have you found any connection between Eric and Roy?"

Kalin admired Ben's abs and imagined running her fingers across the ripples. *Get a grip*. After he dropped his T-shirt, she focused her eyes on his. "Other than his name on the list with dollar values we found in Roy's locker, no." She ignored the sexual electricity humming between them and asked, "What do you think we should do?"

"I'm not sure. Let's talk on the way home."

Kalin returned to her office and shut the door. She sat staring at the view and contemplated phoning White Peaks. Ben had given her space. No pressure for an answer. Smart on his part. She could be stubborn, and if he worked too hard at getting her to turn down the job, she might just accept the position. But since he'd been generous, she had to think about what was best for him and for them as a couple.

She worked in her office until Ben arrived at five thirty. "You ready?"

They walked along the trodden path between the golf course and the ski hill, and Kalin leaned into Ben, letting their arms touch.

"I don't like that Justin is talking badly about you," Ben said.

"It's just chatter."

"What if he's angry enough to hurt you for real?"

"He's never threatened me. It's his manner that bothers me. Even on the night you fought him, I fell by accident. I don't think his goal is to hurt me."

"We should let Fred know Justin and Eric are roomies. Maybe it means something. When Justin's other housemates tell him about the staff check, he's going to be more pissed than he already is."

"I hate looking like I need help, especially in front of my security team, but I'll call Fred when we get home."

Kalin and Ben's fingers intertwined, and they walked in silence to their place.

"Oh, crap. Look," Ben said. Painted in red, 'BITCH' filled the top half of the front door. He ran his fingers through the paint, smudging the letters.

* * *

Fred photographed Kalin's door. Wearing jeans and a flannel shirt instead of his security jacket, he looked like a lumberjack.

"You did the right thing calling me, but I don't understand why you don't want to call the RCMP. Painting your door is a gutsy thing to do during the day, especially when it's well known I live next door," Fred said.

"It's probably a prank," Kalin said.

"You should file a report."

"I think she should, too," Ben said from behind them. He'd just returned from walking Chica, and she strained against her collar to reach Kalin.

"Why did you leave before I got here?" Fred asked.

"Chica's been inside all day. I took her for a quick walk."

"Kalin said you smudged the paint. It was wet when you left. What if whoever did this was still around?"

Ben winced. "I'm sorry," he said to Kalin. "I didn't think of that."

Fred pet Chica. "Would she bark if someone was at the door she didn't know?"

"Usually," Kalin said.

"I didn't hear any barking."

Kalin shivered. "You think she's met the person who did this?"

"Maybe." Fred looked at the snow-covered ground around the entryway. "It's too bad the footprints are such a mess, or we could follow the tracks."

Kalin crouched and buried her head in Chica's neck. How could this be happening? She didn't know what frightened her more, if the painter was or wasn't Justin. Without looking up, she said, "I guess we should tell Miller."

"Did you tell Fred about the staff checks today?" Ben asked Kalin.

"I hadn't gotten to that yet." Kalin summarized the checks she'd done with Tessa.

"You probably can't prove Justin or Eric wrote on your door just because you did a staff check."

"You don't believe her?" Ben asked. "One of Justin's housemates referred to Kalin as a bitch."

"I believe her, but she doesn't have proof. Justin or Eric could say he had no idea she checked their room and took the sheets."

"Then why should I report it?"

"Because then the police can talk to the guys, and whichever one did this will know he can't get away with much."

Miller had disappointed her. After all they'd been through together, first with the investigation into a skier dying on the race course, then with the fire at the resort, Miller actually thought she stole the money. "Can't you talk to Eric and Justin?"

"I will. I'll instruct the security team to monitor them for a while, but you need to be careful."

CHAPTER THIRTY

Skiers and snowboarders were loading at the Alpine Tracks lift station, oblivious to Kalin watching them, when Constable Miller walked to her side. "Have something on your mind?" he asked.

Kalin sucked her lips between her teeth and shrugged. She was still angry with Miller for accusing her of the theft.

"Tessa told me where to find you. I finished taking a report from Fred and want to speak with you before I interview Justin Bradley and Eric Wilson."

Kalin nodded in the direction of the lift station. "That's Justin. The liftie to the left of the chair."

"Has he noticed you watching him?"

Kalin licked her cracked lips. She put her hand in her pocket, searching for lip balm, but came up empty. "I don't know, and I don't really care."

"It's not a good idea to antagonize him."

"I want him to know I'm not afraid of him."

"Maybe you should be." Miller exhaled a heavy breath. "So tell me what happened."

Kalin faced the lift station, avoiding his eyes. "Didn't Fred already tell you?"

"He told me you didn't want to report the door paint to us."

"Fred convinced me you couldn't do anything."

"I'm not buying that. He told me you said you didn't want to make a report before he said you had no proof Justin or Eric painted your door."

"Okay, you've probably figured it out anyway."

Miller tensed beside her.

"It's not what you think," Kalin said. "I'm not confessing. The last time we talked, you practically accused me of stealing the money. I didn't want to give you any reason to be more suspicious of me. If you already think I'm a thief, why would you believe anything I say?"

"You know I have a job to do. Try not to take it personally. I know you've been avoiding me since we last talked. Can you at least summarize your version of events connected to Justin? You know I'll help you if I can."

"Fine." Kalin told her side of the story, right from the first time she'd met Justin.

When she finished, Miller said, "I'll talk with him, but we can't do much unless he admits he painted your door. And Kalin, if you have any new information about Roy, it's in your best interest to tell me. You can't hurt him."

Justin glared at Kalin from his station at the lift. Without taking his eyes off her, he shoveled snow off the ramp before the next set of skiers slid into position, waiting for the following chair.

* * *

"I'll be there in a few minutes," Aiden said. He stuffed his phone into his jacket pocket and left the mountain ops building. He tried to be a good lift manager and give the lifties and ticket checkers a break when they needed one. But did Meare really need a break?

Eighteen-year-old Meare Jensen arrived from New Zealand two weeks ago. She was a late-season hire and had finished her training as a ticket checker yesterday. Today was her first day working at a lift station.

As far as Aiden knew, Meare had never been away from home before, and crossing the ocean was a big deal. She already had a reputation as being a party girl. She called Aiden and asked for a bathroom break probably because she was hung over.

Aiden approached the lift shack. Meare stomped her feet and pulled her jacket collar higher over her chin.

Justin stood with his back to Aiden and his phone tucked against his ear. He wasn't supposed to be using his phone while on duty. After the way he'd treated Kalin, was the guy asking to be fired?

"Wilson," Justin said, then mumbled a bunch of words, like he had some big secret.

The chair swung underneath the Alpine Tracks lift station, and two kids stood at the red line, waiting for the detachable chair to reach them.

Meare stood only feet from him, holding her scanning gun in front of her, waiting to check the next set of skiers for passes.

Justin spoke to Wilson. "We need to move the duffle bag."

Aiden walked to the edge of the maze and headed toward the lift shack. He trudged close enough to make eye contact with Justin.

"Gotta go." Justin tucked the phone into his jacket pocket.

The second Aiden took the scanner from Meare and replaced her at the front of the lift line, she ran toward the crowded foyer and the downstairs bathroom. "Don't talk on the phone while you're on duty," Aiden said to Justin.

* * *

Kalin stood in front of the ticket office. Guests signed up for ski lessons, bought afternoon lift tickets or were heading to the restaurant for lunch. The business of the resort distracted her from her worries.

A teenage girl rushed up the stairs from the public washrooms and skidded to a stop near Kalin.

"Do you need help?" Kalin asked.

"A woman collapsed in the washroom," the girl said.

Kalin jogged down the stairs, pulled her cell from her pocket and called security. Every member of the security team had their level-three occupational first aid, and most of them worked for the volunteer fire department, giving them additional first aid training and experience.

She found a young woman squatting against the open door of one of the stalls. The woman's hands were twisted into tight fists, turning inward into her wrists. She breathed in short rapid bursts and shivered. Kalin knelt behind her, and the woman fell onto Kalin's thighs and leaned against her chest.

"I can't feel my arms or legs," a little girl voice cried at Kalin.

Kalin reached around the woman and held her hand. "What's your name?"

"Meare Jensen."

"Okay, Meare. Help is coming. We're going to take care of you. Can you feel my hand?"

"No." Meare sobbed. "Am I going to die?"

"You'll be fine," Kalin answered, not having a clue what was wrong with her. "Can you slow your breathing?"

Meare made a visible attempt and took a deep, ragged breath.

Kalin held Meare's wrist, searching for a pulse, but couldn't detect one. "Are you in pain anywhere?"

Before Meare answered, she convulsed. Kalin held her tight and waited for the shaking to pass.

Fred arrived, and Kalin glanced at him from her place on the floor. “Call it out.”

He lowered his chin to his chest and used his thumb to hit the transmit button on the radio attached to his jacket and spoke to dispatch. “Call nine-one-one. We need an ambulance. Also call ski patrol and tell them we need an oxygen tank in the women’s washroom, ground floor of the ski lodge.” He turned to Kalin. “What happened?”

Kalin relayed what she knew.

Ben arrived carrying a portable oxygen tank. He put on blue latex gloves, ripped the plastic covering off the mask, pulled the elastic strap free and turned on the oxygen.

Kalin looked at her bare hands and a chill ran through her. Did Meare have anything contagious?

Fred lifted one leg, then the next over Kalin’s shoulder and positioned himself inside the stall. He sat on the edge of the toilet, facing Meare. “Try not to move her. Until we know if she’s injured, you’ll have to keep her still.”

Ben put the oxygen mask over Meare’s mouth and nose and pulled the elastic band behind her head. Kalin used her hands to stabilize Meare’s neck.

“Feel any better?” Ben asked Meare after she’d taken a few breaths.

Meare nodded.

“I couldn’t get a pulse on her wrist,” Kalin whispered.

Ben reached around Kalin, leaning on her back for support, and put two fingers on Meare’s neck. “One hundred and thirty,” he said to Fred.

Kalin stretched her head over Meare’s shoulder to ensure her eyes were open. Wearing her winter ski jacket, ski pants and wool hat pulled down over her ears, and with four people contained in the small space, Kalin was sweating. She couldn’t take her hat off without tipping Meare sideways.

Two paramedics arrived carrying a spine board, and Kalin watched as they packed and loaded Meare, relieved to have someone else responsible for the young woman.

Meare’s roommate arrived. “Aiden called me and asked me to bring Meare’s backpack from the lift shack.” She left with the ambulance and instructions to call Kalin with an update on Meare’s condition.

Kalin stood alone with Ben. Approaching the sink, she turned on the water, letting it get as hot as she could stand against her bare skin. In the middle of washing her hands for the second time, she asked, “What do you think is wrong with her?”

“I don’t know.”

* * *

When they reached home, Ben's wet hair stuck to his forehead, and beads of water ran down his cheeks. Kalin's toque had kept her dry. A storm settled, depositing heavy flakes that were on the verge of becoming rain drops. Higher on the mountain, a couple of degrees colder, snow would be accumulating on the ski runs.

Chica met them in the hallway, furiously wagging her tail.

Kalin turned to the washing machine housed on the ground floor near the garage entranceway. Without caring about the snow dropping on the floor, she stripped to her underwear and threw everything including her ski jacket, ski pants and toque into the washer.

She walked past Ben, stopped long enough to throw him a towel and jumped straight into the shower beside the guest room. Roy's soap and shampoo rested on the side of the tub. The suds bubbled, and shards of glass stabbed her heart, the smell of Roy invading her soul. After a scalding wash, she found Ben sitting at the kitchen table with Chica sleeping at his feet.

She called Meare's roommate but only got her voicemail.

"How about I make us a snack?" Ben asked.

"I'm not hungry. I can't eat until I know Meare's going to be okay. She was so sick and really scared. What am I going to tell her parents if I have to call them?"

Two hours disappeared before Kalin's cell rang.

"The doctor said Meare has a severe kidney infection," Meare's roommate said.

"I don't understand why she was paralyzed."

"He said she was in shock and her body was shutting down. He also said she was lucky she was found so quickly, or it could have been much worse."

"Is she okay now?"

"She'll be fine. She's on an antibiotic drip but can go home tomorrow."

Kalin folded herself into Ben's arms, closed her eyes and told him what she'd learned.

"You okay?" he asked.

"I thought I might not have handled this right. What if I'd done something wrong?"

"You did great. You took good care of her."

"I'm not trained for this."

"This, you are trained for. What you're not trained for is investigating a serious crime. Between the theft and Justin Bradley, something's got to give."

"You know I have to find out if anyone else was involved. What if someone triggered the avalanche? I can't let them get away with that."

"You're talking about murder."

"I am."

Ben took a step away from Kalin and tensed. "You can't investigate a murder. The last time you did that you were almost killed."

"This is different. I need closure. What happened to 'you're here for me'?"

"If you're thinking of taking the job at White Peaks, why worry about what happens here?"

"So that's what this is about. You're angry I haven't decided what to do yet."

"I'm angry…I'm angry because…I'm going to the fire hall. We can talk later."

"You always go there when you want to avoid something. Last year you went half way to Manitoba. Maybe we could just talk about this."

"I need to think." Ben turned on her and stomped down the stairs toward the front door.

CHAPTER THIRTY-ONE

"Damn it." Kalin slammed the *Maclean's* magazine she'd been pretending to read onto the coffee table and startled Chica. What was she going to do about White Peaks? She was getting nowhere talking to Ben, and she had to decide soon.

The home telephone rang, and she glanced at the clock. Eleven thirty. Only security would be calling her at this hour. Her heart accelerated as she picked up the receiver. "Hello?" She cleared her throat and said a little louder, "Hello?"

She listened to long, deep breaths and quietly placed the receiver back in its cradle. As she checked the locks on her doors and windows, Chica watched her, her brown eyes following Kalin's movement, her body resting motionless.

Kalin was becoming obsessed with locks. She hadn't worried about her safety in the city where she was anonymous, just one of many going about her life. In Ottawa, none of her colleagues or employees had known where she lived.

She wished Ben were home. Lately, he'd been spending more time with his buddies than her. He seemed to find one reason or another to hang at his precious fire hall. And going there in the middle of an argument instead of talking to her was not good. Really, not good.

The phone rang again, but this time, she left the handset in place.

The ringing switched from her home phone to her cell. The display told her security was on the other end and not the heavy breather. Security would call her for an emergency involving an employee, and she answered their calls even if she wasn't the on-duty manager. She could add Caller ID to her home phone package or maybe get rid of the home phone altogether.

"There's been an accident at the bar," Fred said.

Kalin mentally braced herself.

"It's Ben. He fell down the stairs and hit his head."

Sweat dampened her pajama top, and her hands shook. If someone had punched her in the gut, her stomach couldn't hurt more. "How bad is he?"

"We called an ambulance and sent him to the local hospital. He looked stable when he left, but a paramedic called a minute ago and told us he had a seizure. He's been put in a chemically-induced coma and intubated."

Kalin slumped into the back of the couch. "That can't be."

"Are you okay?" Fred asked.

"I'm on my way."

"There's nothing for you to do here."

"How did he fall?" Kalin ran up to their bedroom in the loft and began the dance of getting dressed while holding her cell. She squished the phone between her ear and her shoulder and pulled on a pair of jeans. She was going to follow Ben to Calgary.

"Security was escorting a guy out of the bar, and they were having difficulty. Ben tried to assist, and he fell down the stairs."

"Is he going to be okay?"

"I don't know."

Kalin rubbed one hand over her face, snagged her stitches and inhaled deeply. "Anything else?"

"No."

"Call me if you hear something."

Kalin threw on a crimson sweater, the one Ben liked. Without bothering to wipe her tears, she grabbed her ski jacket and ran to her Jeep. Memories of the night Jack died flew around in her head as if a snowstorm exploded in her mind. A police officer standing on her doorstep. Words about a hit-and-run. Not again. Not Ben. Not now.

As she backed out, her headlamps swept over the window beside the front door. Chica peered through the glass. Kalin pulled back into the driveway and got Chica, not knowing what she was going to do with her.

She drove along Black Bear Drive and past Jessica's home. The lights were on. Kalin did a U-turn and pulled into her driveway. She wasn't Kalin's first choice, but where else could she leave Chica. Who knew when she'd get home again?

Jessica opened the door, looking surprised to see Kalin and Chica. Kalin explained what happened and asked Jessica to take care of Chica.

"Of course."

Kalin handed Jessica a key to their house. “Her dog food is in the mudroom in the lower cupboard. She gets two cups a day. Her leash is there, too. I didn’t think to bring any of it.”

“How long will you be gone?”

Kalin hesitated with her hand on Chica’s head. “I have no idea.”

“Leave the dog. She’ll be fine.”

As Kalin backed out of the driveway, a curtain in Jessica’s living room slid to the right, and Simon Crane peeked through the window. She lifted her hand to wave, but the curtain dropped back into place. She almost ran back in to get Chica, but she shifted her Jeep into drive. Just because she’d fired Simon didn’t mean he would take his anger out on her dog. Surely he wasn’t that cruel.

Kalin drove down the mountain, through Holden and got on the highway toward Banff. She didn’t bother to pull over when she called Fred. “Any news about Ben?”

“Nothing yet. Where are you?”

“On the highway. I’m going to Calgary.”

“The roads are slippery, so drive carefully. There’ll be a lot of ice tonight. Call me when you reach Banff. I should know by then where they’re taking him.”

“You must have some idea which hospital.” She pressed her foot on the gas pedal and drove faster. Ice or no ice, she’d get to Calgary in record time.

“He’s being airlifted with STARS. I’d guess the Foothills. The life-threatening cases usually go there.”

CHAPTER THIRTY-TWO

Jessica returned to her living room with Chica prancing beside her. "You were at the bar. What happened?"

"I didn't see much," Simon said.

Chica ran to his side and thrust her head on his lap. He pushed her away. "You know I'm allergic to dogs. She can't stay here."

"I already told Kalin I'd take care of her until she got back from Calgary."

"Why would you do that?"

"Because she's Roy's sister, and she needs help." Jessica grabbed a few mixed nuts from the bowl on the coffee table and munched on them. "Want some?"

"You should be fat with the amount of nuts you eat." Simon pushed Chica's head off his lap. "I can't live with this mutt."

Chica trotted to Jessica and sat on her foot as if making a statement she'd claimed her human for the moment. Jessica wasn't fond of dogs, but Roy had liked Chica, so she could tolerate her being around for a while. "Too bad. You can stay or not. Up to you, but I promised."

"What's with you? Ever since Roy died, you're Miss Nice."

"Are you saying I wasn't nice before?"

"Bad word choice. But you weren't a softy."

Simon rubbed his eyes. They were already turning red and getting puffy. Having no allergies of her own, she didn't stock allergy medicine.

As if to punctuate her thought, he sneezed. He pointed at the keys in Jessica's hand. "Do you want me to get Chica's food and stuff?"

Jessica put Kalin's keys on the mantel. She hadn't asked Kalin, but she assumed because of the late hour, the dog had already been fed. She could wait until morning to go to Ben and Kalin's to get food. "I'll go tomorrow."

Feigning a yawn, she left Simon to the pullout couch, dragged Chica with her and locked herself in her bedroom. She entered the en suite and shut the door. Behind two doors, Simon couldn't overhear her call Aiden.

* * *

Jessica overslept and woke to the sound of Chica scratching at her bedroom door. She glanced at the clock on her wall. Nine-thirty. Shit. She hadn't let Chica out to pee or fed her. She shoved herself out of bed. Chica could run around outside for a minute while she got dressed.

As soon as Jessica shuffled in her slippers from the bedroom into the hallway, Chica bolted to the front door. After letting the dog out, she plodded back through the living room. The pullout was closed, and the sheets were folded in a neat pile on top of the cushions.

Jessica found her cell and turned it on. Simon had sent her a text.

Can't live w dog. Up sick all night.

Jessica's eyes roamed the room. Simon's suitcase was gone. The place was hers again.

She dressed in jeans and a sweater she pulled from her laundry basket. No one cared what she looked like, and there wasn't a person she needed to impress.

Chica barked, and Jessica opened the door to find her wagging her tail. Better get to Kalin's. Jessica reached for the keys on top of the mantel. Her hand stopped midway. She was sure she'd left the keys on the right end. Now they rested in the middle. The empty couch where Simon had slept mocked her for leaving the keys where he could use them. Then she shook her head. She was getting paranoid. What use could Simon have for the keys?

A knock on her front door preceded cold air entering her small suite. Who the hell just walks in?

"Hello?"

She recognized Aiden's voice.

"Where've you been? I've been calling since eight," he said.

"I slept in."

"You ready to go?"

Jessica grabbed Kalin's keys and followed Aiden to his car. Chica ran along beside her.

"She's not getting in my car," Aiden said.

"The whole point is to feed her. If anyone notices us going into Kalin's then we have an excuse."

"She sheds," Aiden whined.

"Let's walk. It's only five minutes."

Neither said a word until they were inside Ben and Kalin's new home.

"Where'd they get the money to afford this?" Aiden asked.

Chica ran upstairs and straight to the mudroom. By the time Jessica reached her, Chica was staring intently at the cupboard. Jessica read the label on the bag of dog food and put two scoops of kibble into Chica's bowl. Chica wagged her tail in time to gobbling her food.

Aiden meandered through the living room. "So what are we looking for?"

"Any hint that Kalin thinks Roy took the money or where Roy might have hidden it."

"Like she's going to keep that kind of thing around."

Jessica filled Chica's water bowl. "You have a better idea?"

"Do you know what room Roy slept in?"

"The ground floor guest room."

"I'll start there, and you check Kalin and Ben's bedroom."

"I'll come with you. One of us might see something the other misses."

They tromped downstairs and into the guest room. The room had been tidied. Jessica stared at the bed. Roy would never have pulled the covers up or tucked in the sheets. Kalin must have done that.

Aiden opened the wall-length closet.

Jessica sat on the edge of the bed, startled at her overwhelming desire to curl up on Roy's comforter.

Aiden placed four books about white-water kayaking on the floor and checked behind the small bookshelf. "There's nothing here, except we know Roy liked reading about kayaking."

"Like that's big news."

"What's with you?" Aiden asked.

"Nothing."

"Let's check the rest of the house. Maybe we'll find something in their bedroom."

Jessica followed Aiden to the top floor. She stopped at the edge of the room.

He went straight to the en suite, opened the medicine cabinet and read the labels.

"That's a bit personal. Do you have to snoop there?" Being in the bedroom was wrong. She'd crossed a line.

“The more we know about them the better. Did you know Kalin takes sleeping pills?”

“No. And I don’t see how that’s relevant.”

Jessica waited in the bedroom doorway, unable to intrude further. Her cell rang, and she glanced at the display. Kalin was on the other end of the call. Jessica’s cheeks heated, and she answered the phone.

CHAPTER THIRTY-THREE

Kalin slipped into Ben's hospital room, tiptoed to the side of his bed and squeezed his hand. He looked small buried beneath the blankets. The egg-sized lump on his left cheek was the color and texture of a rotten apple. An intravenous drip protruded from the back of his hand.

She sniffed at hospital odors she didn't want to identify. Three elderly men, each wearing a powder-blue hospital gown, occupied the other three beds. She ignored them and slid the white curtain around the metal track on the ceiling, creating a tiny bit of privacy.

Ben had come out of the coma the evening before, and she'd spent a restless night in a no-name motel worrying about a full recovery.

She wrapped her fingers around Ben's and waited for him to wake. She'd been in Calgary three days. Two weeks ago, she'd said she would give White Peaks an answer. The only problem was she didn't know her answer yet. She promised herself she'd call by the end of the week.

Ben's eyelids fluttered, and he looked at her through dull eyes. "Kalin?"

"I'm here. How are you feeling?"

"Okay," Ben said in a hoarse voice.

Kalin lowered her head and placed her cheek against his shoulder. Her throat compressed, and her tears ran down his arm.

Ben tried to lift her head, but she only pressed deeper. When she stopped crying he said, "I'm glad you're here."

She raised her head and gently kissed his lips.

He depressed a button on the hospital bed and raised himself to a half-seated position, causing his gown to tighten around his neck and pinch his skin.

She reached forward and released the pressure on his neck, pulling the gown loose, and left her hand resting on his chest. “How badly are you hurt?”

“I guess the doctors were concerned about brain swelling, but I’m fine now. They said they forced a coma to let the swelling go down. My cheek is broken, but nothing else.”

“Do you think someone pushed you on purpose?”

“Not a clue. I can’t remember much. I remember arriving at the bar but that’s all.”

“You don’t think this has anything to do with the theft?”

“I can’t see how.”

“I got a crank phone call right before Fred called about you. It was only deep breathing but pretty creepy since I was home alone.”

“You think it’s related?”

Kalin shrugged. “Who knows? Any idea when you can come home?”

“This weekend sometime. Did you answer about the job?”

“Let’s talk about us when you get home.”

“I can’t wait. Since I woke up, all I’ve been thinking about is us. I need to know if we’re okay. I don’t want you to move even if it’s only during the weekdays.” Sweat seeped from Ben’s pores, and his face turned pasty white.

“Should I call a nurse?”

Ben took a few deep breaths. “No, I’m fine. It’ll stop in a second.”

Kalin held his hand and waited. He fell asleep, and she settled herself in the plastic chair beside his bed.

* * *

Ben’s moan turned into a smile when he woke and his eyes rested on Kalin. “Sorry. I keep drifting in and out. Probably the pain meds.”

Kalin leaned forward in her chair and reached for his hand. “I don’t mind.”

“The stitches on your chin are gone.”

“Yeah. Now our scars match.”

“Where’s Chica?” Ben asked.

“She’s with Jessica. I just called her, and everything is fine.”

“Why’s she with her?”

"I didn't know how long I'd be here, and as I drove past Jessica's, I stopped. I didn't know what else to do with her."

"You did right. Jessica will take care of her."

Ben shifted in his bed. Had someone hammered his cheek? His eyes felt as if they were bulging out of their sockets. They weren't, but that didn't stop his eyelids from searing his eyeballs when he blinked. "We need to talk."

Kalin let go of his hand and positioned herself at the window. "Those are never good words to start a sentence with."

"Seriously, we've been avoiding the White Peaks issue for long enough." If only Kalin would say she'd turned down the job, that they would stay in Stone Mountain and she'd do anything for him and their marriage.

"I haven't responded to the offer yet."

"They must be pressuring you to make a decision."

"They are."

"Have you told Turner?"

"No."

A wave of pain seared through Ben's cheek, and he pushed the magic button on the side of his bed. The medication didn't take long to ease the pain. "Why not? I thought you were going to ask him for a reference."

"I used Gavin Reed instead."

"Turner's going to be pissed if he finds out from someone else."

"I know, but what if we don't go? Then Turner will always think I'm not committed here."

"Are you committed?"

Kalin returned to the side of his bed. "To you. You know that. But we have to look at opportunities that are good for us. We can't just rest on what we already have."

"We could. What's wrong with Stone Mountain?"

"Nothing. I love it. It's just I never dreamed I'd be able to run a ski resort. When I took the HR manager job, I was so excited to be working in a resort, I couldn't believe my luck."

"So what's changed?"

"It never crossed my mind to move until White Peaks approached me. There's something else I haven't told you."

"Why doesn't that surprise me?" Ben smiled to take the sting out of his words.

"I think Stone Mountain might be for sale." Kalin told Ben about the information she found on Simon Crane's hard drive. "If someone else buys the resort, I might lose my job anyway. It's not unheard of for new owners to bring their own senior staff.

Ben swallowed hard. Maybe the medication was making him dopey, but he loved Kalin, and he'd do anything to make her happy. To hell with his own wishes. "Accept the offer."

Obviously the expression on Kalin's face was happiness, and Ben felt like a shit that he'd waited so long to give in. She was everything to him. Their marriage was more important than where they lived.

CHAPTER THIRTY-FOUR

"Are you laughing at me?" Kalin's mom asked.

"I'm laughing with you, not at you." Kalin hit the speaker icon and placed her cell on her desk. The image on her computer monitor showed several skiers about to launch into the Dragon's Bowl.

"You know I'm no good with computers," her mom said.

"I do, but this is easy."

"How is it possible to see people skiing?"

"I told you. It's called a webcam. The camera is at the top lift station and sends pictures to the Internet every few seconds. It's beautiful here, and this gives you a way to see it." Kalin hadn't told her mom about the issues she'd been having or about moving to White Peaks, and the webcam gave her a way to share Stone Mountain without discussing her problems.

"What do I type again?"

Kalin repeated the Internet address. Four o'clock approached, and the lifts were about to close. Darkness would descend soon, and if her mom didn't hurry up, she'd only see a black screen.

Tessa popped her head in Kalin's doorway. In a habitual gesture, she pulled her hair over the battery pack for her cochlear implant. "Simon Crane came to see you yesterday afternoon."

"What did he want?"

"He didn't say. Only that he needed to speak to you personally."

"Can you call him and find out what he wants?"

"I asked him yesterday, but he said he'd only talk to you."

"If he comes back, tell him without knowing what he wants, I won't have a meeting with him."

Tessa nodded and left Kalin to her call.

"Who's Simon Crane?" her mom asked.

"Just someone who used to work here." The view from the webcam showed the area directly behind the summit chairlift and included a portion of the Dragon's Bowl. "Can you see the mountain yet?"

"I can see someone skiing. Is this anywhere near where Roy disappeared?"

Her mom's tone of voice had changed. "It's in the direction of where the avalanche happened, but Roy was farther from the resort. Don't worry. I don't ski in that area." Kalin didn't like to lie to her mom, but she couldn't tell her she'd been in the Bowl with Ben.

"How is Ben?" her mom asked.

"Much better. He'll be home by the weekend." She'd been spending most of her time at work until the doctor discharged him from the hospital. Who wanted to be at home alone?

Kalin clicked the refresh icon, and an image of Aiden popped up on her screen. Every few seconds she refreshed the image, and each time, Aiden was closer to the Dragon's Bowl. She stopped refreshing when he'd gone over the edge and out of sight.

Twenty minutes later, she stood at the bottom of the hill, staring at the darkened runs. Small puddles littered the surface of the snow around the lift station. The warm temperatures were depleting the snow base unseasonably early.

"Kalin?" a young woman asked. "I want to thank you."

"Thank me for what?"

"For helping me last week when I was sick."

Kalin recognized her from the bathroom. "Meare. How are you?"

"Better. The doctor put me on antibiotics for like ten days when I left the hospital. You were so nice to me, and I didn't get the chance to say thanks. It meant a lot that you were there. My mom says thanks, too."

Kalin smiled at her. "It's not a problem. I'm glad you're okay."

Meare chewed at the inside of her lip and scanned the area. "Since you were there for me, I think I owe it to you to tell you something."

"I'm listening."

"Like everyone's talking about the theft, right?"

"Yes."

"There's a rumor that the money was placed in a duffle bag."

Kalin didn't want to add credence to any rumor, so she said, "That's interesting."

"I don't want to get anyone into trouble or anything."

"Meare, if you know something, please tell me."

"Just before I got sick, I heard Justin Bradley on the phone to someone named Wilson. Justin's a liftie. I think Wilson's his roommate. He said they had to move the duffle bag. I didn't think anything of it until I overheard people talking about the money."

Kalin could barely resist dialing Miller's number, but she waited until Meare was out of sight.

* * *

Late Friday evening, Kalin chopped broccoli to add to a beef and vegetable stir-fry. Ever since telling Miller about Justin, Eric and the duffle bag, she'd been worried. Would they come after her? With Ben still in Calgary, she'd asked security to drive her home after work. Once inside, she'd checked that the doors and windows were locked.

Kalin tried to think of something less frightening. When she lived in Ottawa, Kalin and her mom would meet every Tuesday evening, drink a glass of wine, chop vegetables, heat up the wok and stir-fry their dinner, following a ritual where each had her own tasks. She missed those evenings.

Chica sat close to Kalin's legs. Kalin hadn't taken her for a hike before dinner. Going out alone in the dark seemed like a bad move, so she'd let her out to pee, making sure the outside lights were on, and secured the deadbolt once Chica was back inside.

Kalin focused on chopping. The quick bang of the knife against the cutting board satisfied her urge to hit something. Just as the last of the broccoli hit the wok with a sizzle, the front door opened. She turned the gas to low and placed a lid over the wok.

Gripping the chopping knife tight, she walked to the door. Chica was already there, running in circles, barking and wagging her tail. Ben's smiling face lit up beneath the amber porch light.

"What are you doing here? I would've picked you up."

Ben squatted and greeted Chica. "I took the bus. It smells like you're cooking. By the way, if you're mad at me, I need to know, because you look like you're about to stab me with that knife."

"Sorry, I was chopping veggies. How are you feeling?"

"Pretty good."

"The bruise on your face has expanded. Does it hurt much?"

"It looks worse than it feels." Ben touched his cheek. "Do I have time to light a fire?"

"Sure." Kalin left him to stoke the wood stove and returned to the wok. "Are you sure you're okay?"

He crinkled newspaper, added a few logs and lit the fire. "I am. My cheek will heal."

Kalin rested her fists on the counter and stared at him. "You could have died. I've been sick about it all week."

Ben left the woodstove door open an inch to let in a draft. Bright orange flames swirled around the logs and the larch cracked and popped. He returned to Kalin and put his hands on her shoulders. "You came. That meant everything."

She buried her face in his neck. "I know you were trying to help. There's nothing to be sorry for. I only want to explain how I feel. I can't go through it again. I lost Jack and Roy. It's too hard."

"Shh. I'm fine." Ben tightened his grip.

She released herself from Ben's hug, pulled two bowls from the cupboard and set them on the counter beside the stove. "I can't take any more loss. It's too much."

Ben filled Chica's bowl with kibble and placed the dish on the floor. He did this without saying a word. He must have sensed Kalin was building up to something. Chica gobbling her food and wood crackling filled the lull in the conversation.

"I turned down the offer from White Peaks."

"Why? I thought we decided to go."

"I love you. Our life is here."

"What changed?"

"On the drive back from Calgary, I thought about everything that's happened at Stone Mountain. I don't want to start over. I've been having nightmares. I think it's because I'm risking our marriage by forcing a move away."

"That's not true. I'd go with you anywhere."

"I know. And that's why we need to stay here."

"What happens if the resort is sold?"

"I've been thinking about that. Maybe the buyers will want to hire a new president. If White Peaks would hire me as the GM there, I don't see why I couldn't be the president here."

Ben's grin told Kalin all she needed. She heaped the bowls with the stir-fry, put the wok back on the stove and sat across from Ben. "Chopsticks?"

"Sure."

Kalin rested her chopsticks on the ceramic chopstick rest. "I know who helped Roy steal the money."

Ben raised his eyes to hers.

"Justin Bradley and Eric Wilson."

"How do you figure that?"

Kalin told Ben about her conversation with Meare. "I called Miller right after. He'll deal with them."

"You're letting this go?"

"Not quite. I saw something weird yesterday. I was talking to my mom, showing her how to view the webcam photos. I had the images open on my computer and saw Aiden skiing into the Dragon's Bowl."

"So?"

"The lift was about to close, and it was getting dark. Why would he ski in that direction by himself after the patrol sweep?"

"You think he was looking for Roy?" Ben asked.

"Not exactly. What if Aiden thinks Roy stole the money, and he went to look for it? He must know Roy's pack was never found."

Ben fumbled with his chopsticks, managed to get a slice of beef into his mouth and winced when he chewed.

"Does it hurt to eat?"

"A little."

Chica licked her bowl clean and positioned herself underneath the table equidistant from Ben and Kalin.

"I think maybe Jessica and Aiden are up to something. I just can't figure out what." Kalin reached across the table. "I can't believe you still don't know how to use these things. Here, hold the chopsticks like this and relax your grip."

Ben did as instructed.

"You're about to say something," Kalin said.

"How do you know that?"

"Hello? I kinda know you."

"I'm starting to remember the fall."

Kalin held her breath.

"I think I felt someone's hands on my back. Like I was being shoved."

* * *

Kalin loved Saturdays at work. Her job included being visible to all employees. Accounting, IT and marketing shared the administration offices and worked Monday to Friday. The administration building was mostly empty on weekends, making it a good day to be out on the mountain.

She spent the morning in her office. Early afternoon, she got dressed for skiing. Normally the lights on the floor being on energy-save mode on the weekends didn't bother her. Normally she wasn't worried about her safety. She still didn't know who had been looking in her window at night or who had painted her door, and she hadn't heard from Miller about Justin and Eric. She listened for anyone else who might be on the floor. Feeling uneasy, she quickly hauled her gear along the darkened hallway and left for the lift.

The afternoon touring the mountain and visiting lifties at each lift shack sped by. She skied to a stop at the base of the hill, poked her pole into the back of her binding and released her boot with a snap. She'd skied the mountain top to bottom, rode all seven lifts and was fatigued, but her fear of skiing had disappeared like melting snow.

Aiden exited the lift shack at the bottom of the Alpine Tracks ski run. He spoke to a liftie, nodded and removed the first pole in the maze. The liftie stopped the lift for the day, and the wind through the trees filled the space where the hum of the lift used to be.

With her ski boots clomping on the hard-packed snow in the maze, Kalin walked toward Aiden. "Can I talk to you for a minute?"

Aiden lifted one of the maze posts and carried it to the next. "Sure."

"I don't know how to put this without offending you, but I saw you ski into the Dragon's Bowl last night. I know you're searching for the money."

"What are you talking about?" Aiden continued to remove maze posts, and she ran around in front of him.

"I always ski in the bowl," he said

"Not after dark. Stop walking away for a second." Kalin checked the area around her. The sun dipped below the mountain, and darkness would soon follow. There was no one to overhear her. "I want to know what you were up to."

"Don't you want to find Roy's body?"

"Of course, I do."

"I was checking the terrain, looking for signs of him."

Clearly Aiden wasn't going to open up to her, but at least he knew she was on to him. "If you find the money, you have to turn it over to the RCMP."

CHAPTER THIRTY-FIVE

Helen sat in Kalin's office, blinking repeatedly, keeping tears from flowing over her bottom lids. After the phone call from Jessica, she'd left her own office and waited for Kalin to return from skiing. Kalin's winter boots rested askew beside her desk, meaning she would come back to her office before heading home.

Jessica said she blamed Helen for what had happened. Helen didn't want to believe the horrible incident was her fault, but she'd fired Simon. She wasn't blameless.

Carrying her skis and poles, Kalin entered her office and peered at Helen with raised eyebrows. "What's up?"

Helen trusted Kalin and wanted to talk with her. She needed help coping with this, and Kalin was always level headed. She'd know what to do. "Jessica called me."

"What's wrong?"

Helen grabbed a tissue from Kalin's desktop. "Simon Crane tried to commit suicide last night."

Kalin closed both eyes. "No."

"Jessica said it's my fault. Because I fired him." Helen shredded the tissue and let the pieces fall.

Kalin leaned her skis against the wall and passed Helen the box of tissues. "Don't think that. Jessica's lashing out. It's not because you fired him. We fired him together, and we did the right thing."

"But if we hadn't fired him, he wouldn't have attempted…"

"You don't know that. He had other problems. His wife left him."

Helen couldn't imagine facing Natalie after she'd fired her husband for viewing pornography. She guessed Natalie had believed them after all. Natalie was her friend, and she didn't know how to reach out to her. "Which she wouldn't have done if I hadn't fired him."

"You don't know that either. We fired him for justifiable reasons. We have to follow policy. This isn't our fault."

Helen blinked back more tears. "Do you really believe that?"

Kalin reached forward and held Helen's hands. "I do."

"We didn't offer him counseling. We should have."

"That's something we do for people who get laid off. Not something we offer to people we fire with cause. I feel terrible, too, but we didn't do anything wrong."

"Couldn't you change the policy?"

"I can look at it. Simon came to see me the other day."

"What did he want?"

"I don't know. He wouldn't tell Tessa what he wanted. Without knowing, I refused to make an appointment."

"He called me again to ask for his job back. He said there's no way he could work for his uncle in the Laundromat again."

"None of this is our fault. Do you know how he tried to kill himself?"

Helen hadn't asked Jessica. Wasn't there a rule about not asking a question you didn't want the answer to? "No."

"I'll call Constable Miller and ask if he knows."

While Kalin left a voicemail, Helen picked at the folders lying on the surface of Kalin's desk. She read the labels. Helen Armstrong, Simon Crane, Eric Wilson and Jessica Scott. "Why do you have the files for the finance center staff?"

"I took them right after the theft happened and forgot to put them back."

"You suspected all of us?"

Kalin didn't say anything.

Helen handed the folders back to Kalin. "Don't worry about it. I would've, too."

Kalin fingered Simon's file. "I guess I don't need to put this back in the active cabinet now."

"I don't know if his termination papers are in there. They might still be in my office."

Kalin opened the folder and read the first piece of paper. "Did you know Jessica wrote him up for not bringing the finance center receipts to you on the morning of the theft?"

"No, but she was angry at him."

"Do you know why he didn't bring them in?"

"Not really. But it wasn't the first time. Sometimes he went home to bed right after a shift and would bring them to me later. We just never told Jessica."

* * *

Jessica looked around Natalie's condo and noticed all traces of Simon had already been removed. That was quick.

"Thanks for coming," Natalie said. "I think it's best if I handle selling the condo. Simon will be happy you're the agent."

"I don't think he's happy about anything right now." The condo should be easy to broker, and Jessica needed a sale. The two-bedroom unit hosted a small balcony facing the ski hill. Natalie had the patio door open a crack, letting in cold air as if she were removing any scent of Simon. "Have you talked to him since…?"

"I don't know what I'd say to him," Natalie said.

"It's only been a day. Are you sure you want to deal with the condo right now?"

"I need to get this over with."

The appliances had been upgraded from standard to high-end units. The carpet, still luxurious, wasn't worn like condos in the rental pool. Jessica mentally made a list of the attributes she could put in the ad. "I know you're mad at him about the Internet thing, but he made a mistake."

"What is it with you and him?"

Jessica plopped onto the leather couch. She'd been Simon's lifelong friend, but Natalie was his wife. Why wasn't she more upset about this? Selling the condo so quickly seemed cold. "What do you mean?"

"Why didn't you marry him? You two were perfect for each other with your Barbie doll looks."

"Where's this coming from? We've been friends forever. We never dated."

"Simon's been in love with you for years. Didn't you know that?"

Jessica's chest tightened. Was Natalie losing her marbles? "That's not true. He married you, not me."

"He married me for my family money. I guess he thought one day it would be his."

Needing to put some distance between herself and Natalie, she stood and went to the gas fireplace. "You can't be serious."

"I am. You know he hated Roy. He was so jealous when you got together with him. For some reason, he thought you actually cared about

Roy. You seemed so uninterested in all your other boyfriends. He talked about your relationship constantly."

"That can't be true."

"It got worse after Roy died. That's when Simon realized you loved Roy, otherwise why would you be so upset by his death."

"I didn't know. I'm sorry." How could she not know this about Simon? And how had Simon known she loved Roy before she knew?

"There's nothing for you to be sorry about. It helped me figure out Simon would never love me the way I needed. I still had hope, but when the porn thing happened, I knew our marriage was over."

If a person could look sadder, Jessica had no idea how. She couldn't look at Natalie, so she picked up a romance novel from the mantel and fluttered the pages. On the inside back cover, she read a number. A number she would never forget. She looked at Natalie through new eyes. Natalie had the combination to the finance center safe.

Hiding her panic, she kept the conversation on topic, so Natalie wouldn't notice what she'd discovered. "But then why did you marry Simon?"

"I loved him. He was so good looking, and I was blinded by his attention. I thought he liked me enough that we could make it work, but now I know better. The porn issue was a way for me to let Simon out of our marriage."

"Without any money."

"It's not like he earned any himself. You know his history. I supported us through our marriage. I don't think I owe him more."

"But you loved him?"

"I did. But now, no. I want him to be okay but not part of my life."

"He made one mistake."

"It's more than that. Last fall he found a copy of my dad's will. He was looking after my parents' fish, and I guess he snooped. I never told him my inheritance would go into a trust fund that only I could access. He wanted to know if the money would be shared once I got it. That's when I understood he never loved me."

"Are you going to visit him?" Jessica asked.

"I can't. He doesn't need to see me. I can't believe his attempt at suicide was anything more than a grasp for attention. He's too egocentric. If he'd been serious, he would have died."

"That's harsh."

"I know, but he's manipulated me for so long. I can't help him anymore."

CHAPTER THIRTY-SIX

Kalin met Ben in the parking lot near his truck and leaned into him for a hug.

"Hey, what's wrong?" he asked.

She tucked her hands underneath his ski jacket and warmed her palms on his skin. Without letting go of him, she told him about Simon.

"You're not at fault," he whispered in her ear.

She rested her forehead on his shoulder for a moment, then pushed away from him. "I know. I talked to Miller. He said Simon tried to overdose. I feel awful, but I don't know what I could have done differently."

"Who knows how long he's been unstable. He could have been thinking about it for a long time," Ben said.

"Being fired could have pushed him over the edge."

"It could have. But so many things contribute to a suicide. Maybe he did it so his wife would come back. You can't blame yourself."

"He asked to see me. I should've met with him."

"When did he ask for a meeting?"

"The other day."

"He didn't work for the company anymore. You can't meet with everyone who asks to see you."

Clouds full of moisture gathered over the peaks, bringing gloom to the area, matching Kalin's mood. "You're probably right."

"You can't take responsibility for everyone who works or lives here."

"On that subject, I'm a bit worried about Helen. She thinks it's her fault. It's harder for her because of her friendship with Natalie."

"Have you suggested counseling to her?"

Kalin smiled. "No, but I will. That's a good idea. And speaking of ideas, there's something I want to do."

"Now that sounds like trouble."

She explained about finding Roy's bank card in his wallet. "Let's access Roy's account. If he has any money, my mom has a right to it."

"Are you sure that's all there's to it?"

"No."

"Well, let's go." Ben grabbed Kalin by the hand and headed toward the single ATM at the resort.

* * *

Ben and Kalin hesitated at the same time, then laughed.

"We're brave," Kalin said. "Let's get this over with. We'll see if he still had the habit of using Mom's birthday for his passwords and PINs." Kalin inserted the card into the slot and entered the four-digit code. "How much do you think I should withdraw?"

"Nothing. Just check the balance."

Kalin pressed the icons on the touch-sensitive screen and a receipt landed in her palm. "Just over three hundred."

"Are you relieved?"

She'd been thinking some of the stolen money might be in the account and didn't want to admit it. She nudged him with her elbow, letting the contact linger. "Kinda. I knew he didn't have the money, but I needed to be sure."

"You're not convinced Justin and Eric stole the money?"

"I am. But no one's found the cash."

"You still think Roy was involved?"

"I hope not. What should we do now?"

"Do you want to check his storage locker?"

"I left the key at home. Anyway, I don't want to think about that now. Let's do it tomorrow."

They settled into the truck. Ben turned the key in the ignition and put the heater on high. He faced Kalin and held both of her hands. "I know how hard this is for you."

"Without finding Roy's body, I need…If I can get all his things together in one place…" Kalin buried her face in her hands. How could this hurt so much? "Everything that's happened to Roy is my fault." She'd finally said the words out loud. All this time, she'd desperately needed to tell Ben. Her eyes pleaded with him to persuade her otherwise, but she knew in her heart she was to blame.

"How can it be your fault?"

"Roy wouldn't have come to Stone Mountain if I hadn't pressured him."

"I don't think Roy ever did anything he didn't want to do."

"I shouldn't have interfered with him and Patricia."

"You can't blame yourself."

"Yes, I can. I didn't like Patricia. I didn't want Roy to marry her. I tried to find something wrong with her. I told him she'd cheated on him, and I think I was mistaken. Roy never forgave me for that. We never even talked about it. I should have brought it up when he moved here."

Kalin's cell rang.

"Don't answer. Give yourself a break and take tonight off."

She checked the display. "It's Miller." She cleared her throat and slid the answer icon sideways. "Hey."

"I've got some news."

She hit the speakerphone icon, so Ben could hear what Miller said.

"We followed up on your tip that Justin Bradley and Eric Wilson were talking about a duffle bag."

"You found the money?"

"Not exactly. Based on the information you gave us, Turner allowed us access to Wilson and Bradley's lockers. We found a duffle bag in Wilson's. Looks like he was a dealer at the resort. He denied any link to Justin. We've started the deportation process."

"And Justin?"

"We couldn't connect him to Wilson."

"So you're sharing this with me because?"

"I thought I'd let you know Justin's pissed we tried to connect him to the theft. He thinks you put us onto him. I want you to be careful."

"I will. So we're back to Roy doing this on his own."

CHAPTER THIRTY-SEVEN

Kalin dangled the set of keys she'd found in Roy's locker in front of Ben. "If Roy no longer has a storage locker in town, then what are these keys for?"

Ben and Kalin sat in his truck, watching drizzle hit the windshield. After a poor night's sleep, they'd driven to the storage unit and discovered Roy had canceled his contract after only using it for two weeks. The owner didn't know why Roy had removed his things but was happy to get the key back from Kalin.

Ben held out his hand. "Let me see the rest of the keys." He took his time examining each one.

"Did Roy tell you what he stored in the unit?" Kalin asked.

"His kayak was the big thing. He didn't have much else."

Kalin's brain shifted into gear. "He either sold the kayak or stored it somewhere else." She fogged the side window with her breath, then wiped the glass clean. She repeated the process twice. "Aren't the rental kayaks stored in the basement of mountain ops for the winter?"

Ben raised his eyebrows. "You think Roy put his kayak there?"

Kalin shrugged. "Let's drive back up. Maybe one of those keys fits the lock. Would you recognize Roy's kayak?"

"It's not hard. He painted his name on the side. He loved that thing."

Kalin pulled her seatbelt across her chest and clipped it in place. "Let's go."

Black ice speckled the highway. Ben swerved around a corner, the tires slipped, and Kalin held her breath. They were at the edge of a hairpin turn. "Careful."

"Sorry about that." Ben slowed until he had control.

Ben driving at a snail's pace was killing her, but the cliff along the edge of the road leading to white-water rapids kept her from saying anything.

When they finally reached the resort, they entered the mountain ops building, trotted down the stairs and headed toward the back of the room. On his third try, Ben found the key that opened the lock.

The door creaked open, and the room released an odor of damp lifejackets. Kalin reached her hand to the inner wall and found the light switch. Her feet stuck to the floor as if they were caught in deep, wet snow.

"What's the matter?" Ben asked.

"I have a bad feeling."

"It's just a kayak." Ben entered first, and Kalin followed.

Hanging from hooks, kayaks filled one wall of the storage room. Multiple paddles leaned against the wall in a corner. Lifejackets and helmets filled a shelf. Roy's kayak hung on the lowest set of hooks.

Kalin kneeled and slid her hands along the fiberglass. Roy must have had fun in this baby. She wished she'd seen him river kayak.

Ben leaned over her shoulder and looked in the hull. "What's that?"

Army-green material peeked out from behind the seat. Ben shut the door to the storage room.

Kalin's heart sank. She had a good idea what the material belonged to.

Ben kneeled beside her, and they stared at the boat.

She pushed the seat forward and pulled out the bag. The zipper grated as she pulled the tab from one end of the duffle to the other. Along with some of Roy's clothes, another cloth bag filled the space. "This doesn't look good."

"Should we look?"

"No. Yes. I guess we have to." Kalin reached inside the duffle and lifted the second bag to the floor.

The Velcro strap detached when Kalin pulled on it, and the bag flopped open. More money than she'd ever seen in one place filled the bag. It had to be the finance center money. Nothing else made sense. "I don't believe it. He really stole the money. How much do you think it is?"

"I don't know." Ben ran his hand over the cash. "Let's count it."

"I can't believe how much this hurts. How could Roy do this? He knew my career was here. Was this a direct attack at me?"

Ben leaned his forehead onto Kalin's. "Don't think like that. Maybe Roy needed the money for something. I still don't understand why he went skiing that morning."

"To celebrate his newfound wealth and laugh at all of us."

"You don't really believe that, do you?"

"No. But I'd rather be angry than sad."

The concrete floor jabbed at Kalin's knees, and she welcomed the pain. Anything to distract her from the knowledge Roy had stolen the money. She couldn't see any way around that fact. The more the total grew, the faster her heart raced.

When the amount maxed out at just over one hundred thousand, Kalin stood and leaned her back against the wall. She grabbed a lifejacket off the shelf and hugged the flotation device to her chest as if it could save her from drowning. "I knew. I mean I thought…Now it's just real."

Ben stood and hugged her. He whispered in her ear, "Is it possible Roy got this money legally?"

Kalin's laugh erupted, sounding more like a sob. "Thanks for suggesting that, but I can't imagine how. What should we do now?"

"Let's check if there's anything else in the kayak."

Kalin collected Roy's lifejacket and wet suit from the forward half of the kayak and stuffed it into the duffle bag with the rest of his clothes. They opened the door and returned to the employee locker area. Kalin placed the duffle bag on a wooden bench and pulled out her cell.

* * *

Constable Miller stood in front of the neatly stacked money. "When did you find this?"

"Right before we called you," Kalin said.

"What have you touched?"

She nodded in the direction of Roy's kayak. "We removed the bag from the kayak and counted the money."

Miller closed his eyes for a second. "I wish you hadn't done that."

"We didn't realize how much it was," Ben said. "Once we did, we called. We haven't touched anything else."

"What made you search this room?" Miller asked.

"We found out Roy closed his storage unit in town, and Kalin wanted to find where he'd stored his kayak."

Miller finished taking their statements. "I'm going to seal the room and call in my team. In the meantime, make sure I can reach both of you. You may have seriously compromised the investigation."

Kalin and Ben left Miller alone. On their way out, Kalin picked up the duffle bag and slung it over her shoulder. Miller didn't need to know the money had been inside the duffle. The contents belonged to Roy. Now it belonged to Kalin.

* * *

"Are you going somewhere?" Constable Miller asked Paul Turner.

Turner nodded and continued filling a box resting on his office chair. The president's chair would no longer be his position of power. Instead, he'd be reporting to a man who had a bigger office on the same floor of the same building. His autonomy would be gone. It couldn't be helped.

Miller stood with his hands cupped in front of himself, shoulders straight, watching Turner. "Where are you going?"

Turner sighed. He supposed he should tell the cop and stop him from being suspicious. "My son has cystic fibrosis. He's not doing well. I'm moving my family to Calgary where he can get the medical care he needs."

"Are you changing companies?"

"I've taken a position with the Marriott." Turner left unsaid that it was a job junior to his current position, with a lower salary. He scowled and continued packing. With the resort being sold, he'd lose his job anyway.

"I'm sorry to hear about your son."

"Is there a reason you're here?" Turner placed each of his pens in their velvet-lined boxes. His wife had given him one every time he'd been promoted. So meaningless.

"We found the finance center money."

Turner's hand stopped midair, his pen pointing at Miller like an arrow. "All of it?"

"Looks like it."

"Where?"

"In Roy McCann's kayak in the mountain ops storage room."

"Really. Did Kalin have anything to do with the theft?" Turner didn't care at this point. What he did care about was that the money was found before he left the resort for good. Having an unsolved crime hanging over his head would not be great for his career.

"I don't believe she did. She found the money and called me. Ben was with her. We'll continue to investigate, but for now, she's not a suspect."

"What happens to the money?"

"It'll be held as evidence until we complete the investigation. My team is in the storage room now. We'll call it a night and come back tomorrow. Looks like an ice storm is about to hit."

Turner strode across the room, peeled back the flap of a box resting on the floor and slipped a business card from a gold plated holder. "Here. This is my boss at head office. Can you call and give her an update? She'll oversee Stone Mountain until a replacement for me is hired."

After Miller left, the room felt off. He'd been meticulous when he'd taken over the office. His office had been organized. He'd been in control. The chaos surrounding him seemed like an omen of his future life. He had one task left. Pay back the money he'd borrowed from Stone Mountain over the last year to take care of Warren.

He had to leave for Warren and for Crystal, but he didn't have to like it.

CHAPTER THIRTY-EIGHT

Simon stood on Jessica's doorstep. "I need to move back in."

Jessica blocked the entrance to her home. With one foot on the doorsill and the other in the front hall, she held the door tight against her back.

Simon's normally perfect hair poked out at wild angles. His chest heaved. He had nerve showing up unannounced and declaring he needed to move in, but they'd been friends for too long for her to turn him away. He should be at the hospital under psychiatric care, not standing there begging for a favor.

"Aren't you going to invite me in?" He wiped rain off his face and shook his head. Small droplets of water hit the window.

"Of course." Jessica stepped backward. Simon wore faded blue jeans, hiking boots and a dark gray ski jacket. Standard resort clothing, but out of character for Simon. She couldn't believe he would let himself look so common.

Simon moved forward and closed the door. He turned the deadbolt, locking her in the house.

Jessica's hackles rose, and she couldn't say why. "Come on in. I'll get us a beer."

Simon followed her and crashed on the couch.

Jessica retrieved two beers from the kitchen. "Roy did it."

"What are you talking about?"

"Kalin and Ben found the money," Jessica said.

"How do you know?"

"I saw them leave mountain ops. Kalin was carrying Roy's duffle bag."

"Why do you think they have the money?"

"Roy's duffle's been missing since the theft. They must have found it somewhere in the building."

"Where were they headed?"

"Toward their home. And to think, I was going to tell you Natalie stole the money."

Simon straightened and leaned toward her. "That's stupid. As if Natalie could figure out something so complicated."

"She had the safe combination written in the back of a paperback."

"How do you know that?"

"I found the book in your condo when she asked me to put the unit for sale."

"You're selling the unit? That figures."

"What figures?"

"That Natalie would turn to you. She's trying to take everything I have, including my friends."

"No, she isn't."

"Why would she show you the combination? To tell you I stole the money?"

"What are you talking about?"

"She's going to put the theft on me. That way, she won't have to support me."

"Why aren't you surprised about the book?"

"Don't go there."

Jessica tensed. Simon gave off an eerie vibe. Why had she let him in? She'd trapped herself alone with him. In a moment of clarity, she understood. "*You* had the combination, not Natalie."

"What?"

Jessica's chest tightened. "Why did Roy go up the mountain if the money was in the duffle bag?"

"What do you mean?"

"If he hid the money, what reason did he have to go up the mountain?"

"Roy was unpredictable. You know that. Kalin kicked him out the night before he died. Maybe he wanted to blow off steam and went out on his touring skis."

Sometimes Roy slept on a gurney in the ski patrol clinic. When Kalin kicked him out, it was a likely place for him to go. Had Roy seen something he shouldn't have? "How do you know he was wearing his touring skis?"

Simon's cheeks reddened. "I didn't. I just assumed he did."

"Oh, shit."

"What?"

"Somehow you got Roy to go up the mountain. Did you see him take the money? Were you trying to get rid of him so you could have it?"

"What the fuck is wrong with you?"

"You started the avalanche, didn't you?"

Simon grabbed Jessica's arm, wrapping his fingers tightly around her bicep. He yanked her to her feet. "Get your jacket. We're going out."

"Why?"

"If Kalin and Ben have the money, we need to get it."

"I'm not going anywhere with you. Kalin won't keep it. She'll call the cops if she hasn't already."

Tightening his grip on her arm, Simon pulled her toward the front door. Jessica ran her free hand along the entrance side table, feeling for anything she could use as a weapon. Her every fiber screamed.

Simon's eyes followed her hand. "Nice try. There's nothing there." He slid his hunting knife from its sheath. "I said we're going out. Get your jacket."

Jessica didn't move.

"I won't ask again."

With the jagged edge of the blade shining in front of her, she had no choice. She grabbed her jacket from the front hall closet and stepped into her winter boots.

"We've been friends forever."

"I don't give a shit. Move." Simon shoved her between her shoulder blades, pushing her outside before she had a chance to zip her jacket or grab a hat and mitts.

The porch light was off, and she couldn't see through the rain to the end of the driveway. She had no hope someone passing by might see them.

"Go to your left," Simon said.

"There's only forest back there. Let's go find Kalin and Ben." Jessica twisted to the right, but Simon planted his foot against her ankle, stopping her. The rain seeped through her thin yoga pants, freezing her thighs.

"We're going behind the house where we can talk privately."

If Simon forced her into the forest, she'd never get help. She shoved him, gaining a foot of space from him. Lurching forward, she slipped and her bare hands slammed against the ground. Shards of ice cut the skin on her palms, but she ignored the pain and pushed herself to her knees. She didn't make it to standing. Simon pricked the knife tight against her throat. She froze.

"Try that again, and I will kill you." Simon's cold lips touched her ear, his breath burned her cheek, but his whisper couldn't have pierced her more if he'd screamed the words.

"Get up." He dragged her to her feet.

Jessica threw her arm against the house, barely keeping her balance. Blood from her hand left a small stain on the wall.

"Please. Simon we're friends."

"We need to talk where we won't be disturbed."

"We can do that inside."

Simon hit her hard on her back. "No, we can't."

She pitched forward but didn't fall. The pressure of the knife against her back stopped her from running. Keeping the bottoms of her boots flat against the slippery surface, she slid her feet forward. Lifting her feet off the ground meant the possibility of a fall, and Simon might stab her by accident.

Simon grabbed the back of her jacket and stopped. "This is far enough." He shoved her shoulder, twisting her so they faced each other.

"How did you get a key?"

"I stole yours off your kitchen counter. I can't believe you didn't notice."

"What about the combination?" She could see Simon starting to relax. He let the knife hang by his side. His ego dictated he had to brag. If she kept him talking, if she found the right moment, she'd bolt.

"That was easy. Helen tapped it into the keypad every day. I watched her fingers and figured out the pattern. One day she handed me that stupid romance book to return to Natalie. As soon as I was out of sight, I wrote it down." Simon pointed the tip of the knife at Jessica's throat. "Enough with the questions. Who else knows about the money?"

Jessica's eyes followed the blade. "If I had to guess, I would say only Ben and Kalin."

"What about your buddy, Aiden?"

"I don't know."

Simon circled Jessica, pointing the knife at her face. "I'm sick of this conversation. Let's go." He walked behind her, giving her a nudge toward her house.

Jessica's chest heaved. Rain pellets slammed her face and stung her eyes, but she didn't dare close them, even for a second of relief. Staying on her feet meant survival.

A sharp pain sliced through her lower back. She gasped and fell.

CHAPTER THIRTY-NINE

Ben and Kalin slipped and slid in single file along the edge of the road. The ditch gave more traction than the tarmac, and Ben placed one boot after the other on the uneven surface. He stayed close behind Kalin, ready to catch her if she fell. She'd been quiet through dinner at the bar, and Ben had given her space.

Kalin's cell rang. "Hey, Fred."

"The road to town is closed. A car hit a hydro pole. With the icy conditions, the road won't be open again until sometime tomorrow. We're on our own for the night."

"Okay. Call if you need anything."

Fifteen minutes later, Kalin entered the front hall, tossed her wet jacket on the bench Roy built and slogged up the stairs. Ben followed, wishing he could make her feel better. She ignored Chica, turned off her cell and tossed it on the counter. "My head hurts. I need some sleep."

Once in their bedroom, she discarded her soggy jeans in the laundry basket, flopped on top of the comforter on their sleigh bed and curled into a ball.

Ben caressed her cheek. "I'll take Chica for a quick walk. You okay alone?"

"I'm fine. I just need some time."

Ben donned a dry jacket, opened the door and followed Chica outside. The slippery ground didn't affect her, so Ben let her run off leash. He gave her ten minutes outside, then returned home, fed her and checked on Kalin. She was still curled into a ball and breathing deeply, so he let her sleep.

Chica jumped onto the bed and snuggled into the back of Kalin's bare legs.

Ben grabbed dry clothes from the bedroom, gently closed the door and returned to the living room. He picked up his cell on the first ring.

"Jessica's injured."

"Who's this?" Ben asked.

"Aiden. Listen, Jessica just phoned me. She said she needed help. We've got to find her. I can't find anyone else to help me."

"Where is she?"

"She said she was behind her house. She stopped talking. I think she passed out," Aiden said.

"Did she fall or something?"

"I don't know."

"Did you call security?"

"No one answered."

"Try again. I'll meet you in front of her place in a few minutes."

Ben poked his head into the bedroom. Still nestled behind Kalin's knees, Chica rested her head on Kalin's leg. She thumped her tail when Ben peeked in. An open bottle of sleeping pills lay on the bedside table, and he could hear Kalin's deep breathing. In case she woke while he was gone, he left her a note. He picked up the first aid kit and took off.

Ben met up with Aiden in Jessica's driveway.

"Hurry, let's go around back," Aiden said.

Aiden ran behind Jessica's house, and Ben followed.

Aiden fell. He reached down and poked a finger through a hole in his jeans. "I've cut my leg."

Ben rounded him and kept going. "I'll look at it later. Let's go."

Getting a foothold on the ice was difficult, and both fell several times.

Ben's flashlight beam strained to penetrate the rain and fog, giving them only a few feet of visibility before the beam was reflected off a white haze.

Aiden pointed to Jessica's body. "Over there."

Ben handed Aiden the first aid kit and rushed to her.

"Jessica?" Ben squatted beside her and put his hand on her chest. A slight movement. He put his index and middle finger on her neck and checked for a pulse. "We need to get her out of here." He placed his flashlight beside her and positioned himself to lift her.

Aiden didn't move. "Is she dead?"

"No. But her pulse is weak." Ben shouted to be heard above the noise of the wind and sleet hitting the trees. He reached underneath her. "She's bleeding."

Aiden slipped again and knocked Ben's flashlight into the bush. It slid in circles across the ice, shining the beam in all directions. Crawling on his hands and knees, Aiden went after it. The light glowed from underneath a log. "Holy crap." He scrambled backward, taking the light with him.

"Give me the flashlight," Ben said.

"Hold on a sec. Something big is in the trees." Aiden frantically moved the light back and forth. "There."

The light landed on a pair of eyes. He ran the beam along the muscled body that stood out against the fog.

"It's a cougar." Ben stood.

"What do we do?"

"Hold your ground." A minute passed. With the amount of blood seeping from Jessica, she didn't have a lot of time. Ben worked a rock loose with his foot and kicked it at the cougar. The cougar snarled once, and then bolted. "Give me the flashlight."

Shining the light on Jessica's lower back, Ben illuminated a dark patch. "Get me a pad from the first aid kit." He held out one hand to Aiden and pressed the other tightly against her wound.

"I dropped it."

Useless. "Go look for it."

"I'm not going anywhere. The cougar's still around. You go."

"Think. How long ago did you drop it?"

"When I went to get the flashlight."

"Put pressure on the wound, and I'll look for the kit."

"You're not leaving me here."

"Calm down. We're going to be fine. The cougar took off. We need the first aid kit. Okay?"

"Okay."

Ben watched Aiden search the ground. If he took much longer, they'd have to carry Jessica out of there without treating her wound.

"Found it," Aiden yelled.

Ben got what he needed from the kit and placed absorbent pads on her wound.

"Help me lift her."

The path to Jessica's was uneven and slippery, and they did their best not to jar her as they carried her. They were lucky to stay on their feet.

When they finally reached Jessica's, they eased her onto the couch.

"She's not breathing." Ben blew twice into her mouth and pumped her chest for thirty beats.

Nothing.

He blew again.

Thirty more compressions.

CHAPTER FORTY

Kalin sucked air in through her nostrils. She couldn't breathe through her mouth. Something sealed her lips together. What was happening? She desperately needed more air.

Fingers dug into her cheeks, holding her head at a painful angle. She struggled to sit, but strong hands shoved her back onto her pillow. Darkness surrounded her.

"Stop fighting me. I'm not going to hurt you."

A man's voice. Despite the instructions, Kalin bucked and twisted. It was as if the man held her underwater and her body panicked, doing what it wanted to do and not what she told it to do.

The man jammed his knee into her chest, forcing air from her lungs. Mucus stuffed her nostrils, and she sucked hard for air. Bile rose in her throat, and her stomach threatened to vomit.

"I'll let you go if you settle down and promise not to scream."

Her pulse pounded, throbbing up her neck and into her temples. Sweat dripped between her eyebrows and into her eyes. She yanked her arms from behind her back, but something tightened around her wrists, burning her skin.

"The more you struggle, the tighter the rope will get."

She relaxed her arms and the pain subsided. Who the hell was this?

"Don't scream, and I'll take the tape off. If you scream, I'll duct tape your mouth shut for good. Understand?"

Kalin nodded.

The man ripped the tape off her mouth. The burning sensation told her the tape had taken some of her skin with it. She gasped for air, letting her lungs fill.

The man flicked on the bedside light. Simon Crane. She should have known. “Where’s Ben?”

“He left a while ago.”

Please let that be true. The alternative was unbearable. She couldn’t feel Chica near her. “My dog, where is she?”

“You should be more worried about yourself, not the dog.”

“I just don’t understand where she is.”

“She’s asleep on the floor. She’ll be okay. You, on the other hand, after everything you’ve done to me, might not be.”

Kalin strained to see Chica in the darkened corner, barely making out her motionless body. Her heart ached, but Chica would have to wait. “Can I put some pants on?”

Simon’s eyes lingered on her bare legs. “No.”

How could just a look make her feel so violated? The creep had a porn fetish, and now all she wore were panties and a sweater. “I haven’t done anything to you.”

He punched the pillow beside Kalin. “You fired me. It’s your fault Natalie left me, my family is embarrassed by me and I have no money. I tried to warn you to leave the resort. If you’d listened, I wouldn’t be here now.”

The person looking in Kalin’s window and the one who painted her door must have been Simon. “I don’t understand why you’re here. Why am I tied up?”

“I didn’t plan this. You shouldn’t have taken the money. I want it back.”

The mattress slanted toward Simon, and she tried not to slide into him. Her bare legs rubbed against his jeans, and she gagged. “Why do you think I have the money?”

“Jessica told me she saw you take Roy’s duffle bag from mountain ops. She guessed what was in it, and she was right.”

Kalin squirmed under Simon’s grasp. Did he help Roy take the money? And this…this couldn’t be happening. “Where’s Jessica? Does she know you’re here?”

“Jessica doesn’t know anything anymore.”

“What did you do?”

“Nothing she didn’t deserve. She thought you’d turn the money over to the cops. She wouldn’t help me get it back.”

“Is she okay?”

"She had no idea I stole the money. She even believed Natalie took it. Ha."

No matter what she said, he was too far gone to listen. She needed to figure out how to get out of this mess. She needed to find Ben. "How did you get in here?"

Simon rolled his eyes. "You gave Jessica a key when she looked after your dumb mutt. I borrowed it and made a copy. I guess that makes you pretty dumb, too." Simon grabbed the front of Kalin's sweater and pulled her to a sitting position. "I want my money back."

Without hesitating, she swung her legs, caught him with her knee and knocked him sideways. Hurling herself to her feet, she ran a few steps, but Simon's fist slammed into her back, throwing her to the ground. With her hands tied, she couldn't break her fall. Her knees hit first, followed by her chest, then her face. Winded, she lay with her cheek on the carpet. Her nose landed inches from Chica's, and she could feel her slow and rhythmic breathing. At least her lovely dog still lived.

Simon jammed the heel of his hand into her shoulder blades. "Don't do that again."

"What did you do to Chica?"

"I gave her one of your sleeping pills."

"Please. If you let me go, I won't say anything to the cops."

"You still don't get it. You won't talk to the cops again."

"What's that supposed to mean?" Kalin shifted under his weight, her shoulders burning from the pressure.

"Stop moving. You *will* give me the money, and I won't kill Ben just for the fun of it. Or your dog, for that matter."

Kalin's body froze as if her blood had stopped flowing.

CHAPTER FORTY-ONE

Ben had restarted Jessica's heart, treated the wound and placed a blanket over her. He stuck his hand in his pocket, reaching for his cell.

"Shit, I must've dropped my phone. Give me yours," he said to Aiden. He called Kalin, but she didn't answer. Next he called Constable Miller.

"Jessica Scott's been stabbed."

"What happened?"

"Someone stabbed her and left her for dead behind her house. She called Aiden Price before she passed out. When we found her, she was unconscious. Her heart stopped, but I got it going again. I think she's stable now, but we need help."

"The road's closed."

"What about a heli-evac?"

"I'll see what I can do, but it's not likely in this weather. Did she tell Aiden who stabbed her?"

"No."

"Where are you now?"

Ben moved away from the couch, distancing himself from Jessica and Aiden. He turned his back to the figure prone underneath the blanket. "At Jessica's."

"Is Aiden with you?"

"Yes."

"Listen. We don't know if Roy acted alone in stealing the money. You need to be extremely careful right now. Where's Kalin?"

The ice storm had cut them off from Holden, isolated them on the mountain, and he'd left her by herself. "She's at home."

"Alone?"

"Yes." And I left her there. Crap.

"I think things are volatile at the moment, and I don't think Kalin should be by herself. Call Fred."

Ben disconnected. "What's with the poker?"

Aiden fisted the fireplace poker and let it hang by the side of his leg. "What if whoever stabbed Jessica comes back?"

Ben didn't know what to say to that. Water from Jessica's wet clothing seeped through the blanket, leaving dark stains. She didn't deserve this. He called Fred. "I need your help."

"I'm busy. I'll call you back when I can." Fred sounded out of breath.

"Wait. Don't hang up. Jessica's been attacked."

"What happened?"

"Someone stabbed her, and I can't reach Kalin." Ben couldn't believe he'd left her by herself. "She's at our place. I'm going there now. Can you come to Jessica's?"

"It'll take me half an hour. But Ben, you'd better hurry. I saw someone behind your house earlier and thought it was Justin Bradley. I'm with him now. He broke into Kalin's office and tried to steal his employee file, but he swears he wasn't behind your house."

"And I just met up with Aiden, so it wasn't him. Where's the rest of security?"

"With the weather, everyone's busy. There's a three-car pileup near central check-in."

Ben hung up and turned to Aiden. "I'm going to find Kalin. You stay with Jessica. Try to keep her warm. Call Oliver and see if he or anyone else from ski patrol can get here."

Aiden's eyes widened, and his nostrils flared, but he didn't say anything. His heavy breathing was the only sound in the room.

"You'll be fine. Lock the door. And keep calling Kalin until you get an answer."

Ben ran.

CHAPTER FORTY-TWO

"Stop moving. You *will* give me the money, and I won't kill Ben just for the fun of it. Or your dog, for that matter."

"Don't say that." Kalin tried to turn her head and look at Simon, but his knee on her spine and his hand clamped on the back of her neck forced her cheek farther into the carpet.

"You think I won't. Too bad he didn't hit his head a bit harder when he fell."

"You pushed him."

"I want the money. Where is it?"

"I don't know."

"Yes, you do. I already found the duffle bag but not the cash."

"You're hurting me. Let go, and I'll tell you."

A horrid sound burst from his lips. Too hideous to be a laugh. "I'm not letting you go. Where's the money?"

"Did Roy know you're the thief?"

"He must have been taking the shortcut through the admin building. I was literally taking the money from the safe and stuffing a bag when he walked by."

"He didn't confront you?"

"Nope. He kept going. The bastard pretended he didn't see me. Like I'm that stupid. I finished filling the bag and knew I had to get rid of Roy. I grabbed my touring skis from Jessica's office, hid the money on the top of the bull wheel station and started up the mountain slow enough for Roy to catch up to me. I knew he'd follow my headlamp. All I had to do was make him disappear, and he'd be blamed for the theft."

"How did you get into Jessica's office?"

"I stored my gear there. She gave me a key."

"Roy wasn't in on it with you?"

"Hardly. The dumb fuck trekked up the mountain behind me, just like I knew he would. He lost track of me and ended up lower on the terrain. You should have seen the look on his face right before the snow hit him. He had no idea I'd led him up there, so I could kill him. I actually triggered the avalanche by accident. How perfect."

"You left him there."

"Of course. I had my loot to get. I thought it was too dark for Roy to see where I'd stashed the money. I just didn't know the bastard took the bag from the bull wheel before coming after me."

The radio reports had stated there were fresh tracks above the avalanche, and Kalin knew what Simon said was true. "This is crazy."

"It's not crazy." Simon rolled her over. He grabbed her by her hair, dragged her to the bathroom and forced her inside. "You should have kept your nose out of my business and let Roy take the blame."

The pieces were falling into place. The timing of Simon forgetting to bring the receipts to the finance center on the morning of the theft and his attempted suicide all made sense. Maybe when he failed at killing himself, he decided he had nothing to lose and went after Jessica.

"Enough talking." Simon slammed the door.

Kalin needed a weapon. With her hands tied behind her, opening the medicine cabinet was impossible. She turned her back to the door and tried the knob, which twisted but wouldn't budge.

Simon burst in. "Where the fuck is it?"

He held his knife in front of him and advanced toward Kalin. Her eyes glued to the blade. "Why is the blade bloody?"

"Jessica got what she deserved. I want the money, or you'll get the same."

"The police have it," she blurted.

"Explain that."

"After I found it in Roy's kayak I called them."

"You bitch."

"I didn't know what else to do."

Simon paled. "You're finished."

"Please don't do this. I won't tell anyone what's happened."

He jerked the knife toward her.

Kalin edged into the back of the toilet. The porcelain cold against her bare legs. "Please think about this. It's not too late."

Simon shoved his face within inches of hers and held the knife high. "Yes. It. Is."

In desperation, Kalin threw her head forward. The crunch of bones breaking sickened her. Blood and snot spewed from his nose.

His hands flew to his face. “Shit.”

Kalin ran to the living room.

A rumbling growl emanated from Chica.

Simon drew his arm back. Before his hand made contact, Chica leapt between them, snapped her jaws on his wrist and dragged him sideways onto the floor. She let go and retreated, putting her back toward Kalin and baring her fangs at Simon.

He lunged at Kalin, sidestepping Chica. Chica bit his forearm again, and he punched her head. She yelped and let go. The knife flew from his hands and slid across the floor.

Chica ran in front of Kalin, snapping and growling at Simon. Spit flew from her jaws.

Each time Simon stepped toward Kalin, Chica blocked his way.

“Fucking dog.” Simon backed off. He moved swiftly to the sliding glass door and disappeared, leaving the door open and cold wind blowing into the room.

Kalin ran for the stairs leading to the ground floor. Chica stayed and growled at Simon.

“Chica, come.”

Chica ignored her.

Simon grabbed the axe Ben used for splitting wood. He stared at Chica for a moment and then sprinted toward Kalin and her beautiful dog. With her arms still tied behind her back, she couldn’t protect Chica. Still, she ran back to her.

The rainstorm had ended, but the icy surface remained, and Simon pitched forward into the snow. He pressed himself onto his hands and knees, exposing the back of his neck.

In a silent move, a terror-striking silhouette sprang through the air. A cougar clamped its jaws on Simon’s skull. Extended claws flashed, piercing his shoulders.

Simon screamed.

Kalin crawled toward the open door. Without taking her eyes off Simon, she pushed the door shut with her foot just as the cougar dragged its claws across Simon’s neck.

CHAPTER FORTY-THREE

Kalin, Ben and Chica spent the night in a room at the resort. She hadn't been able to face staying in the house, not with Simon dead in the backyard.

Jessica had lived through the night. She wasn't conscious yet, but her breathing was strong. Oliver had arrived not long after Aiden called him and stayed with her. Due to the icy conditions, a helicopter hadn't been able to land.

By morning Kalin felt better, and they drove home, inching along the ice-crusted road.

They stood in the living room and surveyed the damage.

Simon's body lay ripped and partially eaten near the edge of the forest. Ben called Miller and let him know Simon's body was still there, then dropped the blinds on the glass doors.

Piece by piece, Kalin picked up Roy's things and placed them in a neat pile. When she finished, she checked the duffle bag to make sure it was empty. A small pocket was sewn into the inside of the bag and zippered shut. She opened it and pulled out a photo.

Jack and Roy's red faces smiled at her. She remembered the day. The guys had just returned from cycling the Rideau Lakes Tour. Their jerseys were soaked with sweat, and their eyes glistened. She studied the photo. Why would Roy keep this one?

Kalin fed her imagination with a diet of different scenarios, each one spiraling into the one place she didn't want to go. Her stomach knew the answer to her unspoken question before her head did. Her bowels twisted and darkness permeated her as the pieces fell into place. Images of Roy flew at her in quick succession, all of the hints she'd found along the way, thinking she was investigating a theft, not realizing she was solving Jack's death.

Why had Roy reacted so strongly at Jack's funeral? He'd kept a newspaper clipping stating the driver of the hit-and-run vehicle hadn't been found. He'd stored Jack's belongings instead of throwing them away. Miller had been suspicious of something, too.

"Oh, Jack." Kalin moaned. "I need to call Patricia and let her know Roy didn't rob the finance center." She grabbed her cell and headed to the bedroom to make the call in private.

"It's Kalin."

"Did you find him?" Patricia asked.

"No, but the theft has been solved. Another resort employee committed the crime. Roy is innocent."

Patricia released her breath as if in relief. "Thank you for calling me."

"There's something else I need to ask you."

"Sure."

"I found a letter in Roy's things. You said he needed to forgive himself. I'm curious what for."

"Kalin. There's no point in digging into old wounds."

"I need to know."

"What?"

"Was Roy the driver?"

After a long pause, Patricia asked, "What driver?"

"You know what driver. I think Roy killed Jack by accident and never recovered. I think that's why he started using drugs. I hope he came to Stone Mountain to tell me but could never work up the courage."

"You're right. Roy did want to make amends with you. He just didn't know how."

CHAPTER FORTY-FOUR

EARLY SPRING

Kalin revved her ATV engine and waved at Ben to hurry up.

Most of the snow at the base of Stone Mountain had already melted. The terrain in the Dragon's Bowl would be at that in-between stage where there was too much snow to use the ATVs and too little to use the snowmobiles. A formal search for Roy would take place once a bit more snow melted, but Kalin couldn't wait.

She'd tied her snowshoes to the ATV in case they needed to hike. Ben had resisted going, talking about avalanche risk and unstable conditions, and Kalin had said she would go alone if she had to.

Without speaking, they drove to the edge of the summit. They stopped at the entrance to the Bowl. An avalanche sign hanging from an orange safety line displayed a considerable danger warning. The sign would stay there until ski patrol officially opened the area for hiking. With the chair lifts shut for the season, they didn't want anyone entering the terrain without their knowledge.

"Are you sure about this?" Ben asked.

Kalin strapped on her snowshoes and ducked the line. "Does it look stable to you?"

Ben surveyed the area and reluctantly nodded. "Let's go to where we found the boot buckle."

The sun shone and warmed Kalin's cheeks. Rocks and grass broke through in random places, and the soft breeze ruffled the blades.

"Do you wish you'd taken the job at White Peaks?"

"No. I made the right decision."

"Even though you didn't get Turner's position after he left?"

"The new owners want their own person in charge. I get that. At least I get to keep my job."

"When's your new boss get here?"

"She arrives next week."

Ben stopped and put his hand on Kalin's bicep. "Wait here."

"What do you see?"

Ben pointed to the side of the run. In a snowbank, a portion of red material broke through.

She stepped forward.

"Kalin, don't."

She locked eyes with Ben. He was right.

He caressed her cheek with the back of his hand. "Let me do this for you. He might be…You don't want your last memory to be of him buried, do you?"

Kalin waited while Ben walked toward the discovery. He knelt beside the mound and gently wiped away snow. After a moment he stood and returned to Kalin.

"It's him."

Ben pulled her into his arms and held tight.

Kalin believed Roy hadn't meant to kill Jack. After the accident, he'd changed. He'd suffered because of what he'd done, but hadn't had the courage to admit to Kalin he'd killed her husband. And could she blame him?

She tucked her face into Ben's neck. She didn't want Roy to be dead, but finding his body would give closure to her mom and stepdad.

"Are you okay?" Ben asked.

Killing Jack had ruined Roy. Kalin had finally recovered, but Roy would never have the chance. She needed to forgive him, just as she needed to let Jack go. Without knowing who'd killed him, she hadn't been able to put him to rest. Ben deserved all of her, not just the portion she had left over from Jack, and so she said a silent goodbye to him and let her heart fill with Ben. "I will be."

Ben called his boss. "We're in the Dragon's Bowl."

~ * ~

If you enjoyed this book, please consider writing a short review and posting it on your favorite review site. Reviews are very helpful to other readers and are greatly appreciated by authors, especially me. When you post a review, drop me an email and let me know and I may feature part of it on my blog/site. Thank you.

Kristina

KMStanleyWriter@gmail.com

Message from the Author

Dear Reader,

AVALANCHE is the third book in the Stone Mountain series. What most people don't know is that I wrote it first. Then I wrote DESCENT and BLAZE. The story fit better later in the series, and so I rewrote it. AVALANCHE is the novel closest to my heart since it's the first story I wrote, and I think that gives it a special place.

I was the director of security at a ski resort, the best job of my life, but the stories and people in DESCENT, BLAZE and AVALANCHE come from my imagination.

Stone Mountain and Holden do not exist on the British Columbian map. I made up the towns and the characters. For those of you from the area, you may see the resemblance to Panorama and Invermere. I love the area and wanted to write about it, but didn't want to be restricted by an actual place. My imagination needed more freedom to get the story out.

If you'd like to connect, send me a tweet @StanleyKMS telling me you've read AVALANCHE, and I'll follow you back. I can also be found at www.KristinaStanley.com.

With all my heart, I thank you for reading AVALANCHE.

Kristina Stanley

Novels by Kristina Stanley

Descent

Blaze

Avalanche

About the Author

Kristina Stanley is the best-selling author of the Stone Mountain Mystery Series. Her first two novels garnered the attention of prestigious crime writing organizations in Canada and England. Crime Writers of Canada nominated DESCENT for the Unhanged Arthur award. The Crime Writers' Association nominated BLAZE for the Debut Dagger.

Her short stories have been published in the Ellery Queen Mystery Magazine and *The Voices From the Valleys* anthology. She is also the author of THE AUTHOR'S GUIDE TO SELLING BOOKS TO NON-BOOKSTORES.

Before writing her series, Kristina was the director of security, human resources and guest services at a resort in the depths of the British Columbian mountains. The job and lifestyle captured her heart, and she decided to write mysteries about life in an isolated resort.

While writing the first four novels, she spent five years living aboard a sailboat in the US and the Bahamas.

Find out more about her at www.KristinaStanley.com.

57876392R00136

Made in the USA
Charleston, SC
27 June 2016